Ka
En
20
nev

As a journalist she has lived and worked in Kashmir, Iraq, Qatar, Finland, the UK and India – where she freelanced as a radio reporter for the BBC World Service and wrote the occasional article. She most recently worked as a news producer for Al Jazeera English, before leaving to write her second novel.

ASHRAM

MURDER
in the
ASHRAM

Kathleen McCaul

piatkus

PIATKUS

First published in Great Britain as a paperback original in 2011 by Piatkus
Reprinted 2012

A CIP catalogue record for this book
is available from the British Library.

ISBN 978-0-7499-5363-8

Typeset in Sabon by Palimpsest Book Production Limited,
Falkirk, Stirlingshire
Printed and bound in Great Britain by
Clays Ltd, St Ives plc

Papers used by Piatkus are natural, renewable and
recyclable products sourced from well-managed forests and certified
in accordance with the rules of the Forest Stewardship Council.

MIX
Paper from
responsible sources
FSC® C104740

Piatkus
An imprint of
Little, Brown Book Group
100 Victoria Embankment
London EC4Y 0DY

An Hachette UK Company
www.hachette.co.uk

www.piatkus.co.uk

For my mum and dad, James, Gerard and Mary

SAVA ASANA – CORPSE POSE

SAVA OR MRTA MEANS A CORPSE. In this asana the object is to imitate a corpse. Once life has departed, the body remains still and no movements are possible. By remaining motionless for some time and keeping the mind still while you are fully conscious, you learn to relax. This conscious relaxation invigorates and refreshes both body and mind. But it is much harder to keep the mind than the body still. Therefore this apparently easy posture is one of the most difficult to master.

B.K.S. Iyengar, *Light on Yoga*

1

The train horns woke me up early again. I didn't mind so much. It's cheap, living round the railway and at night, when I can't sleep, those trains keep me company, calling out to one another like whales. It'd been a night of strange dreams: helicopters, bottles of wine, friends and betrayal. Friends that turned into other friends, an uneasy sense that some people I trust I shouldn't, a frustration with the world and everyone in it.

Sunlight seeped through my thin curtains. Drops of sweat were already forming in the small of my back and sliding down my thighs.

It was my birthday. I was twenty-six. I felt bad about turning twenty-six. I had made a big five-year plan for my future on my twenty-first birthday, but nothing had worked out the way I had thought it would.

It was too hot to lie in bed. I rolled off the mattress and into the bathroom. It was steamy in there before I even turned on a tap. The water was scalding. I peered at myself in the mirror. I was completely naked; I couldn't sleep with anything on in this heat.

So what had twenty-six years done to me? I turned round to inspect my bum. I'd had a tattoo of a Celtic cross done in a Cardiff Goth parlour when I was fourteen in a fit of Welsh mysticism. It was so tacky. I hated it. But it did provide an interesting way of weight watching. It stretched when I had been eating a lot of sweets and cakes, which sometimes I did. At the moment it was rather a skinny-looking cross. I had lost my appetite in the summer. And I was always going to be small however much the cross bent and bowed.

My hair was a short red mess behind my crumpled, bed face. I was very brown on my face and my hands and my feet but everywhere else I was deathly pale. It's not a good place for all-over sunbathing, Delhi.

I wanted a coffee but knew it would screw me up, make me hyper all morning. I'd have a milkshake instead, a treat for my birthday, to cheer myself up. I could have my mango too; it was just ripe yesterday, perfect for this morning.

But in the kitchen, every surface was black and moving. Ants swirled thickly over the surfaces and swam along the floor. Slamming the kitchen door in shock, I wiped my forehead. Stephen's fault, I thought darkly. How many times did I have to tell that guy not to leave food out in this heat? There was only one thing to do; go in, boil water, kill the buggers.

Actually, I enjoyed sluicing the scorching water over their marching trails, seeing them sweep along the surfaces like little broken boats. Destroying their whole world made me feel quite empowered. It did occur to me that this was murder, but they were so small and insignificant, it didn't take much to push that to the back of my mind. By the sink was a ball of writhing black, an ant Mecca. As I killed more and more ants, the mass thinned out and dirty yellow began to show through. After my last kettle of hot water I inspected the centre of the massacre. It was my mango! Stephen had taken my mango! He knew I'd been saving it! And then he'd just left it out! There were only a few strings of yellow flesh still clinging to the skin, peppered with ants so greedy they'd got stuck. I was pleased – they deserved it.

I threw open his door but he wasn't there. It was just his unmade bed as usual; clothes all over the floor, his guitar, the fan still going, wasting our electricity.

'Stephen!' I shouted, flipping off the switch.

I wandered into the lounge and the newspaper flew past me, lobbed through the balcony doors by a boy on his bike, like every morning. It hit our one palm, messing up the spiky shadows on the wall. I opened up the *Hindustan Times*. Twenty-sixth of March. Elections. Heatwave. Delhi hits fifty. A fucking heatwave. In India. Nine o'clock in the morning and I was already slippy like a snail trailing sweat across the marble floor. Gross.

I flicked through the news, looking for a story I might be able to follow up. Nothing. I threw the paper on top of the dusty pile I stored under our coffee table. I don't know why I bothered storing them, I never once looked at them again. I felt depressed. I had no story to work on today. No ideas. No commissions. Nothing at all to do but contemplate the failure of my five-year plan.

I'd had such a great start as a reporter, fantastic. I'd been sent out to cover the courts on my first day of work experience at the Cardiff *Echo* as a fresh graduate.

I went with Stew, a veteran reporter who dressed in winkle-pickers and drainpipes and had a cover band that played Queens nightclub every Saturday. We dropped in briefly on the big trial of the guy who'd raped and killed a teenage girl in the woods a few months earlier, but after Stew got a couple of quotes from one of the solicitors on the case he told me to go home because he had a gig rehearsal.

So I went to the bus stop and smoked a cigarette while I waited. Some bum with a dirty Welsh rugby shirt on came up to me to cadge a fag. I gave him one but he coughed and didn't inhale. He didn't seem as completely out of it as most tramps around the bus station. Some of them were so flamboyantly fucked they made White Lightning cider seem like a positive lifestyle choice. This guy was young and awkward.

I asked him if he had had any sleep. He shook his head.

'Are you OK? I mean, you don't look like you're used to this. Do you need a cup of tea?'

He started crying. I patted him on the shoulder. Eventually he confessed he had been living rough for nearly a week, had lost his memory and had no idea who he was other than his name was Rhys Williams. He was petrified. I got my first story prickle. Rhys Williams was the young Welsh rugby captain who'd gone missing after ten pints on the town last Friday. The whole country was trying to find him, his fiancée had been on TV constantly, sobbing and wailing. I peered closely at him. Yes, that was Rhys, a load more hair, not looking at all his clean-cut self, but that was him. The tramps wouldn't have been able to focus closely enough to report him.

'Don't worry, I know who you are. I'll look after you,' I said.

I put my arm round him and we walked over to the police station, with a quick detour to the Cardiff *Echo* office for a photo and an interview. I was offered the job of trainee reporter at the end of the week.

This seemed the best job in the world for someone as nosy as me. I just had to talk to people all day, about their lives, their problems. I had seemed to have a talent for getting stories out of people. I looked too innocent to judge them, I think. Or maybe too dumb.

My editor told me I could do whatever I set my mind to. I believed him and made a plan. I told everyone I would be a foreign correspondent for the *Daily Telegraph* in five years.

But five years were up and I wasn't working for the *Telegraph*. I wasn't a correspondent for them or anyone else. I was living in Delhi, trying to scrape a living as a freelance journalist and not die in the summer heat.

I cranked up our clunky old computer to check my emails and got a little rush of optimism. Maybe today I'd get a good article commission. Your birthday should be a lucky day. And yes – there was an email from *Vogue*! They'd responded to my pitch! But no. They didn't think a feature on Indian fashion designers was right for their next issue.

There was another email from Guy Black, on the foreign desk at the *Telegraph*. I'd had a coffee with him before coming to Delhi; he looked after South Asia and was keen on picking up new stories not on the wires. He was around my age; we'd got on quite well. He said he envied me going off to free-lance, but really we both knew he was better off with a staff job on a national. He'd be a correspondent in no time.

I got another little spell of cheer as the computer loaded his email up slowly. An article for the *Telegraph* would be way better than working for *Vogue*, any day. They did real stories about people, not just frocks.

But Guy didn't think my piece on Delhi sewage workers was right for the *Telegraph* either – they'd liked the pitch but they weren't going to commission it as a full story. He'd give me a call later to go through it. I sent him a cheery note back trying to sound carefree and easy.

I was anything but carefree. I'd been freelancing in Delhi for months now and was having real trouble selling articles. All the national newspapers had correspondents. I'd done a few things for Asian magazines but nothing that really mattered. I had some savings but these were running out fast. India wasn't as cheap as it once had been. The whole thing was exhausting; it gave me a gnawing feeling that perhaps the future wasn't going to be as fulfilling or as important as I had thought. That maybe I wasn't better than the Cardiff *Echo*; that maybe I shouldn't have quit my job there. That maybe local journalism was really all I was cracked up for.

I thought maybe I would have some emails from my friends back home, wishing me happy birthday. But they seemed not to have remembered. I was amazed at how quickly I'd lost touch with everyone. After the first few quick notes saying 'Good luck!', 'Miss you!', 'Let me know how you're doing!', all contact seemed to have faded away. I was out on a limb here.

My best friend from school had written though, Beth. Of course she'd remember today. She gave me a big happy birthday in capital letters and then moved swiftly on to her promotion and pay-rise. I was jealous. She had a boyfriend and was going on holiday to the Maldives. Scuba diving. I'd sneered at her when she said she was going to be a solicitor but her life was going great now.

There was an email from my dad.

Ruby love,
Happy Birthday. I hope that the sky is bright and blue in Delhi
to celebrate your birthday. Here in Wales it is grey, like it was
on the day you were born. But that day I soared high above
the low clouds and will do again today just with the memory.
There is a book in the post for you. I know your mother has
sent you something too.
Love,
Dad

I rubbed my nose, feeling a ripple of distant affection. I could just see him there writing it, in his reading glasses, his lips loose with concentration as he peered at the computer screen. He'd be running his hands through his hair, which was going grey at the temples now, as he looked out of the window to check the sky.

Dad was very sensitive to the sky – he was dangerous when there was a low orange sunset and tired in the grey. When it was blue he was happy, he was wistful. He'd be happy just staring into the blue for hours – he saw things in it. He was very romantic for a physics teacher.

There was no email from my brother. I wasn't surprised. He was kind of wild and didn't think about things like birthdays. He was four years younger than me and had inherited the bits of my parents I hadn't. He was pale and tall like my mother, but had my dad's black hair and eyes. I was short and olive skinned like Dad but with Mum's red hair. I wished it had been the other way round. Rhys was lethargically romantic and took over the world from his bed while I was just kind of impish and healthy looking and always worked hard. Not cool.

There was no email from Mum either. She'd get round to it but it would take a day or two for her to work out the date.

There was an email from Stephen. I was still mad at him for eating my mango but I knew straight away it would be the best email of the day.

Ruby Jones, you harlot, happy birthday . . .
I imagine you've just got up and are grumpy because it's hot and you haven't got any article commissions and it's your birthday and you think you look like shit.

I laughed.

Well, I can't do anything about the heat – sorry – it's hot here
– get used to it.
See ya tonight lovely,
S. x
P.S. It's the day before your birthday – I'm in the lounge, going
out now – might be back tonight – dunno. If I don't see you
before this evening – I'm taking you out to the Oberoi for
cocktails. Don't worry about money – I got this one. And I
made you some mango milkshake – in the fridge . . .
P.P.S. You don't look like shit. You're beautiful.
P.P.P.S. I can't believe this email won't have cheered you up –
but if I haven't managed to work my magic on you – practise
your headstand.

I smiled and rolled my eyes. So I would get my milkshake
after all. What a flatmate. He was the only friend I really had
at the moment – but he was so funny and crazy and cool that
one was all I really needed. He really looked after me. He
was subtle about it too; didn't let on he knew how much I
relied on him here in Delhi.

I'd been at Oxford with Stephen; we'd both done English.
We hadn't been friends though. I'd seen him in lectures and
always thought he'd looked so full of himself, in his cracked
leather jacket and cashmere scarf.

But I'd met him again in Delhi at a yoga class in my first
week here. A couple of Swedes who were staying at my hostel
kept raving about Shiva yoga and I'd tagged along to see what
the fuss was about, and for a bit of company. There was already
a crowd shoving and jostling to get into this famous class by
the time we got there. These two blondes had thrown themselves into the fray but I hadn't been so enthusiastic. I hung
back. And that's when I'd found Stephen, smoking a cigarette,
leaning against the wall of the ashram, in his old leather jacket.

10

I'd been incredibly glad to see a face I recognised. The city was a jam-packed struggle of cars, dogs and humans with nothing in the writhing mass that cared about me or even knew me. I gave him a big kiss.

He didn't react to this. Just gave a half-smile and looked at the smoke blowing out the corner of his mouth. But I think he was pleased to see me too.

'People say Oxford's glory days are over and I'm inclined to agree. But it does teach you manners,' he said, nodding over to the elbowing yogis.

He gave me a cigarette and we chatted. He'd been over here for about six months, doing a PhD on a Fulbright scholarship. It turned out he had a spare room in the flat he'd been living in. He gave me the address and said I should come and have a look if I was sticking around the city. Nizamuddin Shrine. I said I'd take the room there and then. I had no other choices and I liked accidents like that.

Nizamuddin Shrine, a centre of Sufism, known throughout the Muslim world. It had sounded idyllic but I thought I'd landed up in some kind of pilgrim hell when I first got there. My Hindu rickshaw driver wouldn't even attempt its muddy lanes so I'd struggled on foot through open-air butchers, men selling dirty garlands of roses and little fires where paraplegics, druggies and the most miserable immigrants hung round waiting on scraps of Muslim charity. It was a bit like an Islamic Glastonbury.

The strains of 'Little Wing' floating down from my new home did nothing to reassure me. I was not into Jimi Hendrix.

He opened the door.

'Hey – I'm in the middle of something – make yourself at home – the room's there,' he said, turning back to the living room.

My new room had been grimy; the window sill silted in dust. I'd felt flat in the room's grey light. I wandered out into

11

the warm yellow lounge, where I found this strange guy standing on his head tapping his toes to 'Purple Haze'.

'What the hell are you doing?' I said.

'Do you mind; I'm trying to meditate,' a mumble came from his squashed throat.

'What? To Jimi Hendrix? Come off it.'

'It's my headspace – don't kill it.'

I shrugged and turned to go back to my room. What a weirdo. Who the hell had I moved in with? I'd never liked him in uni, why did I think he would have changed?

'I bought some English scones for you from the embassy. Make a cup of tea, I'll be done in a minute,' he mumbled again.

My ears perked up. I loved scones, loved cakes and biscuits too. I'd tried the Indian sweets but they were too brash a sugar hit for me, left your teeth aching and your appetite dead. I wondered if he had remembered the iced bun I always brought to the modernism theory lectures to get me through the boredom.

Making a cup of tea for us both settled me in; Stephen would have known that instinctively. I took a nose through his cupboards too.

The kitchen was empty apart from a congealed bottle of soy sauce and some dusty cornflakes, but my new flatmate had bought cream and jam for today. Such effort for a stranger made me want to cry. I let myself feel a little homesick for the first time while the kettle boiled.

He rolled up a spliff after tea. I pulled out my bottle of gin from duty-free, which made him really happy. He ran down to the pilgrim hotel on the ground floor to get some cans of tonic water and some tiny round lemons. It was late by the time we went to bed, the shrine lights were off and packs of dogs were barking in the dark. We'd become friends. I'd even

12

agreed to give yoga another try, to join the Shiva centre Stephen told me had saved his life at university.

I learned later his tendency to overdramatise, in dress and stories. Yoga hadn't quite saved his life; more helped him negotiate a difficult growing up period. Stephen had been a lonely fresher, struggling with his identity and his sexuality. He was half Indian and half English but knew nothing about his Indian side; didn't know his father at all. New friends, constantly asking where he was from, rammed home to him the fact that he simply had no idea. Trying out Shiva yoga had been a first attempt to learn something about the country that claimed half his blood. And then he found it calmed him, gave him space alone to be himself. He told me it made him realise he didn't need to answer anyone's questions, said he had enough of his own to worry about.

His PhD research subject is 'Homosexual tantra in the Vedas and beyond – a comparative analysis of male love in Hindu literature'. He fashions himself as some kind of gay-pride Hindu guru, with a pink om T-shirt and long hair. He tells people he has yogic blood in him and always ends up chatting in a headstand at parties. He is such a show-off. He went to Eton and Oxford, not some levitation yoga school in the clouds. He's ashamed of that part of his background, I think. He had a rough time with his parents both gone – his grandparents brought him up. They send him parcels and I've seen photos of them. They seem nice, old, but he doesn't mention them much. Not exciting enough for the myth of Stephen, probably.

Despite my reservations about Stephen's status as a spiritual leader, I took his advice. I tried to flip myself up into a headstand. After falling down a couple of times, I gave up and did it against the wall. The streams of sweat did a U-turn, running down my legs and my stomach and my throat

13

into my mouth and eyes. They tasted salty like tears. Just as I was calming down, my phone went. I swore; collapsed in a heap.

The number coming up was Shiva yoga centre. It would be Rani, our teacher there. I couldn't believe he was phoning. I stared at my mobile. Maybe today really would turn out to be a lucky day.

Rani was another reason – maybe the biggest reason – I was feeling bad this morning. I was interested in him. No, wait, that is an understatement. I was completely infatuated with him. I'd spent the past few weeks mooning in bed, dreaming of our life together. How happy we'd be when Rani finally plucked up the courage to leave the ashram and sweep me off my feet. I had had it all planned out. He wouldn't be a yogi completely any more because he would have to break his ashram vows to marry me. But once we were married I would give up journalism and we would move to Goa and set up a yoga centre/guest house and live there in some kind of shanti hippy sexual nirvana.

It hadn't worked out like that at all – the whole thing had been a bloody disaster.

Stephen said that I should get over it; that my utter dedication to Rani was simply a bad case of Orientalism.

'You only like Rani cause he's exotic, Ruby. He represents the dusky, sexual East which will release you from your fettered English upbringing. You're like one of those bloody memsahibs,' he'd said to me.

'I'm Welsh. You're the one with the dodgy English schooling, not me. I was going to raves and taking pills while you were probably getting buggered in the toilets of your dorm.'

'No need to be rude about a good education, Ruby. I'm just saying you should analyse exactly what you see in the guy.'

14

'Apart from the fact he's the most gorgeous guy I've ever met?'

'Look, that's true, he is incredibly hot, but you shouldn't get so obsessed with someone just cause of what they look like. There's got to be more than that, Ruby. What is it? What do you see in his *soul*?'

'Oh shut up with that spiritual bollocks.'

'The Rig Veda says that thought gives rise to desire. Think.'

'I don't know! He's charismatic. He's got this energy all round him that makes me crazy. And he's so lost-looking; no one can get near him because he lives this life of a monk. I thought that I could help him, that I could change him and make him happy.'

Stephen had rolled his eyes at this.

'I'm going to have to murder you for your inane female tendencies,' he'd said and rammed his pillow over my face.

I'd really had to fight to get him off me. I laughed at the memory as I picked up the ringing phone.

'Hey, Rani,' I said as casually as I could, hearing the nerves tighten round my voice.

'Ruby.' He sounded choked.

'What?'

'It's Stephen.'

God. Always Stephen.

'What?'

'Stephen . . .'

'What's he done?'

'Stephen . . . The police have been here . . .'

'Oh, what the fuck? Has he been caught with drugs? Shit – typical – on my birthday too.'

'No, it's . . . it's . . .'

I heard his phone clatter to the floor.

'Rani?'

'Ruby – it's Swami Shiva.'

I got a lurking feeling. There must be something going on if Swami Shiva had deigned to talk to me.

'Swami, what's going on?'

'Ruby, I'm sorry. The police have just been to the centre.'

'Why?'

'They pulled a body out of the Yamuna River today and they found Stephen's yoga membership card.'

'No . . .'

'Is Stephen with you now – at the flat?'

'No . . . but he said he might be out.'

'I'm sure it's not him – I'm sure he's fine – but we need to go and do an identity check on the body. I'm sorry.'

'I just got an email from him, it's not him.'

'Yes, yes, he is probably fine, but we need to do this. We'll let you know as soon as we know it's not Stephen.'

'I'll come with you.'

'There's no need.'

'I'm coming – I can't wait here.'

Swami Shiva paused. 'Where do you live?'

'Next to Nizamuddin Shrine. Do you know it?'

'Of course. We'll pick you up on the way – we'll be about an hour.'

I lurched out of the room to the balcony. I called Stephen several times. His phone was turned off. I tried Rani. He didn't pick up. I called the centre. It was engaged. I threw my phone on the floor and it clanked loudly.

I left it where it was; went back inside. I sat on our sofa and watched the phone, still and small in the morning sun. I picked up a cigarette packet. Took one out, put it in my mouth. Put it back. Got up. Sat down again. The doorbell rang. I didn't answer it.

My hands were shaking but I wasn't really worried. I knew

Stephen was still alive. He had such a powerful presence I could feel him wherever he was in the city. I would have known instantly if something bad had happened to him. I began to pray, murmur some pleadings to a childhood God. God was with Stephen. He was the hero of his own epic and it had only just begun. I never knew someone so obviously destined to pack their life to the brim with stories.

At midday I was still sat there on my own. I phoned Rani. It was engaged. The sun was white and strong now, throbbing through the sky, burning my face. I got up and pulled a blind down. My phone jerked to life outside on the floor. It must be Stephen; he'd tell me he'd been mugged. Someone had taken his card and he was OK, he'd just been out all night. Bad luck for the person who took his card. The phone burned hot against my ear from sitting in the sun.

'Hello?'

'Ruby, it's Rani – we're outside.'

I could see Swami's sleek black Mercedes, gleaming amongst the goats and the bashed-up rickshaws. Swami's driver Raj was talented. It was a feat to negotiate the hustling side streets round Nizamuddin Shrine on foot, let alone in a car like that. I picked up my keys and my Ray-Bans and raced down the dark staircase two steps at a time. A hand covered in boils grabbed my ankle as I stepped outside. I screamed, jumped back.

It was Hassan, a man with no legs who wheeled himself round the shrine lanes on a broken old board with wheels. He lived off the leftovers from snack stalls: honey sweets stuck to the bottom of giant sizzling woks or burned bits of cold pakora. Stephen paid him to keep an eye on his motorbike. I gave him ten rupees.

'Sorry, Hassan. Have you seen Stephen? Where's his motorbike?' I pointed to where it was usually parked.

17

Hassan shook his head. Shrugged. There were just chickens pecking in the space where Stephen's Enfield usually stood.

Raj was leaning up against the wall, smoking a bidi, waiting to open the door for me. I scanned his face for worry, but he looked the same as ever.

It was cool and shady in the car. I could see Swami Shiva and Rani in the wing mirror. Rani was fidgeting, moving his long arms and legs around, restless. I tried to catch his eye in the mirror but he was avoiding looking at me. Swami was as still and as calm as usual. His long beard shone, his white robes were pressed. He nodded to me gently. The leather seats were pale and luxurious. It was the first time I had been in a car like this in India, but these two yoga gurus looked very used to being driven around in an imported Mercedes.

'Raj – the police morgue, please,' said Swami.

We drove quietly over Delhi's flyovers, weaving in and out of the smashed-up metal buses, trucks, cars, rickshaws. We crossed over a black, stagnant river with huddles of plastic homes around it. It usually stank, but Swami's AC protected us from the fetid sewage. I could still see the women with wild hair and mad eyes though, rocking their babies. We stopped at a traffic light where a starved, grey-haired old man lay comatose, his ribs and knee joints glinting in the sun.

The poverty bothered me even less today than it usually did. It had been shocking at first and I had shed a few tears but after a few weeks Stephen said I was getting boring and I should either go and work with a homeless charity or get used to it. I got used to it. Sometimes I would get flashes of guilt and give out a bit of change to assuage my conscience but mostly I just ignored it. Life shits badly on some people – there was nothing much I could do to change that. Of course I felt it deep down. Extreme poverty, suffering up close makes you question everything: society, religion, the idea of what one deserves and doesn't deserve. But I tried to keep the surface of everyday life as smooth as possible and remember relativity.

I noticed Swami Shiva didn't wind down the window to give out any money to the beggars either. He just stared blankly out with none of the compassion he displayed in the ashram.

The Delhi police morgue was a low grey building, waving in the white heat. Bidis, fag ends and burned matches marked the way from the car park to the entrance, where flowerpots held a few wilting marigolds and thousands more cigarette butts. Swami walked towards the door as he always did, peacefully and deliberately. It was the gait of a man who had fulfilled his life's missions. Following him reassured me. Swami had said at his last lecture that if one had a good open heart you couldn't be harmed by the world, it couldn't hurt you. Stephen had the most open heart. It would be someone else in there.

It was dark inside the morgue; an embattled AC groaned. A lethargic receptionist jumped up when he saw Swami Shiva. A policeman came out to greet us just a few moments later.

'Swami Shiva, an honour to meet you, sir. Inspector Mukerjee here.'

The inspector pumped Swami Shiva's hand. He was a barrel-chested man with slick black hair and a moustache. His eyes were large and a startling liquid blue. He filled every crevice of his khaki uniform and topped it off with a silk cravat.

'My wife is a great fan of your books – a great fan of you, sir. She goes to your centre regularly. We've even visited your retreat in South India, sir. You completely cured her wind problem – we had terrible trouble with it – the cinema was a nightmare. But she did your 'Yoga for Digestion' course and she was cured! She thinks you're a saint, sir – she won't believe you were here today,' he said, continuing to shake Swami's hand.

19

Swami smiled a small smile. The inspector looked around at Rani and me standing together. He recognised the fear on our faces, remembered what we were doing here in the morgue.

'Ah yes. Do you know Stephen Newby personally, sir?'

'Not so well, but I do. My apprentice Rani is, ah, close to him. And this is Ruby, who lives with him. She wanted to come with us,' said Swami.

'Good. I am sorry to put you all through this. Please come this way.'

The room was small and cold and hummed quietly. A bare bulb hung over a white-sheeted body. Rani grabbed my arm, looked at me for the first time that day. An electric shock went through me. I was disgusted with myself. Here I was, about to identify a dead body and all my own flesh could think about was sex. How utterly inappropriate.

'Ruby, I'm scared.'

'It's all right, Rani – it's not going to be him, don't worry,' I whispered, squeezing his hand. I considered the best case scenario here. Of course it wouldn't be Stephen, but the awful, intense experience of witnessing death would bring me and Rani closer, culminating in us comforting one another in bed together later. Oh Christ. I couldn't believe I had just thought that. I was one fucked-up selfish human being. I said sorry to God.

'Are you ready for me to show you the body?' asked the inspector.

Swami Shiva nodded.

He pulled back the sheet. I heard Rani wail. I smelled the stench of river sewage. There were weeds woven through the man's matted hair and a clean red gash on his forehead. He was naked; he wasn't wearing Stephen's usual beads. He was so much paler than Stephen. Stephen was nutty brown; this man was waxy pale.

20

I dropped to my knees and retched but nothing came out. Rani was beside me, clutching my arm. He put his hand to his mouth like he was going to be sick too, but all that came out was a dry, scratchy burp. I heard Swami Shiva tell the inspector it was Stephen. It was Stephen.

2

I was in a room with a window. Some time must have passed: the sun was lower and deeper; the shadows falling across the room were long. Someone placed a plastic cup of tea in my hand. The thick surface scum made me sick and I felt a strong urge to throw the scalding tea over the inspector. Rani twisted his yellow yoga shirt round and round in his hands. Swami had his hand on Rani's shoulder.

It was Stephen in there. That was his face, white because his heart had stopped beating. That was his hair, all wet from the water. Stephen was dead.

I wasn't crying or anything. I was just sitting there. I couldn't process this. It was jamming me up, crashing my system. There was some part of me inside whacking the escape button over and over again, but nothing was happening. There was no escape.

'Have you any idea why Stephen would be on that bridge?' asked the inspector.

'He liked sunsets. We watched the sunset there a few times,' I said. He'd got the habit off a Sikh friend, Hartaj, who was religious about his sunsets. Hartaj had told us the sunset was one of the best from that bridge and we'd been down a couple of times together.

'Was this an accident, Inspector? Did he fall in?' said Swami.

'It's unlikely. It's very difficult to fall in the Yamuna. The municipal authority has fenced over every bridge in the city, to stop people throwing in river idols.'

'River idols?'

'People worship the Ganges. They worship the Yamuna too. They throw coconuts, statues, candles, all sorts in the river. It's clogged up already and this just makes it worse. The river authority tried to stop this but you know people are ignorant. They wouldn't stop so the bridges all got fenced over. And the fences had some more positive effects. Suicides and river deaths have fallen by half since they were put up a couple of years ago. As I said, it's very difficult to fall into the Yamuna. Was Stephen in any kind of trouble that you know of?'

Stephen was secretive. Stephen lived wildly. But I didn't think he was in any serious trouble. I shook my head, glanced at Swami.

'Stephen could be obstinate, but the only person Stephen had got into trouble with recently that I know of was myself, actually, Inspector,' said Swami.

'What about?'

'It was a small private matter – something to do with the centre.'

Rani moaned and began to sob and wail.

The inspector looked at Rani and then across at me. My hands were shaking and my tea had slopped over my skirt. I noticed the wet patch before I noticed how it was scalding me.

'You're all in shock. I'm going to go down to the bridge with Forensics. Try to get some witnesses. I'll begin interviewing you all properly tomorrow. Do you know his parents, Ruby? The embassy will need to inform them as soon as possible,' said Inspector Mukerjee.

'He doesn't have parents,' I said.

The inspector looked up.

'His mother is dead; she died in a car crash. He doesn't know who his father is.'

Mukerjee shrugged. 'Unlucky family. Mukesh, Probir, you go down to the embassy and inform them of the death.'

He turned to two young men sitting in the corner of the room whom I hadn't noticed before. One was skinny and small; he looked like he had an overactive thyroid. The other had rolls of fat around his belly. He had small, intelligent eyes. They both nodded enthusiastically.

'Inspector. Do you think . . . could Stephen have jumped?' asked Swami.

'Suicide, you mean? Unlikely. The boy had his shoes and socks on. The psychology of a river suicide usually means they take their shoes and socks off. And again, the fences make it much more difficult to jump off the bridge. But this doesn't stop everyone, of course. And the bridge, it's known as Suicide Bridge actually. It's where a lot of young women go when they find themselves in bad marriages. Do you think he had a reason to take his life? I'm sorry to ask.'

'No! Of course not! It's my birthday – we were going out for cocktails tonight,' I said.

God. We should be at the Oberoi bar now. Me in a strappy dress, Stephen in his jeans still, but being glamorous with his credit card. We'd be drinking cosmopolitans. He'd have eyeliner on and his hand on my leg under the table, trying to slide it under my skirt. Stephen wasn't as much of a queen as he liked everyone to believe.

'I think that's enough for today. I have all your numbers

24

and addresses. We'll speak tomorrow,' said the inspector.

The door burst open and a small man with an ancient camera launched himself into the room. He looked very excited; started babbling at Swami Shiva.

Swami looked at the inspector.

'I'm sorry – my Hindi isn't fluent – what is this good man saying?'

'Of course, sir – being from the South, from Kerala, isn't it? Hardly anyone can understand Javid's gutter Hindi. He's the morgue photographer. He wants to have a photo with you, for the office.'

Swami Shiva loved to have his photo taken; the walls of the Shiva yoga centre were covered with pictures of him with ministers, ambassadors, pop stars. He never refused an interview. But now he frowned slightly. 'Not today, I'm sorry. If he would like to come to our centre another time I would be happy to have my photo taken with him.'

'Of course, Swami, very inappropriate.'

The inspector shouted something at Javid, who backed out of the room shamefaced.

'Inspector, one thing before we go. I imagine the media will be very interested in this case,' said Swami.

'British Asian murdered in Delhi. Yes, most probably.'

'I would appreciate it if you could try to keep the Shiva centre out of this as much as possible; my students are all going to be very upset without the added pressure of reporters hounding them.'

'Within reason, yes, of course, sir. I've only got the greatest respect for your yoga network – helps so many people,' said the inspector, standing up.

Swami asked me to stay at the ashram for the night but I said no. I wanted to go home. It was dark by the time Raj dropped me back at Nizamuddin. I wandered through the flat, dazed. I watched myself, amazed at how normal I was acting. My emotions hadn't caught up with the facts yet. There was a disconnect in my head between what I knew and how I felt, which was just kind of numb.

I looked in the fridge for something to eat as I almost always did when I came home. There was nothing but the mango milkshake Stephen had made me. Curdled now, greeny milk on top, lumps of mango pulp at the bottom. I took some bread out of the freezer and toasted it, then made some tea. We – I – didn't have any milk so I put a lot of sugar in it. It made me feel sick. I had sharp stabbing pains in my stomach. I got myself a gin. Stephen had taken the last of the ice and not filled the tray up again. I tried to summon my usual surge of annoyance with him but it wouldn't come. It was impossible to will him back by getting angry. I had the gin warm and without lemon.

I lit a cigarette and stared at the moon coming through from the balcony. It was whole orange, small and mean. I put on some music; some Janis Joplin Stephen had been downloading.

The gin loosened me up a little, eased the shock. But I could feel hysteria rise to replace it. I drank more gin. I had to get a grip. What did I need to do? I should call someone.

Who? My parents? No. I couldn't handle that now, not now. Stephen's grandparents? Fuck. I should have told Inspector Mukerjee about his grandparents. Of course they were his next of kin. They'd brought him up. His grandmother sent Stephen parcels of food from Fortnum and Mason. His grandfather was a diplomat too; Stephen picked up everything through the embassy here. My mind had just gone blank back there in the morgue. I should call the inspector to let him know as soon as possible.

But just then my phone went. I jumped.

Zero, zero, four, four – an English number. Was it Stephen's grandfather? Already? Did they know yet? He must do. The embassy would know. I stopped the music, wiped my eyes and picked it up.

'Hi, Ruby,' said a chirpy, satisfied voice. 'It's Guy here from the *Telegraph*.'

Guy. Of course, he'd said he was going to ring.

'Hi, Guy.'

'Are you OK to have a chat now?'

'Not really, sorry.'

'What's up – are you OK?'

His British voice was bittersweet. The familiar tones were painful because they reminded me of home. It struck me that home wasn't ever going to be the home that I left. It would be different with Stephen dead. I would be different at least.

'Yes, fine . . . no . . . actually . . . no . . . I'm not OK.'

'Ruby? What is it? Look, your article wasn't bad. It was good actually; those men really let you into their lives. But sewage workers aren't really for *Telegraph* readers . . .'

'It's not that . . . it's . . . it's my flatmate. He's just been found dead.'

'Jesus. I'm so sorry. Were you close?'

'I'd been living with him a few months. I mean, he was my best friend here.'

'British?'

'Yeah – well, half British – British Asian.'

'Was it an accident?'

'They think it might be murder.' I heard my voice rise to a warble.

There was a pause on the phone. Guy spoke very gently, very quietly to me.

'That is so terrible, Ruby. I am so sorry. That is terrible. Have his parents been told?'

'No . . . no . . . he hasn't got any parents.'

'Poor guy. Poor guy. What was his name?'

'Stephen – Stephen Newby,' I said, beginning to cry a little with the sympathy.

'What? Stephen Newby? Are you sure?'

'Of course. Of course I am. I saw his body, Guy.'

'Fuck. I went to school with the guy. Shit. Stephen. What was he doing in India anyway?'

'He was half Indian. He was doing a PhD. And trying to find his father.'

'He was half Indian? He kept that quiet at school. I mean he was dark, but he could have been anything: Italian, Spanish. There's so much Eurotrash at Eton,' said Guy.

'Eurotrash?'

'Sorry. Sorry. That was insensitive. It's just Stephen being Indian – no one ever knew. I mean his grandad is Sir Newby. There isn't a more respected career diplomat in his genera- tion. He was ambassador in Panama after my great-uncle. I met his grandparents a few times at school functions. Nice people. They'll be devastated. But it's weird the embassy haven't put out a press release. Especially for a diplomat's grandson; did you let the police know that Stephen's grandfather was a diplomat?'

'Actually my mind just went blank in there. I was in shock. All I could remember was that Stephen's parents were dead. I didn't say anything about his grandparents.'

'Ruby, I'm going to phone the embassy. I'll phone you straight back. OK?' he said.

I nodded and he put the phone down. It rung again five minutes later.

'They don't know anything. The police hadn't informed them about any British death today.'

'The inspector on the case, I remember he told his juniors to do it.'

'Probably didn't think it was that big a deal if he didn't have any next of kin, thought they could leave it for today.'

'Did you tell them?'

'Well. Ah. Not exactly.'

'What do you mean not exactly?'

'I just asked if there had been any British deaths in the past twenty-four hours. Said I was checking up a possible lead. They said they hadn't heard of anything.'

'Why didn't you tell them?'

'Shock?'

'Don't fuck around, Guy.'

'OK, look. The embassy haven't been informed. That means only you and I and the Delhi police now know about this death. It's not going to be on the wires till tomorrow.'

'And?'

'This is completely exclusive. This is something even Eddie couldn't get,' said Guy.

Eddie Challan, the *Telegraph* correspondent out in Delhi. He'd come from Iraq where he'd broken some amazing stories. People talked about him like he was a god at the *Echo*. I'd eaten up everything he'd written. All the small personal stories he'd done as well as the big ones. He'd moved to Delhi round the same time as I had, confirming just how far away from my five-year plan I was. There was no way I was ever going to be able to compete with someone like him for a job.

'It's not just me who knows. There's Swami Shiva and Rani – they're yoga gurus here.'

'Yoga gurus?'

'You know, teachers.'

'Yoga instructors?'

'Well, yeah, but also, you know, spiritual leaders.'

'OK, whatever. Would they talk to the press?'

'No, definitely not. Swami asked the inspector to not involve the press if it was possible.'

'Ruby. You're a fucking genius. This is a massive scoop. The grandson of one of the biggest diplomats in the world has been murdered in Delhi. Sir Charles helped put together the Kyoto protocol. He left the Foreign Office and became huge in climate change policy.'

'We don't know it's murder – and Sir Charles has nothing to do with it.'

'OK – dead in suspicious circumstances. And Sir Charles has everything to do with it because he is Stephen's guardian. And you know, he's due in Delhi soon, for a climate change conference. Fuck, this gets better. But the main point is no journalist but you and I know about it and won't find out about it until we get tomorrow's paper out with an exclusive, which you're going to write.'

'Guy, are you kidding me? Are you completely out of your head? This is my friend. This is my best friend who died. I'm not going to use his death for an article. I'm going to put the phone down and call Inspector Mukerjee and tell him who Stephen's grandparents are. Then I'm going to phone the embassy.'

'Ruby, don't – listen to me. Think about it. You need a break out there. It's practically impossible to get commissions as an unknown freelancer. How much is your rent? Are you making it each month?'

'Stephen's university pays the rent on our flat. He's got one of those cultural exchange fellowships. I pay for bills.'

'That's going to stop now, isn't it?'

'I guess.'

'I'll get you a fee of a grand for four hundred words on this.'

'No.'

'I can probably stretch to two if you're going to be so sensitive.'

'It's not about the money, Guy! You're crazy.'

'You're right. It's not about the money. It's about the fact that you will have had the biggest break of your career and you're completely at the centre of the story. That won't be the last commission. You'll get them flooding in from other newspapers for first-person pieces. The *Telegraph* will have to put you on some kind of exclusive contract to keep you and then they'll get you to do other articles and before you know it you'll be a correspondent for us.'

'No. And what about Eddie? He'll be fuming at you if you give this story to me. He should have it.'

'Well, actually he's got typhoid – he's in hospital. Which makes this now triple lucky for you and me. If he was around he'd get all the glory as usual. But now we need someone to fill in for him. If you write this article, it'll be you, and I'll get credit this end for sorting the whole thing out. You refuse this, you've refused your big chance. They don't come along too often. Some people don't ever get one. I'm jealous, to be honest with you. I wouldn't waste it.'

I put the phone on the seat beside me and put my head in my hands. God. I couldn't believe I was even thinking about it. I'd made a mistake not telling Mukerjee about Stephen's grandparents. That was from shock. But this wouldn't be a mistake. This wouldn't be about shock. This would be about me being cold and ambitious and making a break out of my best friend's death. It was sick.

31

'No, I'm not doing it.'

Guy let out a sigh. 'Then I guess I'll just have to do it. I haven't got so much to go on as you so it won't be as good. It won't be personal. But it will still be an exclusive.'

'You can't do that, Guy. Anyway, I'm going to call the embassy right now.'

'They'll all have gone home now, Ruby. The press secretary told me they were about to close the office.'

'Are you really going to write it if I don't?'

'Yes.'

I knew then I would end up doing it. I'd mentioned Guy Black to Stephen and he'd spat Black out again. He despised him. Said he'd been a bully and an opportunist. Said he picked on people's weaknesses. Said I shouldn't have anything to do with him. I could see now he was right. But I didn't want my friend's death written up by Guy Black. He wouldn't have wanted that.

Stephen had always said I should take every chance I could.

There was something else here too. I should be the one to tell his story. I needed to be the one to tell his story. I'd wanted to know things, to investigate so many stories before, but none more than how Stephen had died.

Guy was still waiting on the line.

'Hey.'

'Hey.'

'You're a real bastard, Guy, you know that.'

'Look – it's tough, Ruby. I don't want to be sat at this desk for the next ten years.'

I didn't say anything.

'Are you going to do it?'

'I'll try.'

'Good girl. Well done. You've made the right decision. If I know Stephen he'd be proud of you.'

'Would he? I don't know.'

'I think he would. Now, what did I say – four hundred words for two grand? I'll get finance to OK it and, when you send the article, send your bank details too. We'll transfer it directly to your account at the end of the working week.'

Easiest and hardest money I've ever made. I couldn't say I didn't need it.

I sat down at my cranky computer. I opened Word and stared at the blank screen, the only light in the dark room. I began typing.

'Stephen Newby was a great friend . . .'

I'm not writing an obit . . .

'Stephen Newby's death is a great tragedy . . .'

I deleted it.

That's editorial. He wants facts. Simple facts. I went to the kitchen and poured myself another large gin. I thought it would help me but it just made the room rotate slowly. I sat in front of the computer sipping it quickly nevertheless. My hands shone a greeny white, like ghost's hands. The bones of my wrists were showing through. I closed my eyes. None of this was real. I could feel Stephen here now, slouching in his leather jacket and beads, shabby and glamorous.

I spun my head round. But he wasn't there. There was nothing there but darkness. This was crazy. What was I doing writing this story? What kind of animal was I? My friend had just died, maybe even been murdered. I reached for my phone to call Guy back. I couldn't do this.

But I had a text message. From Stephen. Fuck. He was alive? That wasn't him in the morgue. I let out a sob of desperate relief. But I clicked the message open and saw that it had been sent yesterday, while he was still alive.

*Ruby – I need to talk to you. It's about my father. This is a
big story. Call me when you can. S.x*

'Fuck . . . had you found him?' I murmured.

Stephen had never been told who his father was. His mother
hadn't told his grandparents and she had died before Stephen
had been old enough to ask her himself. All he knew was that
his father was Indian; that his mother had returned from a
gap year in India pregnant. His grandparents had told him
not to mention it in school. He'd kept quiet when school
friends talked about their dads. He just shrugged his shoulders, said his dad had died with his mum. The other boys
would leave him alone, shy away from their usual prodding
questions. It was too much for them to even contemplate:
Mum and Dad dying.

But at university Stephen had studied literature and got
mixed up in the post-colonial crowd. He studied Fanon, Camus
and Dubois; Gil Scott Heron and V. S. Naipaul too. He wrote
his dissertation on 'Rushdie and midnight's grandchildren. The
epic extended'.

Suddenly the colonial world of his grandfather's embassies
in which he grew up was the enemy. The murky part of his
past was the thing to embrace. Stephen resolved to find his
father. He applied for a Fulbright scholarship to study a PhD
in India simply as a way to get over here. And of course these
academics had loved his louche charismatic style. He got
funding and a place at Jawaharlal Nehru University and his
mission had begun.

He'd been in India a year and his PhD was coming along
swimmingly, but he'd hardly got anywhere with the search
for his dad. Stephen got morose about it sometimes. A lot. It
wasn't something he'd have committed suicide over, though.
Just something that got him down.

But this message from him now, had he found his father? He'd found a story – was it something that would get him into trouble? Could that be the reason he ended up in the Yamuna? In the police morgue? Cold, with weeds in his hair? Had someone shut Stephen up? Was I paranoid? Of course I was. My friend had just died.

I was getting weird twinges, though. Like there was something up. Fuck it. I'd make his story as salacious as possible. Then the whole world would want to know how Stephen had died and we might have a fighting chance of finding out what the hell happened.

Stephen would have appreciated that; he liked the grubby side of life. I sat down at the computer once more, drank my gin and began typing.

ILLEGITIMATE GRANDSON OF TOP DIPLOMAT SIR CHARLES NEWBY FOUND DEAD

By Ruby Jones

The illegitimate grandson of renowned diplomat Sir Charles Newby, one of the architects of the Kyoto Agreement, was found dead in Delhi yesterday morning. Stephen Newby, 27, was pulled from the Yamuna River that runs through the city and identified through a membership card to a yoga centre he attended regularly.

Stephen was on a mission in India to discover the identity of his father. His mother, Claudia Newby, who died in a car crash in 1988, became pregnant while on a trip to India and had never revealed who his father was.

Stephen was openly bisexual and took an active part in Delhi's burgeoning gay scene. He was the recipient of a Fulbright scholarship to study for a PhD at Jawaharlal Nehru University into 'Homosexual tantra in the Vedas and beyond

– a comparative analysis of male love in Hindu literature'.
   The police are treating the death as suspicious.

I clicked Send, turned my computer off, gulped down the rest of the gin and collapsed on my bed.

3

I dreamed through the train horns and the call to prayer from the mosque next door.

I woke abruptly, my eyelids jerking open, around midday, my hangover sledge-hammered by the heat. Brutally, the events of yesterday dawned on me. I lay in bed, horrified, but with a glimmer of hope that this was the dream and my dream was reality.

I got up and went into the living room. My glass, sticky with hot finger marks from last night, was on the table. It wasn't a dream. I checked my emails, like I did every morning. One from Guy.

Thanks for all that – the stuff about his father and his grandfather made the story – my editor's really pleased with you and me – more commissions to come soon I am pretty sure. Breakfast news and Radio 4 led with Stephen's death in the morning – it was a quiet day in Westminster admittedly but this is still a real coup. His grandfather was

interviewed on Today. *He hadn't been informed until the story broke over here but he held it together really well. Speak soon.*
G.x

Another email from my mad mother.

Ruby, my darling,

I am SO SO sorry I forgot your birthday! I just hadn't realised the date! I was writing all day – an ode to SPF 50 for the Vogue *summer issue. By the time your father got home from work and asked about your birthday it was far too late to phone – midnight over there in Delhi – I know you're a pretty sensible girl and would be tucked up in bed by then!*

We saw your article in the newspaper today, darling. Crazy! Are you OK? Is that your friend? I think I remember you mentioning a Stephen. Funny name that, isn't it? For a diplomat's son. Anyway, Daddy and I are thinking of you.

Have you got your birthday card yet? I'm so sorry, I think I posted it a little late and it might not have got to you in time. It's a beautiful one though, made by an artist friend of mine who lives in the Brecons – the paint is all made from woodland plants! Look out for it! Happy Birthday Twenty-six – gosh, it's quite old, isn't it?

Mum x

This was so typical of my mother – worrying about my birthday card and the death of my friend in the same breath. She was kind of out there mentally – the real world just bounced off her.

Mum was a very, very minor modern poet. She'd had two small collections published by the Arts Council in Wales and would have an occasional sonnet or something printed in a women's literary magazine called *Phetus*. Mostly she wrote poems to commission and small pieces for women's magazines.

Sylvia Plath was her heroine. When we were children she'd regularly recite bits of *Ariel* to us while our fish fingers or our sausages were burning up in the oven.

I think it was the combination of the constant taste of charcoal food and images of red stigmata that made me turn to journalism. I loved words but I wanted them to communicate facts, reality. Concrete things that everyone knew mattered and wouldn't require so much ardour that I'd mess up my tea.

I hit Reply.

Yeah – he was my flatmate actually, Mum. I'd told you about him but I wouldn't have expected you to remember. Write a poem about that – finding your friend dead in a river in Delhi.

(He was named Stephen after Anna Karenina's brother – it was his mother's favourite book. To be honest with you I don't think it's as flaky a name as Ruby. At least you didn't call me Ariel . . . that's a blessing at least . . .)

As soon as I had sent it, I felt bad. I was taking out my guilt, my upset, on my mum. She hadn't done anything wrong. She'd be really upset by that email. I wrote another.

Mum, sorry, I shouldn't have been so horrid. I just feel really bad at the moment, you know. I'll talk to you soon. Don't worry about me too much. R. xx

She'd understand, she never bore grudges. I got up from the computer and walked out onto the balcony. There were a couple of TV cameras outside my house already. I found the *Hindustan Times* stuck in our palm and unrolled it.

GRANDSON OF FORMER BRITISH AMBASSADOR FOUND DEAD IN YAMUNA was the headline.

I went back inside and turned on the TV. BBC World. A sharp-suited youngish presenter with coiffed hair was coming to the end of her link. 'Where our correspondent, Mike Hughes, reports . . .'

The television switched to a man of about thirty in shirt and tie standing on a bridge in Delhi, some grim, dusty buses, a few cyclists going past behind him.

'This is Wazirabad Bridge. It's the main trunk road north from Delhi and for these commuters making their way home from work, it marks the end of the city. But this bridge marks other ends too – it's known as Suicide Bridge. Police say at least three or four women throw themselves off the bridge each month, to be found floating in the weeds of the Yamuna River below.'

The shot switched to a smooth and relaxed river, ducks lazily swimming, the water glistening. It looked idyllic, but even without it being a suicide spot I knew it stank. The Yamuna was one of the most polluted rivers in the world.

Mike continued as I watched the ducks quack and dive happily. 'These women are mostly desperate young brides or wives who can no longer live with abusive husbands or mothers-in-law. But yesterday, garbage pickers who trawl the Yamuna for rubbish, made a shocking discovery. The body of a young Englishman – Stephen Newby.'

I switched to NDTV 24-7 – the main Indian news channel.

A grey-haired man in an expensive suit was holding a press conference; it looked like somewhere in London.

'I will find out what happened to my grandson. Nothing will replace him. The idea of Suicide Bridge is rubbish. Stephen was a happy and well-adjusted young man.'

'Sir Charles, did you know your grandson was gay?'

'No comment.'

'Sir Charles, could you explain about Stephen's search for his father?'

'No comment.'

The screen switched to outside the Houses of Parliament where the Indian correspondent was standing.

'Despite his pleas for help concerning Stephen's death, Sir Charles refused to answer any questions about Stephen's search for his father, intriguing the British press further. This story doesn't seem likely to slip away. Prithvi Suri, NDTV 24-7, London.'

We were back in the studio, to yet another stylish, suited presenter.

'Indian police announced the launch of a full investigation early this morning,' revealed the girl in a tinkling voice.

I switched the TV off and closed my eyes. I was watching Stephen's life being rolled up into a suspicious homicide and spat out on every news channel. Shit. It had worked. It was a scandal. I'd broken an international news story – my best friend's death.

I felt sick. My hands were shaking. I got out a cigarette and smoked it sitting on the edge of the couch, tapping my foot. As soon as I saw Sir Charles up there, old and broken and fending off bloodthirsty hacks, I knew I had made the wrong decision to write that story. I should have called Inspector Mukerjee up as soon as I had remembered. A worm of guilt wound inside me, boring a hollow in my stomach.

And Sir Charles wasn't just reeling from the shock of Stephen's death but the revelations about his grandson's sex life and also this search for his father. No one but Rani and I had known about this mission. Stephen had kept it from his grandparents; partly because he was bitter they hadn't made his mother explain who the man was in the first place, partly because they were old and he hadn't wanted to upset them.

The doorbell went. It was Inspector Mukerjee, in his cravat and his Ray-Bans. He looked cool, but when he took off his glasses his eyes were bloodshot mad.

'Ruby Jones – I'd like to see your passport please.'

I took it from under my bed. He flicked through it quickly till he came to my visa.

'I thought so. This is a tourist visa, not a journalist visa. You're not permitted to report in India. I'm arresting you for breaching visa protocol and withholding information essential to a homicide investigation. We're going to the station.'

I slumped in the front seat of the inspector's white car. We crossed the Yamuna and I noticed the fences on the bridge for the first time. They reached up six feet high. How could Stephen have fallen in? He must have been thrown.

It was late March. The leaves had fallen off the trees lining the road, leaving only stark branches. One dead-looking tree had opened up in bright red flowers. The buds were the same size as hearts. Cars ran over the falling petals, mushing them to a fleshy warm pulp in the intense midday sun. The car's AC made me shiver.

I usually took a cardigan with me for AC but the inspector had been so angry I hadn't thought about what clothes I was putting on. A pair of super-light jeans, a creased grey shirt from my laundry, an old pair of sandals; I'd at least remembered a long blue headscarf to keep the sun off my head.

We arrived at the main police headquarters. Ten floors of barred dirty windows; the kind of place you could disappear in. Bored men milled around the entrance, leaning on old Enfield rifles. We climbed in a rickety lift to Inspector Mukerjee's office.

'I'm afraid my AC is broken. I'm waiting for it to be fixed,' he said.

It was hot like a sauna; extreme and awful after the arctic car. I suspected some kind of temperature torture to soften me up for questioning. There was a lack of air and light. I found it hard to breathe. Office chairs scraped against the floor and the sound grated in my ears.

But Inspector Mukerjee didn't look any happier than I was, mopping his glistening brow with a white handkerchief. Struggling to open his small window, he pushed hard against it. It flew open but an outside electrical cable crossing the window shut it straight back again. Swearing in muttered Hindi the inspector sat down heavily on his chair, leaned back and stared at me.

'I've been in the Delhi police force for over twenty-five years. In that time, I have had to arrest a number of British citizens, usually for drug possession, or smuggling. Your embassy always takes a British arrest very seriously and it's not often or for long these people stay in a Delhi jail. But I think the embassy may quite like to forget about you. Indeed, I think they would thank me for putting you away.'

'Because of my article?'

'That article is proof you've been working as a journalist here under a tourist visa. I can arrest you and put you in jail and then deport you or I could simply deport you. The police here are usually too busy to be chasing every student wanting to write little things for their college magazine about this beautiful country. And even I am not going to stop a young woman trying to write some worthy piece on our great India. But this! This! What were you thinking? Why didn't you tell me Sir Charles was Stephen's grandfather yesterday? I would have got the investigation under way much quicker! You made me think he was a poor orphan!'

43

'He is . . . he was!'

'My dear, he is no such thing. He is not only a British citizen but the grandson of an incredibly powerful international figure. Sir Charles was due to make a guest appearance at the Delhi environment summit next month. You know the subject? Saving the damn Yamuna River! They've had to cancel the whole thing now out of respect! Crores down the drain and me getting the blame for the whole thing! I've had the ambassador and the chief of police on the phone all morning. They all want to know who the hell Ruby Jones is.'

I felt the blood rush to my face.

'You know the poor man found out about Stephen's death from reading your article? Sir Charles is most, most upset, very shocked and very, very angry. He's threatening to send Scotland Yard here to oversee the case. If that happens I myself will be in deep water. If there is one thing our politicians don't like it's when the Britishers start sticking their nose in Indian affairs again, thinking they still run the show. Looks bad on us, like we can't manage, which we very much can!'

I sat mute. The inspector stared at me. I was terrified. But at least Mukerjee's outburst appeared to have calmed him down a little. His cheeks were deflating and his eyes were less red.

'But weren't your assistants supposed to inform the embassy?'

The inspector growled. 'They thought stopping at the chicken roll stall was more important and the place had closed by the time they got there. They thought it could wait till tomorrow. It clearly couldn't,' he said. 'But this isn't the point. Let me find this article of yours now.'

He started up his computer and peered at it in the curious way my dad did when he was Google-searching. As if he were leaning over the edge of some wishing well that might contain the source of all knowledge, but might just as easily contain some goblin that would pull him down and drown him.

I guessed the inspector was looking for my article online. The internet is a bloody disaster if you make a mistake as a journalist. My story on Stephen would never go away. It would be archived for ever for the world to use against me and copy and paste onto other websites and chat forums where people would dissect my lines and throw mud at my callousness. Maybe I was being slightly paranoid, but the fact was you couldn't get away from anything you'd written with a byline now. Gone were the days when yesterday's news was today's fish and chip paper.

The inspector read out parts of my own article to me now.

'What exactly did you mean by bisexual? What is this "scene" you say he was part of?'

It wasn't much of a scene – more a scattered group. The cultural co-ordinator at the French embassy was a raving Bengali queen who used to go after rickshaw drivers. Half the male teachers at the British Council were gay. There was a German and Nigerian couple at Delhi University doing PhDs in male Asian sexuality who were supposed to have the best parties in Delhi. Their group had slightly more frisson than most ex-pat circles and Stephen enjoyed this. He'd had very liberal attitudes towards sex. He'd happily sleep with most people who came his way. He saw it as a way to connect and get to know them and a way to view the world.

'It wasn't anything dangerous – just some foreign men having parties.'

'What did they do there?'

The inspector spoke with a tone of repulsion and wonder. I would have found his attitude funny at another time.

I shrugged. Stephen had taken me along to a couple of

these nights. There had been a lot of wine, sitar music, kissing. After a while he told me I should probably leave, or, if I stayed, I should be very open-minded. I left.

'Was it just foreigners or were there locals too?'

I knew the German couple had once taken along their driver, Shiv. They had told their liberal friends they'd opened Shiv's eyes to gay love. When they got ready to leave, the driver was found in the kitchen buggering the host's cook. Stephen had been in a fit of hysterics when he told me, but the incident had been too absurd even for the German academics and the host of the party had not been pleased at all. The driver stayed with the car after that.

'Mainly foreigners, I think.'

'Did Stephen have a boyfriend? Anyone who might be jealous of him? Anyone who might commit a –' the inspector searched for the right words, seemed embarrassed '– crime of passion?'

'Well . . .'

There was someone in particular. But he was the gentlest person. He couldn't have hurt Stephen. And to be put under suspicion, even just to be exposed as gay, would break him into pieces.

'There is someone?'

I had an urge to tell the inspector what I knew. I found it very difficult to keep anything private or secret for long. I had an insatiable urge to gossip about everything, however serious it was.

But I shook my head. This was too, too serious. The inspector looked at me closely for some time, suspecting I was lying. His phone went, some cheap Bollywood ring tone, saving me for the moment. It made me think of the text sitting in my phone from Stephen. I should tell the inspector about that – about the news of his father.

'Yes, yes, bring him up straig▨
and biscuits, please, too.'

'Inspector, I've got something to show ▨

The inspector turned to me once more. 'No.▨
is here – he wants to talk. You will have to wait; b▨
you're minutes away from being charged with obstructing
investigation and working illegally. I'm thinking about
deporting you as soon as possible.'

Probir, the inspector's assistant, brought Swami Shiva in. I
recognised him from the morgue, the fat one. The smell of
stale sweat wafted over me as he came into the room. I got
up and stood by the window. I could see Raj far below. He
was watching the black Merc, smoking his bidi as usual, patient
in the shade.

'Sit down, Ruby,' the inspector barked, oblivious to the
stink of his assistant.

Swami Shiva was wearing small wire glasses and holding
a computer printout of my article.

'I have something to tell you, Inspector. I don't think it has
anything to do with your investigation at all but it's better
you find out from me than from anyone else,' he said, looking
at me.

4

Rani and Stephen in love – or at least in lust. It seemed impossible. But then so had the heat. It'd all started with the heat.

February had been bliss: balmy sun, dusty light, not a better place to be in the world than Delhi, or that's what it felt like then. But soon enough the sun got vicious. It beat down harder every day, shocking even locals with its ferocity.

At first Stephen and I took refuge in the shady parts of Lodhi Gardens, but after a week of this terrorising heat, leaves fell dead off the trees leaving only brown tindle on parched lawns. The very air seemed to catch fire, wavy with fumes and wailing prayers round our flat. Stephen and I sat there like hot rats suffocating every evening, until his grandfather got us passes to the British embassy pool.

It claimed to be Olympic size – Stephen said it wasn't. Nevertheless, it was big, large and blue, banked with lawns fed by constant sprinklers. The air was greener and cooler by the pool; swallows swooped low on the surface.

A stone laid by George Freeman-Thomas announced the pool open in 1935, a secure period before war or independence. The pool had lived through tumultuous times but you got the sense this place had always retained its calm, kindly used and lovingly looked after. Tiled in turquoise, the wooden changing rooms were polished and contained an abundance of large bald towels in faded stripes. Waiters dressed in overwashed white would bring you tarnished silver pots of tea or cold lemon drinks.

This was a quiet, fusty type of privilege, one you couldn't buy at the new five-star hotels. It was the jewel in the British diplomatic crown; a pass to the pool curried more favour than a million dinner or cultural evening invites. They were limited and given to a few other high-profile embassies and senior Indian politicians. And somehow Stephen had wangled it too.

There was a small cafeteria selling deep fried bread and other Anglo-Indian snacks, with a hall attached, where dance, meditation and yoga classes were held. That's where we met Rani. He taught a small class three times a week. Stephen was over the moon when he found out. Rani was one of the top teachers in India; a legend in himself. He'd been left as a baby at the gates of Swami Shiva's second centre in Kerala, just after a tropical storm. It was assumed his father had died at sea and his mother could no longer look after him. Either way Swami Shiva took him in. Rani grew up in the ashram and began to show huge talent for yoga practice. He became Swami Shiva's adopted son and his protégé.

Rani mostly taught at the Delhi Shiva centre, but his classes were always heaving with people. The Shiva network was a charity; the cheapest yoga classes in Delhi as well as some of the best. It was tough to get a place, there were always queues outside the classes, and once inside you spent a lot of time avoiding arses and elbows and flying legs. It was a yoga sweat shop. Stephen and I had met trying unsuccessfully to get into one of these classes, hanging back from the crowd. Stephen had practised Shiva yoga for years; it had been the cheapest and biggest class in Oxford too. The embassy paid a lot of money for the appearance of this small, quiet yoga group.

We got into a pleasant evening rhythm. Yoga with Rani, a swim in the pool, then tea and a snack in the café. The rest of the class were older, ambassador wives or ambassadors themselves, who usually rushed off to functions or their children after the class, on the phone to their drivers as soon as Rani had bowed his head for the final prayer. But Rani would swim after class like us and we got to know him. It was very quiet in the evening, with only a few solitary swimmers in the dark. We skulled around the shallow end chatting, the light strips above the changing rooms shimmering on our skin.

Stephen invited him to join us for tea in the café and he shyly accepted. Stephen's grandfather had sent him English chocolate that he wanted to share. Rani refused at first, saying chocolate wasn't a pure food, wasn't allowed in the ashram. But Stephen insisted.

'They put loads of chemicals in the chocolate here, to stop it melting in the heat. This is pure, it's delicious,' he explained.

In the end, Rani couldn't resist, scraping off the wrapper that had melted into the chocolate and groaning with pleasure after his first bite. We laughed at him but Stephen and I were smitten with Rani; both claimed wildly to be in love with him on our journey home. He was humble, poised and completely untouched by the outside world, fame or appetites. So unlike Stephen and I – I worried we'd corrupt him.

In return for our small tea offering, Rani politely invited us back to the yoga centre for dinner. We ate simply, brown rice and yellow coconut dhal, sitting on the floor with Swami Shiva in the private ashram kitchen. Stephen was star-struck; it was like meeting a film star for him. But Swami was easy and interested in our lives. He was less earnest than Rani and wore his fame with humour, telling us about giving some famous movie star and his wife a yoga lesson on their tour of India. The hot food wasn't agreeing with the young starlet and she had kept on letting out the most enormous belches and other unmentionable sounds.

Chewy, who managed the ashram kitchen, joined us. He was from Honolulu; he had chin-length grey-blond hair, very brown skin, a Hawaiian shirt for every day of the week. He made the best cheesecake in India, according to Swami and Rani. His latest was kiwi and pineapple, which we ate while he told us about the book he was writing.

'It's called *Join a Cult and Double Your Money*,' he told us.

'Is the Shiva network a cult?' I asked.

'No way, man, Swami Shiva is one of the good guys, he rescued me,' said Chewy.

'Who from?' I asked.

Chewy had joined a cult in Hawaii when he was seventeen and spent fifteen years meditating, drinking and lusting his way round the world. It was run by a former San Franciscan ballet dancer, who called himself Swami Jimmy and claimed to be a reincarnation of Isadora Duncan. Swami Jimmy was a raving queen with a love of boys and diamond jewellery. He'd decided Chewy should take a vow of poverty around the time he was coming into an inheritance. Jimmy spent it all in an afternoon at Tiffany's. He had a troop of boys he would travel round the world with, meditating, getting drunk and sending them out to work. When the group came to India, Chewy met Swami Shiva who invited him to stay at his ashram. Chewy never left. Years later Swami helped him sue the guru, now working as a yoga teacher in LA fitness, claiming he had been defrauded though mental manipulation and brain-washing through starvation and sleep deprivation. He won twice as much as his inheritance – hence the title of the book.

'This man was a hypocrite. The main thing is you live as you teach. This is the most important thing,' finished Swami.

We loved meeting Swami Shiva and he seemed to enjoy meeting us too.

'I'm happy you've made friends with Rani. It's hard for him in the public eye so much – hard for him to make friends here in the ashram. The embassy pool is a nice, quiet place for him to relax,' he said.

Swami invited us to the Shiva centre's Holi party which they were having in a couple of weeks. Holi marked the beginning of the Indian summer and was one of the biggest festivals of the year. Everyone throws colour over each other and drinks bhang, a kind of weed that gets you really high.

Stephen and I cackled at this on the way home.

'I can't believe the Swami Shiva was talking about getting caned like that . . . next thing he'll be telling us how he and Rani often smoke crack before class,' I joked.

Stephen laughed, shook his head, ran his hand across his mouth in thought in this way he had that I liked.

'It was a nice day. He's so cool, man. I love him. He's so famous. He's incredibly rich you know, Ruby, but he keeps his feet on the ground. He still eats on the floor in the kitchen. He lives what he believes, you know? The simple life. I respect that. And I can't wait for the Holi bhang,' he said.

I laughed.

'Yeah, that's living what we believe . . . ?! Hey, you know the *Telegraph* want to look at that feature I did on the sewage workers?'

'They do? That's wicked, Ruby, well done. Things are going so nicely at the moment, aren't they? I'm very happy.'

Stephen put his arm round me and smiled into the hot breeze coming through our rickshaw.

*   *   *

It was hottest a few days before Holi. The papers began screaming about a heatwave and even a cool dip couldn't tempt diplomats away from their AC. The pool was empty and no one but Stephen and I turned up for Rani's class. Stephen said we should take advantage of the quiet – do some diving, let off some steam from the heat.

I went in head first. The water rushed past my head. There was a glugging sound in my ears as I swept to the bottom of the pool for a moment of quiet, completely alone. Stephen bombed or belly-flopped. Rani held his nose and did a kind of ballerina jump in the air, looking scared before he splashed down into the water. Not much like the fisherman's son he was supposed to be. We dived in over and over again, working ourselves up into a childish frenzy, laughing and joking, pushing one another in and leaping after each other. We were being rambunctious, but in a dark, empty Delhi swimming pool you can do what the hell you want. I dived after Rani and met him at the bottom of the pool.

It was inky down there and you had to squint against the chlorine, but I was used to that. In a faint, shaky slant of fluorescent light, I saw Rani moving around under the surface, finding his bearings, sparks of froth spangling from his slender moving limbs. I grabbed his arm and pulled him to me. His eyes were clamped shut but he seemed to gasp – bubbles swelled up in silver bursts from his mouth. It felt like an invitation to kiss him. I nervously swam my lips towards his. He took them instantly, pushing his wet tongue inside my mouth. Tasting of human and chemicals, we sucked our way to the surface.

My heart was bursting when we broke the surface, flailing through the white splash. The wave subsided and we faced one another, dripping wet and warm. Rani's eyes widened in horror.

'Ruby!' he exclaimed.

'Who did you think it was?' I said. That was not the reaction I'd expected.

'Hey you two!' Stephen shouted, on the edge of the pool, his tummy slightly sticking over his too-tight brown trunks. He dived into the pool and the ripples ran through Rani and I as we trod water, avoiding each other's eyes.

I confided in Stephen that evening, blushing into my pillow as he sat rolling a spliff on my bed. I was horrified; I meant nothing more to Rani than any of those sighing girls at the centre. Stephen just laughed and laughed. Then he stopped, looked thoughtful.

'You know Rani's a girl's name?'

'No it's not!'

'It is, Ruby – you don't know any Hindi at all. It means princess.'

This pissed me off. Stephen didn't think I was any good at languages and told me so. In fact it was quite clear he thought himself much more intelligent than me in most ways.

I had tried to learn. I had picked up some kind of rickshaw Hindi by sheer will to communicate and get to know the men that drove me around the city. I could find out the basics: where they lived, where they were from, if they were married and how many children they had. I'd had a couple of conversations with Swami Shiva's driver Raj too. But after the initial few sentences, I stumbled, I forgot the vocabulary I had learned, I mashed up the grammar in my mouth. Stephen, on the other hand, had a ferocious memory and had mastered huge amounts of vocabulary. The words slid off his tongue easily and I'd been very jealous of this. I wanted to talk to people.

'I know more than you think, Stephen, I just don't like speaking in front of you. But anyhow – why the hell would Rani have a girl's name?'

'He was left at the Shiva centre with a bracelet saying "Rani" – probably his mother's – but the monk who found him just called him Rani. And it stuck. He's pretty like a girl anyway.'

'He's beautiful – I'm devastated,' I cried.

'Oh shut up, Ruby, you'll get over it. You've got tons of men to choose from. I've seen you flitting those little green eyes of yours all over the guys from *Outlook* magazine at Baci.'

'They're not all from *Outlook*, some of them are from NDTV actually.'

'Whatever, they're all nice cool guys, why don't you hang out with one of them? You might get a job out of it too.'

'I could get a job at one of those places anytime.'

'Why don't you then?'

''Cause that isn't part of the plan, Stephen – I haven't got time,' I said.

'That is totally your problem. You pluck these ideas out of nowhere, fix them in your head and then you just go at them hammer and tongs without stopping to think whether they are really the right thing for you; like this five-year plan, like Rani.'

'Yet again you think you have the solution to every problem I have, that if only I was you I would be fine. Just fuck off, Stephen. You think you're so much better than me but you're not exactly playing happy families with Daddy now, are you? How's your mission going?' I said.

His face fell. He was hurt. I felt bad.

'I'm sorry. I just – you always think you know more than me,' I said.

'OK, fine, but surely even you can see that you and Rani together is insane? It will never happen, Ruby!'

'But I'm in love with him. I think about him all the time!' I wailed, leaning on Stephen's chest, half in jest. We needed to lighten the situation.

Stephen patted my head and handed me the spliff and we lay there chatting until I fell asleep.

I avoided the swimming pool for a few days in shame but couldn't refuse the Shiva centre's Holi celebration. I can't stand to miss a party and this looked set to be a big one. The build up to Holi was wild. Teenage sweethearts flirted outrageously, lavishing green and yellow and red upon one another's uniforms. Grown men manhandled each other by the side of the road, smearing colour onto one another's faces. Stephen went to Bogle Market and bought special Holi paint – gold – expensive and rare.

'Why did you buy that? There'll be loads of powder at the centre.' I asked.

'It's going to give me special powers,' he said with a leer.

'What? Tell me what you're up to.'

Stephen just shrugged and wouldn't say anything, however much I nagged him.

The morning of Holi, thumping spiritual music woke me up early. I couldn't tell where it was coming from. I sat on the balcony eating a mango, watching ice-cream sellers, with their bike fridges, line up like an army ready to go into action.

Stephen jumped me from behind, stealing half my mango, kissing me with sticky lips.

'Holi hai!' he wailed. 'I think I'm going to douse you in turquoise. It'll go very nicely with your red hair, won't it? Anyone ever tell you you've beautiful hair, Ruby?'

He sat down on top of me and I noticed he had an erection.

'Stephen! What the hell?'

'Sorry, sorry. I think it's the heat making me horny. Do you want to do something about it?'

I thought about it for a moment. I went through waves of

fancying Stephen and he was always up for anything but we'd managed to keep simply friends and that was precious.

'No, no I don't think so – come on, we've got something good, we shouldn't spoil it.'

'Still pining after Rani, I see. Well, your loss.'

He got up and went to the bathroom. He seemed pissed off. Things between us had been so easy but it was getting a bit intense. And I was jealous of him. I hadn't told Stephen because I didn't want to encourage him but I knew Rani thought he'd been kissing Stephen at the bottom of that swimming pool. And there'd been a lot of passion in that kiss.

Swami's driver Raj picked us up. There were no taxis; even the rickshaw drivers were off enjoying themselves. The usually rammed roads were empty; shadows and sunshine flickered across the tarmac. It was the sides of the roads that were mayhem today. Piles of coloured powder – turquoise, apple, lemon – kicked, thrown, rolled in. Middle-aged women, whom you felt should have known better, covered in head-to-toe strawberry. Marauding gangs of yellow boys with supersoakers of vermillion.

My mouth was dry as we drove up to the centre. I didn't know what to expect from the party or from Rani – it would be the first time I'd seen him since we'd kissed in the swimming pool. But I needn't have worried about some awkward quiet. The courtyard of the centre was a mass of writhing, coloured people. Silvered Japanese girls wearing goggles. Punjabi guys whose skin was now as bright as their turbans always were, in red, pink and blue. Tall, gangly Pollock-esque ex-pats. One guy completely black, a lurid look in his eye and a can of Day-Glo spray paint in his hand. He grabbed me and dumped me in a pool of emerald water. I emerged bright green. I looked over at Stephen. He was fuchsia, laughing and loving it.

I saw Rani appear through the crowds, yellow and white in kurta pyjamas. He laughed and doused Stephen with red. He saw me, shyly nodded his head and after a second's hesitation picked up some blue powder from piles at the edge of the grass and ran towards me, dousing my head in a cloud the colour of the sky. I laughed, screamed, told him to get off. Stephen galloped over, dousing us both in purple. We ended up on the floor hitting each other with colour. We'd made up; we were friends, no more, no less. Relieved and sad, happy and disappointed, I went off with them both to get bhang lassis. Volunteers were filling up plastic cups with this dirty white bitty liquid from steel vats.

'You think this will get us stoned, Stephen? I can't believe there's anything in it at all if Rani's drinking it.'

Stephen opened his eyes wide and his mouth wider, croaked out a villainous 'Holi hai,' and drank the lot down.

'Ruby, it's the one day in the year when it is completely religiously acceptable – no, sorry, mandatory – to get off your face. Even grannies get stoned on Holi,' he said, wiping his mouth.

I threw the foul-tasting mixture down my throat.

I joined couples dancing round a paddling pool of pink. One girl sidled up to a gangly ex-pat and leaned blue all over him. The black man pulled a shy bystander onto the dance floor with a fluorescent squirt and a hand. A toddler weaved in and out of people's legs, throwing white speckles over everyone. I couldn't tell who was Indian or English or anything.

After two or three bhang lassis, my hands were tingling and I couldn't stop winding my tongue round my mouth. This stuff was strong after all. I sprawled out on the grass by the guy who had thrown me in the paddling pool, who was fast asleep now. The dance floor was emptying; people were flaking out in the shade, eating samosas. I looked for Stephen and Rani. I couldn't see them at all. I imagined they were together somewhere. Jealousy worked up inside me and grabbed me round the throat.

It was then I saw Swami Shiva. His white robes doused in pinks and reds and oranges. He looked on fire, dignified, unlike the rest of us crazed toddlers. He was looking for something. He saw me and walked over. I tried not to seem stoned.

'Ah, Ruby, have you seen Rani?' he asked.

'I think he's with Stephen,' I replied.

Swami frowned. 'Where's Stephen?'

'Er, I'm not sure.'

'When did you last see him?'

'With Rani,' I said unhelpfully.

'Hmmm. They haven't left, have they?'

'No – maybe they're in Rani's room,' I said.

As soon as I'd said this I regretted it. Sometimes there was no filter between what I said and what I thought. The middle process between thinking and speaking just disappeared and that's mostly when I got into trouble. I had a feeling this was going to be one of those times.

'Let's go and see,' said Swami, fixing me with his eyes, making it impossible to do anything but get up and obey him.

We walked over towards the dorms quickly, my heart thudding. They wouldn't be there. They wouldn't be so stupid. Anyway, it's pretty innocent to be just sitting with a student in your room. God knows enough people looked like they needed to crawl into bed right now. But the urgency in Swami Shiva's walk made me nervous.

Gold powder speckled the entrance of Rani's room, like confetti. Swami noted it before opening the door.

A line of gold led from the entrance of the room to the desk, then to the walls and then to the small single bed where

Rani and Stephen were sleeping naked. They were covered in handprints of gold: on their chests, on their arms, on their legs, on their behinds, on their faces. They glistened in the low afternoon sun and the long shadows of Swami and I, still as statues, fell across the two of them. Gradually, Stephen's eyes began to flicker open softly, adjusting to the light. He looked up and met Swami's gaze and mine.

Swami explained what he had seen calmly and clearly to the inspector. I tried to imagine how he felt about what he had seen. On the day, he had stared for some time before slowly turning around and walking away. I didn't know what he had planned to do about it; what he planned to do before Stephen had died, that is.

The situation must have stumped even Swami Shiva. Staying in the ashram meant no smoking, no alcohol, no meat, no onions or garlic and definitely no sex. And there was his adopted son, his protégé, caught with not only a pupil but a male pupil at that.

Inspector Mukerjee was clearly shocked by Stephen and Rani's affair. His face was solemn and he sat dumb for a while.

'Well, er, I guess the best thing is to begin interviewing people at the yoga centre?' was all he said eventually.

Swami had closed the centre to the general public straight after the police had called yesterday, but he could gather the residential students in the main hall for questioning.

'Can I go home?' I asked as Mukerjee was busying himself with his Ray-Bans and his gun.

'You're coming with us. I haven't decided what exactly I am going to charge you with yet. Anyhow, you might be useful. You seem to know a lot more than you're letting on, more than anyone in fact.'

'You can't just drag me around with you!' I said.

'Would you prefer me to put you in a cell? I haven't the time to charge you now and I'm not letting you get away with this,' said Mukerjee, with an arched eyebrow.

'You can't just dump me in a cell! Swami Shiva?'

'Why don't you just come with us, Ruby? I am sure that Rani would appreciate seeing you whatever.'

'Make yourself useful to me now and maybe I'll forget about the visa, Ruby. What is that phrase you Britishers like? You scratch my back, I'll scratch yours?' concluded the inspector, striding out of the door with his hand on his gun holster.

'Fucking idiot,' I muttered under my breath, but followed on.

The inspector let me ride with Swami Shiva and Raj at least. I had the whole of the back seat to myself. Swami sat in the front of the car, which was unusual. He talked fast to Raj all the way. I tried to listen in but couldn't pick up a word. I felt shit about this until I realised they were talking some Southern Indian dialect with nothing whatsoever to do with Hindi. They were both from Kerala; they were talking Malayalam.

I waited in reception with the inspector while Swami went to gather the students, surrounded by photos of world leaders and pop stars visiting the Shiva centre. I liked the picture of Rani helping Fidel Castro into a headstand best.

Swami Shiva put his hand on the inspector's shoulder to usher him into the hall.

'Inspector, I'm sure this incident on Holi was a one-off. Rani and Stephen were simply misguided ... frustrated, perhaps. It would have blown over. But this, this thing, is a serious sin here in the ashram. I would be very, very grateful if you didn't mention it to the students.'

'Where is Rani?'

'I've sent him to the temple to do bhakti for Stephen. I'd prefer it if you didn't interview him quite yet, he is very delicate and I am not sure how Stephen's death has affected him. It has been very difficult to begin the conversation, as you can imagine.'

'Of course, Swami – within reason, I can hold off interviewing him, but if he was having relations with Stephen he is going to be a prime suspect before long.'

Swami nodded slowly, closed his eyes. He seemed very tired, like my dad did when school called about my brother, saying he'd been caught smoking or with a girl again.

'At least he knows to use protection, at least we taught him that,' Dad would say, shaking his head.

I doubted Swami Shiva had ever spoken to Rani about this sort of thing and now it was kind of too late.

I walked towards the hall to sit in on the interviews but the inspector turned round to stop me.

'You're here so I can keep an eye on you and make sure you don't get into any more trouble. I don't want you having any more information then you've already got. You wait here,' he said.

'But you said I could be useful. Look, I've got something to show you anyway. My phone . . .'

'Do as you're told,' he snarled.

I decided it would be best not to argue this one.

I slumped down in one of the reception chairs and watched the inspector through the hall door window talking to the rapt group of students. They were a mixed bunch. A gaggle of Japanese girls all in matching yellow Shiva centre T-shirts, tied up with knots at weird angles. A few middle-aged Indian men and women, a tanned Israeli couple in fisherman's pants with om patches, two tiny wiry old white women and one billowy, large English lady who usually had a shining smile on her face, though not today. There was also a handful of Delhi students. Chewy was there too, his hair was tied back with an elastic band. He was wearing a grey shirt with flamingos on. The only one missing was Tito, a big, tattooed Brazilian guy who was studying Hindi at Delhi University. He was away in the mountains. Someone would have to tell him about Stephen, he wouldn't know yet.

I wandered out to the centre's garden. It was peaceful. Wind chimes rang in a hot breeze which smelled of smoke and sandalwood. Raj was lighting incense sticks to a small Ganesh shrine.

He bowed down low, praying. For Stephen, I thought. Stephen had loved Raj; practised his Hindi with him whenever he could, always made a point of asking him how he was. Raj had enjoyed the attention and invited Stephen, me and Tito to dinner at his home.

Raj didn't live at the ashram as most of Swami's employees did; he'd chosen to live outside and get extra pay. It wasn't much more but he and his wife Sita were saving to buy a house. Sita had thick, thick hair down to her waist and huge black eyes. Laughing and fluttering around like a bird, she'd talked non-stop in Hindi, ignoring the fact that we couldn't understand half her views on Swami Shiva, on house buying, on their twins, on Pakistan and on where to buy South Indian spices in Delhi. Tito did a good job of keeping up and translating. She'd slapped him playfully on the back for his efforts, taken an interest in his tattoos. He had one om sign on his upper arm and some lines from the *Bhagavad Gita* just below his neck.

She laughed at it, clearly approving.

'What does it mean, Tito?' Stephen had asked.

'It's a line from the Gita I like. About work. No work stains a man who is pure, who is in harmony, who is master of his life, whose soul is one with the soul of all. Everybody's defined by what they "do" now. We forget that it's only a small part of our soul,' he said.

'Sita obviously likes that,' I noted.

Tito laughed. 'I think she sees the quote differently. She thinks it's about not getting into trouble or something,' he said.

I didn't really understand this but I loved her mischievous, vivacious streak. Sita had made the whole evening a party. She brought out some strong Kingfisher beer from her icebox and poured it into steel cups. She even had a sip herself from Raj's. At the end of the evening Tito rolled up a joint. I thought this might be going a bit far but he winked at her and she chuckled slyly.

Sita stopped talking only to serve us all elegantly with long thin dosa pancakes. By the end of the meal Stephen and I were both in love with her. Raj drove us home and we told him he was a very, very lucky man. He'd ducked his head in shy agreement. Stephen had said we should invite them back for fish and chips but that wasn't going to happen now, of course.

I didn't want to disturb Raj at his prayers, so wandered further out to the quiet road the centre was on. Left led to the main road, right to a dead end where an old banyan tree grew. I turned right. Branches spiralled around the thick trunk, reaching down into the ground, a forest in itself. I liked this tree very much. There were pieces of ribbon, fabric, tied to it, where people had made a wish, an offering to the banyan.

My mother had told my brother and I stories about this huge variety of tree when we were young. How the banyan's branches dived down to the underworld, picking up ghosts and goblins, who would climb up into the world and live around the trunk. This was a place souls hung out. People in

India worshipped the banyan, told stories of demons and gods, sitting in its shade. Mum had enchanted us with incense, just like the kind stuck now in the tree's tentacle roots, and told us those same stories, of lions breaking out of pillars and flying mountains.

I sat down among the branches and closed my eyes. Mum had educated us with many legends – from Wales, from Norse, from Africa, from the Bible and the Torah – but none had delighted me as much as the *Ramayana*. The little child god Krishna was vibrant blue and wild, while Jesus was wrapped in pale swaddling. The Welsh myth *Mabinogion* evoked a bizarre and magical landscape, but I'd been born to the Welsh mountains; Merlin and King Arthur were like next-door neighbours. Monkey gods and lords with elephant heads were more exotic. They lingered in the back of my mind like the spirits round the banyan tree.

When reporting at the *Echo* had become mundane, when the late-night deadline tea that had at first been so exciting dried into irritating morning rings on my desk, I'd decided to quit and move abroad to make my name and India was the first place that came to my mind. It seemed to my editor I had plucked the destination for my new life from nowhere. But I think the Hindu gods had worked their magic on me years before.

My editor had tried to persuade me to stay. He thought I was being impetuous. That I hadn't planned my trip properly. That I was being foolhardy just upping and leaving with no contacts and no job prospects out here. But I assumed everything would work out very well if I simply embarked honestly on my adventure with a good heart and a little tenacity. Because when you're good, good things happen, or so it had seemed up until a few days ago. That's what all my mother's legends had taught me.

And now? Well, with Stephen's death, the legends suddenly lost their power. They were just stories now. Or lies. Nothing to believe in, at least. I'd meant to tie my headscarf to the tree, as a prayer for Stephen. I thought maybe I'd be able to feel him around here, maybe we could talk. But I didn't feel him, no I didn't. I would keep my scarf for myself; it would be more use stopping me burning up in the sun.

I felt bad. I felt really angry with myself for being so soft and believing in goodness just because nothing really bad had ever happened to me. Now my best friend was dead and I was on the brink of being arrested, things didn't seem so simple. I had been spoiled. I should have been more prepared for life. You only have to look out of the window of a car in Delhi to know believing in any moral universe is bullshit. How exactly did that naked baby lying on the side of the road by a rubbish dump deserve such a nursery? What about the man with no hands and one leg who stands in the middle of oncoming traffic in the hope someone will stop to give him a rupee? How exactly had he provoked the gods into pissing on him so utterly? Life suddenly seemed scarily and nastily random.

I opened my eyes. I didn't know how long I'd been lying under the banyan tree but I figured I should make my way back. There was a rickshaw rank by the centre; I went towards it, angry at the world and Inspector Mukerjee most of all. Who was he to bully me? Drag me around with him? If he wanted to put me in a cell he could put me there. I wouldn't be threatened any more.

But the drivers weren't in their vehicles – they were all having paan at the small stall opposite the centre gates. By the time I noticed where they were I had thought better of my impulse to run away. I needed to be clever. I shouldn't make things any worse for myself. I didn't know if I wanted to leave India now or stay, but best to make the decision for myself, not get thrown on a plane by a pissed-off policeman, disgraced by the wrong visa.

I wandered towards the sleepy-eyed, nut-bellied paan wallah, shining in the afternoon light, like a little god himself. A paan wallah makes paan, a chewy affair of betel nut wrapped in green leaf that is taken all over India as a breath freshener, digestive and a mild high. A lot of people have a particular way they like their paan, with cinnamon or fennel, a little coconut, easy or heavy on the betel nut, rose or tobacco powder. Girls more often have it sweet with candied fruit or something. Making a good one is considered an art and this guy was particularly good. His tiny workspace was fastidiously arranged. Bottles were polished and lined up in order of size. He was a man who cared for his possessions. His ready-made tinsel strings of digestives, nailed to the wall, glowed behind him.

There were three drivers crouching on their haunches, chewing and spitting and engrossed in their Hindi newspapers. As I arrived they stood up, made room for me. One of them put his newspaper out for me to sit on. I refused, motioned that I would stand. But he insisted, pressing out the front page in the dust.

'Hang on,' I cried out, grabbing the paper off him.

I couldn't understand the Hindi typescript at all but the front-page picture made it clear what the story of the day was. It was a grainy photo of Stephen, smiling and happy outside Humayun's tomb.

I had taken that photo, on a day we had spent there. How had they got this? How could they use it like this without my knowledge or permission? I felt invaded. I saw a Facebook stamp at the bottom. They'd ripped it off Stephen's profile. I remembered now; he'd used it as his home-page picture.

67

Anger rushed through me. I began to sweat with indignation. But I quickly deflated. This was no worse than what I had done. And Sir Charles would have felt a million times worse than I could ever feel when he read my story, read that his grandson was dead. Guilt grabbed me round the waist again and squeezed me sharply.

I asked the men the name of the paper but someone called my name before they had a chance to answer.

'Ruby – come here, please.'

Inspector Mukerjee was standing at the gate with Swami Shiva and the students behind him. I left the stall and went over.

'Ruby, why didn't you tell me Stephen had a motorbike?'

'What? I don't know, you didn't ask me.'

The inspector growled. 'Come with me to the garage. One of these Japanese girls says she saw it in there. I need you to identify it as Stephen's.'

It wasn't there. There was nothing in the garage but the black Merc. We all stood around it like muppets, looking at our faces in its shining paintwork.

The inspector's eyes were beginning to widen and become dragon-like. He turned the full blast of his angry stare onto me.

'What? Don't blame me – I didn't mention it. Who said it was here?' I defended myself.

'I . . . I thought I saw it this morning,' said Kiki.

Kiki was meek and polite and not the sort of girl to make things up. She was incredibly shy; I imagined it had been very difficult for her to say anything at all.

'Perhaps, Kiki, you might have thought you'd seen it, when it was really another time? It's all very confusing at the moment,' said Swami Shiva.

'It's a possibility,' agreed Mukerjee.

The inspector only talked directly to Swami, treating the rest of us as if we were a class of small children.

'Yeah – but where is Raj? The Mercedes is here but he has disappeared,' I chipped in.

No one said anything, just kind of cast their eyes around for him.

'Why don't we ask the paan wallah – he's been there the whole time,' I suggested.

We all turned to look at the chubby wallah, picking his ears contentedly.

'Good idea,' the inspector said, grudgingly.

We trooped over.

'Ah, Swami, will you take a paan from me, please?' said Mukerjee.

Swami laughed a little shrilly. 'Ah, no, no, thank you, Inspector. Paan unfortunately is classed as a form of intoxication. Culturally acceptable and mild, but an intoxication nonetheless.'

'I'll have one,' I said. I liked paan. I liked anything that got you a bit fucked and I needed something to take the edge off right now, definitely.

The inspector turned towards me, getting that dragon look again, but then he let out a long breath. 'I guess you've earned it just now. You're at least starting to help me, not get in my way.'

The inspector ordered two paan and stood chatting with the wallah as he daubed red betel across two large leaves, picking and shaking his various tins, finally presenting us with two large green triangles.

The inspector popped it in his mouth and chewed thoughtfully and dramatically. Everyone was waiting for him to say something; I think he was enjoying his moment in the spotlight, he glanced around him ever so quickly to take in his audience.

'What did he say about Raj, Inspector? I got some of it, not all,' I said.

'He saw him drive off on a motorbike about half an hour ago. This man said Raj left just after you went off and fell asleep under the banyan tree. He said I should warn you to be careful sleeping under there; if you're not aware you could be carried off to the underworld.'

I wasn't sure if he was joking or serious. I think he was serious.

'OK, I will,' I answered solemnly, nodding to the paan wallah, who nodded solemnly back.

'Anyhow, he saw Raj drive off. He called out to him to see if Raj wanted a paan, but he ignored him, just went on,' said the inspector.

One of the Japanese girls began translating for the others. Soon they were squawking quietly together, which set the whole group off in a chorus of languages. Swami, Mukerjee and I stood thinking in silence.

'This is all very strange,' said Swami Shiva. 'Really I don't understand why Raj would have gone off without telling me. But I think perhaps I know why he has Stephen's bike. I think maybe he was helping him repair it. Yes, I think he mentioned that to me a few days ago.'

'He should have told someone he had Stephen's motorbike when he was found dead,' said the inspector.

He was still chewing the last bits of his paan. He stuck his tongue in his cheek and then spat red liquid out with a disgustingly loud belch. Swami Shiva flinched.

'I'm going to find him,' he said.

'Of course you should go to the garage and find him. Do you know what he looks like, Inspector?'

'No, I don't. Ruby, you'll have to come with me. You know the bike too.'

'What? I'm not your assistant.'

'Well, you're technically still under arrest, so it's either coming with me or dropping you off at the jail for the night while I go looking for Raj on my own.'

'You can't keep using that excuse to drag me round!' I said.

'Why not?'

I couldn't think of any reason so I found myself driving off with the inspector once more.

5

'Do you know where he lives?' Mukerjee asked me.

'A slum resettlement colony in the north, Dakshinpuri.'

'In Dakshinpuri? That's not a great place to live. Why does he not live at the ashram?' he said, inspecting his moustache in the wing mirror.

Dakshinpuri looked like hell from the outside, it was true. But once in its alleys, the place had a worn charm. Close calm quarters. The sounds of eating, talking, the day's cricket match on a radio floated out from the tightly packed homes.

Sita would have wholeheartedly agreed with the inspector though. The most enthusiastic speech she had made for us the night we visited, translated through a half-smiling, half-frowning Raj, was on her dislike for her colony and her house. There was no running water. The people in Dakshinpuri were all from the bad states, from Uttar Pradesh and Bihar.

Their house was just a plaster room divided by a thick blue nylon curtain with fluorescent flowers. The whole family, Raj, Sita and their three children, in the same place, eating and washing and sleeping. In Kerala, Sita's family had a house with four bedrooms. Raj explained Dakshinpuri was temporary, that they were living here because it was cheap and they could save more money to buy a house or flat in one of the new apartment blocks being built outside the city, maybe even in the new city, Gurgaon. Sita liked Gurgaon, liked the malls there.

'His wife and he are saving up for a house of their own, they're saving money by living in Dakshinpuri,' I told the inspector.

He frowned. 'Dakshinpuri is very close to Wazirabad Bridge. There's a temple on the south side of the bridge and the slum on the north side. Let's go there.'

'We're not going to the garage?'

'I want to talk to his wife first anyway.'

'Why?'

'Wives give good leads. They give away information they don't know is important. The very sight of a policeman usually makes them quiver with guilt even if they know nothing,' said the inspector, chuckling.

'And home is the first place people head in any stressful situation, so it's good to know where he lives,' he continued.

'You're talking about Raj like he's a suspect. He's Swami's driver for God's sake.'

The inspector arched his eyebrow. 'A holy man like Swami devoting himself to God does not necessarily mean all those around him are saints too. Look at Rani even, doing sex. With a man. There's one thing you learn in this job, it's not to go on first impressions. Instincts? Yes. Surface appearances? No.'

'It still doesn't make sense to turn Raj into some prime suspect without even talking to him first.'

'That's exactly what we're trying to do now. Talk to him. However, speaking as someone with fifteen years' experience

73

in homicide, sneaking around with the motorbike of a suspected murder victim does warrant suspicion.'

Mukerjee gave another chuckle and a little sigh of self-congratulation at his skills of detection. I didn't believe Raj had anything to do with Stephen's death but I wanted to get Stephen's bike back at least.

We turned towards the Oberoi flyover, past upper-class Khan Market and the Lodhi Garden tombs to the sprawling colony of tiny huts that had sprung up next to a north Delhi motorway and called itself Dakshinpuri.

Raj had led the way gracefully through his neighbourhood alleys on our first visit. I clumsily tried to remember his path, turning this way and that. People knew one another, I asked directions and eventually we came to his tiny bungalow. Sita was on the doorstep, throwing one of her twins up in the air and catching her just in time. She was laughing and so was the child. The other twin was clutching round her ankle, wailing to have a go. It didn't look like she knew Stephen had died, but then she must have done, Raj must have told her.

Sita saw me and broke into a wide smile, perching the kid on her hip and wiping the sweat from her brow. She looked like a child herself. Her smile dropped for a split second when she saw the inspector behind me, but it quickly reappeared, more beaming then ever. I wondered if the inspector noticed.

He puffed out his chest and put on a serious face, speaking to her like some pompous headmaster.

She didn't quiver with guilt. She was made of better stuff than that. Sita fluttered her eyes in thought, shrugged, glanced through her door, looked at the inspector and invited us all in for tea.

She shouted something out to the inspector as she checked in her milk can.

'Raj has gone to the dairy for some more milk, but we have

enough for tea,' said the inspector, scanning the small home. He picked up an envelope on the bed.

It was thick and padded with spidery Hindi letters written upon it.

Mukerjee stuck his hand in the envelope and stopped in his tracks. He looked inside the envelope and his air of astonishment grew. I looked around at Sita; she was standing with the twins, her eyes wide, watching the envelope. I couldn't work out if she knew what was in there or not.

'Something new, after fifteen years' homicide experience, Inspector?' I said.

He lifted a dragon eyebrow at me and pulled out a thick wad of banknotes. 'There's hardly a case that didn't involve this stuff.'

'Wow! Cash! But there's a lot of it, isn't there?' I exclaimed, delighted.

Sita put her hand over her mouth, her eyes widening in what could have been shock, fear or pleasure. Probably a mixture of all three, her mind whirring through possibilities.

We all stood there for a moment just looking at the money. The handful had hardly made a dent in the envelope. This really was a load.

'There must be three or four lakh in there,' said Mukerjee. 'What the hell is Raj doing with this kind of money?'

Mukerjee fired some questions at Sita. She shrugged, looked happily amazed; drunk on the idea of sudden riches. She leaned towards the envelope and made a swipe at it. It was hers after all, I guess.

Mukerjee leaned back, swung the envelope out of her reach.

'Oh no. This is evidence until we know what Raj is up to. It could be something to do with Stephen's case,' said the inspector, in English, I noted. Sita didn't speak English so that must have been for my benefit.

'Come on, let's go. Let's go find him at the dairy,' said the inspector, striding off, putting the envelope under his arm.

Sita shrieked after him. I followed after Mukerjee but turned to shrug an apologetic goodbye. Her face didn't look so pretty now, distorted with having so much so quickly and then having it all taken away again.

'What is she saying?' I asked.

'She wants the money back! Feisty little one, that one! Very attractive, Raj is a lucky man,' said the inspector with another one of his chuckles. He really was an oaf.

'Well, why are you taking it? It's not yours.'

'Because I want to know where the hell it is from! What is Raj doing with this amount of money and Stephen's motor-bike? Come on. I want to get to the dairy before he leaves. I warned Sita not to phone him, said I'd be back to arrest her if she did. I think she knows I was serious but I don't want to take too many chances.'

6

Raj shopped in Jangpura, a Punjabi neighbourhood of small streets, dead ends and tiny shops. When we arrived there, Stephen's red Enfield was parked outside the market.

'That's it,' I said.

'You sure?'

I nodded, it was a Chattisgarh number plate; Stephen had picked it up on an opium trip to the state and managed to drive it back smacked out of his head. He was always doing things that no one else would dream of and surviving. Then he fell in a river. I guess he used all his luck up too quickly.

The inspector turned off the ignition. 'Can you see him?'

There was a line of women with steel cans at the Mother Dairy, collecting milk before the milkman pulled down his shutters at five. Raj wasn't there. He wasn't at the fruit stall either. Then I saw him standing in line at the government wine and beer shop, his milk can already filled, white droplets sliding down the sides.

'He's there, at the wine and beer shop. That's weird,' I said.

'Keep your head down, I don't want him to see you.'

'Why not?'

'I want to see where he's going, what he's up to.'

I slid down my seat. I was enjoying all this intrigue, despite myself. It was like some C-class Hindi detective film or something.

Raj drove off with the milk can slung over his arm, clutching a brown paper bag filled with some bottles. It wasn't a lot compared to what you saw some men balance on the backs of their bikes – anything from beds to bales of hay to families of five, babies dangling by the exhaust.

We followed at a distance, through Bogle Market, in and out of pomegranate and pineapple carts, steel utensils shops, men selling underpants and oily makeshift garages.

We turned right from the market on to one of the big new roads, weaving between trucks, beat-up metal buses, brand new four-by-fours and a bee swarm of green and yellow rickshaws. We lost Raj.

'Damn. Damn,' breathed the inspector.

We got caught between two battered private buses racing each other along, vying for customers on the same route. They were lethal, these buses, always knocking people over and killing them, causing accidents daily, but they gave way for us.

'Traffic police are as important as homicide here, they share the same offices in Karol Bagh,' said Mukerjee.

We saw Raj again as we turned left under the railway bridge, going towards Civil Lines. We all got caught in a jam, waiting for the lights to change. The inspector put on his Ray-Bans and shrugged his shoulders a couple of times; he revved the engine as the train hurtled past and we got ready to go.

Suddenly we were on Wazirabad Bridge; the bridge Stephen

was supposed to have fallen from. This was out of town; the traffic was thinner.

'If we carry straight on we'll reach his neighbourhood. That's where he's headed,' said the inspector.

But Raj wasn't going home. He turned off after the bridge down a lane going towards the Tibetan colony, Majnu-ka-Tilla.

I knew the place because a few people who went to the Shiva centre stayed there. They wore 'Free Tibet' T-shirts, ate flabby steamed dumplings and smoked charas spliffs, gazing out over the river. You couldn't see the rubbish or smell the Yamuna stench from the guest-house roof terraces apparently and people said it was safer to smoke at Majnu-ka-Tilla. The colony was really a glorified refugee camp and the police hardly bothered to go there, only once in a blue moon to take bribes for the smuggling to and from China that went through the Tibetans.

The lane narrowed quickly to a dark path of hard baked earth between houses. We parked up and walked through swarms of flies, buzzing and knocking into each other and us.

'From the river, the sewage,' muttered the inspector.

'It stinks,' I said, putting my hand over my mouth. Stephen was sensitive to smells; I hoped he hadn't choked on this. I hoped the flies hadn't buzzed around him like this.

We saw Stephen's Enfield once more, parked outside the Smiling Buddha guest house. The inspector guided me into a dark chai shop opposite and ordered two teas. He sat silently sipping from a dirty little glass, his sunglasses still on, despite the shade. There were large sweat patches under his arms. Raj came out of the Smiling Buddha with a short Tibetan woman in traditional dress. She seemed to be giving him directions. He gave her some cash and wheeled the bike down the side of the guest house.

'He's going down to the river. We'll watch what's he's doing from the roof.'

The woman lifted her apron up in shocked defence as we marched into her grimy, cheery guest house. The inspector put a finger to his lips and walked straight up the stairs. The light was turning grey up on the terrace, the prayer flags dark shadows, flapping hard in the wind. We could see Raj clearly. He'd pushed the bike down to an old ghat. It would have been used for Hindu river worship, but the Buddhist Tibetans had abandoned it. I could see even from our vantage point that it was covered in bird droppings.

'No one to do proper pooja in this stinking colony,' said the inspector.

Raj took out his bottle from the paper bag and began pouring the contents over the bike. It looked liked one of those super-strength country-made liquors.

'He's going to set fire to it. To destroy the evidence,' said the inspector. He lifted up his barrel chest to heave a revolver from its holster. He took aim quickly. The shot rang out and echoed all around that sparse place. Raj screamed out once and dropped to his knees.

I ran down to find Raj writhing on the ghat, blood seeping out of his leg and onto the stone steps, mixing with the bird shit. His mouth was open and he looked like he was screaming but no sounds were coming out. His skin was contorted and stretched out of any recognisable shape by the pain. I didn't help. I just stood there, looking at him, amazed by how red the blood was. He didn't register me. His eyes were clamped shut. He kicked out his leg, knocking over Sita's milk that was still with him. It poured down the steps into the river, mixing with the blood to make a vibrant creamy pink.

Inspector Mukerjee was close behind. He wasn't thrown at all by this sight and took control in a way I never could. Behind my fear, hysteria and sickness, a small part of me noted that he did his job well. He'd picked up some sheets from the hotel and wrapped them tightly round Raj's leg, talking all the time in low calm Hindi, not in the pompous police tone he'd been using with me.

'Ruby, come on, don't cry – he's not going to die. I need your help to get him to the car. Take him under his arm. Good girl,' he said.

The three of us limped back to the car, Raj now moaning steadily, intoning prayers. The inspector lay him down on another sheet in the car before giving the Tibetan lady a flick of notes. She looked satisfied, happy to profit from this trauma.

'Bitch,' I said as we drove off, to no one in particular. I was mad and taking it out on her.

Raj grimaced and thrashed in the back of the car. He began to shout out. I didn't know if he was shouting out with the pain or anger. Was he shouting at me? Maybe he was calling me a bitch. I started sobbing. The inspector calmed us both, speaking in quiet Hindi and English alternately, while speeding fast to A and E.

The inspector took charge in the hospital too, shouting orders to nurses as we entered the ward. They rushed over to help and he went with them into an emergency theatre. I followed but was stopped on the way by a hospital orderly and taken to a cavernous waiting room.

I sat on a hard plastic chair in a line of hard plastic chairs. It was gloomy now and the room I sat in was huge and dark, like some vaulted Spanish cathedral. There were a few people sat far apart and alone on chairs, but more were on the floor. Families had set up camp down there, with cooking pots, paraffin stoves and cushions, like they were in the midst of some kind of pilgrimage, or a caravanserai. Their intimate movements were very dimly lit by far off electric light bulbs casting thick and wide shadows onto the walls. It felt like a scene of black enchantment. I would have thought I was dreaming except for my pounding headache and the taste of medicine and death in my mouth. I sat for some time in a daze, exhausted, without speaking to anyone, until I heard my name.

'Ruby. Take this.'

It was Inspector Mukerjee. I was relieved to see him. He handed me a plastic cup of machine tea, breaking whatever spell I'd come under. I blew on the froth, sipped it. The synthetic cardamom and sugar made my teeth sting, but it was good for me.

'What are all these people doing? It's like they are camping out or something.'

'They are. They're from the countryside. They've brought their relatives for treatment and they are waiting for them. They could be here for weeks. They won't go home without them, be it in a coffin or in a wheelchair or well and walking. That's the country way,' he said.

'Where's Raj?'

'He's having an operation on his leg now. He'll be fine, on crutches for a few weeks, but other than that fine.'

'Why did you shoot him?'

He took a sip of his own tea, watched a father and child passing food between one another, before answering.

'I was called out to a bank robbery once. Most of the customers had escaped and the robber was holed up in the safe. I was with a stake-out crew outside. A man with a gun and a bag of money suddenly burst from the bank. We all shot. He was in pieces in seconds. It wasn't the robber. It was an unlucky customer used as a decoy. I'll never forget the screams of his son and his brother as they ran to him through the gun smoke. I have been a very, very careful shooter since then. But I thought it was necessary today. Raj was about to burn Stephen's motorbike. Not only is that incredibly incrim-

82

inating behaviour, it would mean I'd lost an essential piece of evidence. I wouldn't have been doing my job if I'd have let that bike get burned.'

'Where is it now?'

'Mukesh collected it, it's at the police garage.'

'Have you spoken to Raj?'

'Not yet, I'm going to wait for the operation to be over and then we'll take him in for questioning. But he's looking to be in over his head with this. I can't work out exactly what has happened here but by the end of the night I'm pretty sure we'll know and it'll be a guilty plea. He'll go down.'

I started crying. I still couldn't believe Raj had anything to do with Stephen's death, but the money, the bike, the burning, everything seemed so suspicious.

'But what about Sita? And his children? He's got three, you know. The youngest is just a tiny baby.'

The inspector looked at me with a sorry frown, hovered a hand over my knee, but withdrew it, thinking better of the gesture. He sighed. 'Ruby, how old are you?'

'Twenty-six.'

'Hmmm. You seem younger.'

'Act it too.' I grinned through my tears.

'Listen, Ruby. This job is not pleasant. I deal with death and I deal with grieving people. I lock murderers up and their families grieve sometimes as much as the victims. It's hard. It's never simple. There is so much good in the worst of us, and so much bad in the best of us.'

'But Raj, really, I know him. I don't know what's going on at all here, but Raj is a good guy. He's noble, you know, kind, he cares about the ashram and his family. He's not a murderer. Stephen and Raj – they were friends.'

'Ruby, I'm sorry to say but you don't know this. We can't know every side of people, even those closest to us. And this man, how well did you really know him? You'd been to dinner at his house once. You had been driven in his car. But of course he would present his best side to a friend of his employer, a white woman at that. And you can't even speak his second tongue properly, let alone his mother tongue. How can you think you really know him?'

'I just . . . I just feel it.'

The inspector groaned with impatience. 'This isn't about feelings. It's about doing the job you've been given. It's my job to make sure homicide does not go unpunished. Because if it did, where would we end up? It's the conviction we need, for justice and to serve as a warning. I might not have liked your article, but I'll let you know, I understand that you needed to write it. Because if journalists didn't write about what they know, what would happen then?' he said.

'I'm sorry about it. I wish I hadn't written it. It wasn't essential,' I said.

'Well you caused us some bother but if we get a guilty plea now from Raj we can put it behind us. I won't be charging you with visa breaches, since you ended up helping me quite a bit. But make sure you get it sorted out before you write any more articles. I've got the number of someone in the External Affairs Ministry who can help you.'

'I don't know if I want to write another thing in my life.'

'Come on now. You're a good journalist. You'll be great if you keep at it. You've certainly got an eye for whom to talk to; I would have walked straight by that paan wallah and he was key. Come on, I'll drop you home. It's going to be a while before the anaesthetic wears off Raj and I can talk to him. I've got a long night,' he said.

7

It was over by the morning. The police released a statement claiming Raj Simhan had admitted he was guilty of Stephen Newby's death. They would still be collating evidence and statements but they had stopped looking for the man responsible.

The *Hindustan Times* did a double-page spread with graphics showing times and locations. I watched Inspector Mukerjee announce the case closed on TV. He looked delighted.

Swami Shiva declined interviews but issued a statement of deepest regret and said that his Delhi centre would remain closed until Stephen's burial.

Sir Charles was getting into Delhi that afternoon to arrange the funeral, which would take place on Friday, in three days' time. He wanted to meet me; I was to see him at his hotel in the morning for breakfast. I should have been petrified but I just felt numb. Guy got in touch, asked me to do a first-person account of the arrest, said it would be a killer article. He apologised immediately for the bad pun but I still refused; I told him I needed to sort out my visa first, but I really wasn't interested anyway. I wasn't sure I'd be telling the right story.

Raj was an instant celebrity. A photo of him in shades smoking a bidi by Swami's black Mercedes became the icon of the 'Stephen Newby Murder'. Raj was good looking, which must have helped his fame. His age was given as twenty-nine. Just three years older than me. I hadn't realised he was so young.

Headlines Today had a creative reporter who explained that given Stephen's background it was most probable that Raj was having 'dangerous liaisons' with Stephen and the murder was 'as the French say, a crime de passionelly'.

Every news channel, every newspaper, every website had a version of Raj's statement. I pulled it out of a copy of the *Hindustan Times* and folded it carefully into a notebook.

It had been another hot day. I was sitting outside under a tree. The students were in the middle of afternoon meditation. I was smoking some bhang. I don't usually smoke but it had been left over from Holi and it was too hot to work in the garage just then. Then it all went quiet. There'd been a power cut. The coolers stopped and all I could hear were birdsongs and chimes.

The local dairy sells off their ice cream for half price in a power cut to stop it all just melting away so I went to get some. I was a bit high but not too much and it wasn't a long way.

I pulled the car out but didn't look both ways. The centre's at the bottom of a dead end. No one comes that way unless they are going to a class – it's gridlocked just before it starts and silent when the students are in the hall. But I heard something smack into the car. I stopped and got out and saw

Stephen's motorbike spinning on the ground. Stephen was by the wall. He'd hit his head and there was some blood running out of his nose.

I thought about calling Swami Shiva. I heard the coolers had started again. They roar so loud no one had heard anything. Then the chanting started and I decided not to bother anyone. I put Stephen's bike in the garage and put him in my car to take him to hospital. I wanted to take him to A.I.I.M.S. hospital, the one near Panchsheel Park all the foreigners go to. But the traffic was so bad because of the flyover they are building there. I was stuck. I didn't want anyone to see Stephen so I put a towel I had in the front over him. I got out of the jam and stopped on a side street to see how he was. I pulled the towel off him and he hadn't been breathing. He was pale. There was no sweat on him and there should have been. It was so hot. I got scared. He was dead. I drove around with him under the towel till it got dark. I headed home to ask my wife for advice and when I got to the bridge, no one was on it at all. I thought I could just throw him in. He was dead anyhow. He would be in the holy river. I hadn't done it on purpose. I had done my best to help him. I didn't want my family to suffer. That's why I tried to hide it. I didn't want my family to suffer.

Flashes in my mind of Stephen's heavy body being heaved over the fence, his beads getting caught on the wire, made me sick to the stomach. Had Stephen really been dead? He was by the time the rag pickers found him in the morning.

How useless. How utterly useless. This story was stupid. Stupid. How could Stephen die in such a pointless way? And how could Raj act so idiotically? Even if he was stoned, it just didn't make sense to me how he could ever think throwing Stephen into the Yamuna was the proper thing to do. But then, as Mukerjee had pointed out, how much did I actually know about the man, or this country? Violence erupted suddenly here; a quiet scene could turn into a riot in a flash and people would die. I didn't really know how a man from the South, living in Dakshinpuri, valued the life of a white man.

Still, I couldn't make sense of it. In the very coldest terms, it didn't make a satisfying story. It didn't fit with the characters I had known. Mukerjee didn't think my judgements had foundation because I was foreign, but I knew people. And people didn't change that much from country to country. Everyone needed to sleep, to eat, to fuck, had families, friends, some kind of way to fill the days.

Raj wasn't stupid; he was intelligent. He looked after his children and worked extra hard to fufil his wife's dreams of owning a house. I didn't believe he would ever throw anybody or anything, dead or alive, unceremoniously over a fence into the Yamuna. He was Swami Shiva's driver; he'd been schooled in ashram ceremony and practised his prayers properly. He'd believe Stephen would need cremating or burying at least, with proper rites.

But then again, how do you know how you'll act in such an extreme situation? I'd acted in ways I didn't think myself capable of in the last few days.

Then there was that text message Stephen had sent me. About his father. I had a shocking thought that perhaps Raj was Stephen's father. But of course he couldn't be – he was only a few years older than Stephen. They just seemed much further apart in age because Raj lived a grown-up life and Stephen had no more responsibility than a teenager.

I cast my mind back to the morgue. I tried to force myself to visualise Stephen's body. Had there been bruises? Bruises that would show he'd been knocked down by a car hard enough to kill him? I just couldn't remember. There could have been, but my knees had given way within seconds of registering Stephen's face and all I had seen was the floor.

8

I hadn't much time the day Raj was charged to really think the whole thing through. The phone rang constantly: my mum and dad telling me to come home, friends asking me how I was, but mostly journalists, wanting an interview, talking with sickly, affected sympathy.

It was nearly dinnertime by the time I'd fielded all the calls. I was about to turn my phone off when the ashram number flashed up. It was Chewy. He said Swami Shiva wanted to see me with Rani. I took a rickshaw over straight away.

The air was dusky and smelled of coconut curry as I arrived at the centre. Pan clatter and laughter wafted from the kitchen, people happy at the simple thought of eating. I marvelled at that.

I walked across the ashram's grassy courtyard towards the low concrete dormitories at the back, painted pink, for residential yoga students. Rani lived in one of these basic rooms.

The light was fading; his desk light was on. I could vaguely see his silhouette through the mosquito screen, lying on his small single bed, knees bent up, hands resting behind his head on his faded yellow pillow, staring at the ceiling. There was his wooden desk, on top of which I knew were just two or three books on yoga, the *Bhagavad Gita*, a clock, a reading lamp. His threadbare red yoga mat was always on the thin space between his bed and his desk.

I knocked on the mesh door and went in, lingered by his desk. I had never been in his room alone. The first time I had seen it was on Holi. The gold paint had all been cleared up since.

'Are you all right, Rani?'

He continued to stare at the ceiling; there was no acknowledgement of my presence. But as I'd stepped into the room, a volt went through me so vivid I didn't think it could be me alone feeling it.

I sat down on the bed and took his hand and had a second rush. The last time we had touched was holding hands before Stephen's body had been uncovered. That wasn't a moment a body forgets.

Rani linked his fingers through mine, but continued to stare at the ceiling. I lay down next to him and put my hand on his forehead. He curled into a ball around me and began to cry. I put my arms round him.

So much intimacy, so much energy between us; when we were strangers, really. And as I kissed his forehead and shushed him quietly I realised I had even less idea of what was going on in this guy's head then ever before. I hadn't heard him speak since the morgue. His last words to me had been 'Ruby, I'm scared.' I'd told him not to worry, but then we'd both seen Stephen's features in the dead man's face and had collapsed onto one another. I can't remember a word Rani had said since then. His thoughts were more deeply embedded than ever, despite our legs and arms being twined together on his tiny bed.

I'd wished for the unknown dead body under the morgue sheet to bring Rani and I closer and well, I had got my wish. Stephen's death had brought us to this point.

Guilt. I felt a lot of guilt lying there. It should have been Stephen there with Rani. Stephen had been the one he really wanted.

Rani and Stephen. What had brought those two together? I'd thought it was their bond of lost fathers and exotic backgrounds. Stephen had said grandly they both came from the orphan tradition. Just a week or so ago I'd felt terribly left out and had fantasised about some tragic, glamorous background that would qualify me for their club, for their shared 'tradition'. My mum was a poet, it was true, but she was a resolute mother with a sensible, kindly husband. I remember an enchanting childhood full of colour.

Now something really terrible had happened to me and to Rani that we could share. But there wasn't anything romantic about it. Desperate grief had forced Rani to throw his arms round me, and I'd accepted his embrace knowing this. These kisses were guilty and seedy and full of pain. I pulled away. He had kissed me in the swimming pool, when he'd thought I was Stephen, differently, with a happier passion.

'Rani, Rani, Swami Shiva wants to see us.'

'I don't want to go anywhere, I just want to lie here.'

'How long for, Rani?'

'For ever. I don't know. Until he comes back.'

'He's not coming back, Rani.'

'Then I don't want to get up.'

'Please, for Swami Shiva, let's go. Or he'll come and find us here and that won't be good.'

That seemed to do the trick. Rani dragged himself out of his bleak bed.

We walked to Swami Shiva's quarters. Wooden floors, big

windows shielded by bamboo blinds. Orange cushions scattered over the floor. A low green-oak bed. It felt more Buddhist than Hindu, except for the brass om sign and the many photos of Swami and his students. This room was more sophisticated than the cheery yoga ashram reception. Swami was sat on his green bed, dressed in white as usual, his eyes closed, meditating.

I looked at the photos while I waited for him to come out of his trance. I liked the old black and white ones of Swami as a young man teaching a small class. Short-haired and supple-muscled, unrecognisable as today's grey-haired wise man. There was a nice one of Swami demonstrating an elegant tree with slender branch arms. The class gathered round him were mostly women, like now, when Rani taught. They wore baggy harem pants instead of high-tech yoga gear, but the girls in the pictures had the same dazed, adoring concentration I had seen in class and perhaps had on my own face, heads leaning forward, devoted eyes set on Swami. It looked like he'd had as many admirers as Rani. I would have fallen for him probably.

There were more recent photos too, even one of Stephen and me, at the last headstand workshop in the centre. There was Stephen, slightly lopsided in his jeans, feet floating in the air, for once free of his dirty Converse trainers, and there was me next to him. I felt loved. Swami must really care for us, his students, to have our photos up there in his private room.

When he came out of his meditation, Swami invited Rani and me to sit. Swami continued to sit in lotus postion, as did Rani. I tried to, but then settled for crossed legs and a bent back.

'Thank you for coming, Ruby.'

'It's not a problem, Swami.'

'This is a terrible day. One of the worst days.'

'I know, I know.'

'First Stephen and then . . . I mean I just cannot believe this. Raj has been driving for me for nearly ten years. And before that . . . well, I know his parents, his family in Kerala.'

'I still can't believe his statement. I don't believe it. Don't you think it needs more investigation?' I said.

'Ah, Ruby, you're a kind girl, a good soul; you don't want to see the bad in people. But I went to see Raj and Inspector Mukerjee today. To see for myself if this statement is correct. Raj stands by it.

'Who knows what a man will do when confronted by death, when confronted with losing everything. Only God can know. We only know Raj in this life. We do not know his past lives. Evil will find ways to penetrate a person when he is weak, in shock.'

'I guess.'

What Swami said kind of made sense, in a religious way. It didn't make me feel better or reassure me though. Rani didn't say anything. He was just sitting there, straight-backed as usual, but with roving eyes, his insides all bent up.

'What's going to happen to him?'

'Well, as he's pleaded guilty he'll get manslaughter. Some kind of deal the police often make. His sentence, I don't know. The inspector told me if it's ten years; he may get out in five. Mukerjee also told me that he'd had to confiscate a large amount of money from his wife,' said Swami.

'Yes – I was there. What was it?'

'Ah. I'm not quite sure. I assume it's Raj's savings. He's been saving hard to buy a flat for them all in one of the new colonies. This is what I wanted to talk to you about. I don't want Sita to suffer because of Raj's mistake. I want you and Rani to go down to Dakshinpuri tonight and give her this money. It's what Raj had made and a little more. Enough for the deposit.' Swami handed us a brown envelope, very similar to the one Inspector Mukerjee had taken from Sita in the first place.

I'd seen Sita on TV earlier. She'd been petrified, dragged to the door of their house, the white lights of the cameras reflecting off her skin and saucepan eyes, their youngest child screaming in her arms. Scrums of people ogled round her door. It was a day out for the crowds, like some medieval beheading.

'I don't want to go,' said Rani.

'Rani, why?'

'I don't want to help her, or him. They killed Stephen.'

'Sita had nothing to do with Stephen's death, Rani.'

'They all killed him. They killed him,' repeated Rani.

Swami frowned, his voice became low and quite hard. 'Rani, this is not the way to remember Stephen. You must learn to forgive even the most heinous crimes. If you do not keep your heart open and whole through this trauma, your work in the ashram is hypocrisy. Your life as a yogi is not true. You must not bind to yourself any joy, be it material or physical or personal,' said Swami.

Rani flicked his eyes up briefly and then to the floor. But they had stopped roving around. Swami once again had brought him back to normality. He had power over Rani like a father.

'OK. I'll go.'

'But where's this money coming from, Swami?' I asked.

Swami gave a small smile. 'Anonymous charity.'

Anonymous charity was a quirk of the Shiva network; a part of their finances that was never revealed.

Swami published the network's annual accounts every year. This wasn't a legal obligation, but various celebrity gurus from the 70s had fallen hard from grace, even been sent to prison, for fraud, extortion and tax evasion. Swami said publishing all his incomings and outgoings helped him use his earnings in the best way.

Swami might preach simplicity to his students but it was clear that the Shiva network made a lot of money. The accounts always made the news in India and were scrutinised for some days. He'd be slightly criticised in editorials for his Mercedes and his business-class flights but columnists acknowledged these were minor expenses compared to what the network made and ploughed back into its members and its charity work.

The one thing journalists really did make a fuss about was a tax-free 'Anonymous Charity' lump of money which the Shiva network said they donated to individual cases they felt worthy of assistance. Swami Shiva had come to an agreement with the Indian Inland Revenue about this and refused all accusations and calls to reveal the benefactors. I knew at least one of them now – Sita.

This was another scoop, at least in India. The family of a murder suspect was now going to receive money from the Shiva network. I could just see the headlines – SWAMI SHIVA – ANONYMOUS MURDER PAYOUTS.

But I would keep his charity anonymous. Sita needed all the help she could get. I looked over at Rani. He was taking no notice of our exchange but lying on the floor staring out of the window at a pair of lovebirds playing in a banyan tree.

'Maybe I should go on my own, Swami? Is Rani up to coming? He looks like he needs some looking after.'

Swami looked across; frowned. 'He will go. He should behave with discipline now. He should not retreat into his mind like this. A student of the Vedas should not be so attached to life. I've taught him this. Our soul never dies, only our physical body dies. We should neither fear death nor look

96

forward to it but revere it as a most exalted experience. Life, death and the afterlife are part of our path to perfect oneness with God. It's important for Rani to learn this through self-less karma,' said Swami. But he didn't sound as convinced as usual.

9

So I found myself once more in the lanes of Dakshinpuri, this time with Rani in tow.

It was dark now and wives were scrubbing the evening entrance to their homes clean. Bare bulbs buzzed, spreading dim light over people washing themselves and their dishes outside. Doors were open, letting in the slight night breeze after the baking hot day. There were few fans here – I imagined you'd just have to get used to dripping in sweat.

We found Raj's wife crouched down in her tiny kitchen area, her crying baby slung on one arm. She was trying to feed the thing from a steel plate of mashed-up rice and milk on the floor. The curtain was pulled back. Raj's toddler twins were lying on the large bed, which was also the sofa, table and safe, on the other side of the room, watching an Indian soap listlessly.

Sita recognised me as I bent down to call through the door. She wailed, pounced and grasped me desperately. When we'd come round to dinner her strong hands had grabbed my cheek playfully, now her fingers coiled round my arms. It hurt and it scared me. I wanted to prise her off and run away. But I saw Rani backing out towards the door and that made me mad at both of us.

'Rani, you're weak,' I spat, putting my arm around Sita and sitting her on the bed. She gave up her grip in a fit of sobbing, crying out in Hindi. I think she was saying her life was fucked.

I was repulsed by the scene; repulsed by my ineffectual pity. I wished she would stop grabbing me; I hated her for the severe guilt that was brewing inside me. But I hadn't done this to her. It was her husband who had ruined her life.

'Give her the money, Rani,' I said, eventually.

He brought out the envelope and handed it to her. Sita pushed it away, yanking her hair and screaming.

Rani was pale and kept opening his mouth and then closing it again and shaking his head.

'What's she saying, Rani?' I asked.

'She doesn't want money, she wants her husband back. She's saying he would never have done anything to hurt anyone, especially not Stephen. She doesn't believe he made that statement.'

I guessed this was noble of her but I just felt angry. Angry she couldn't have seen how lucky she was when everything was fine. I wanted to shake her and say how does Dakshinpuri look now? Now how does the brand-new flat seem? Like a dream come true? If Raj and Sita had been living at the ashram maybe this wouldn't have happened. I wanted to scream and cry and wail and moan about Stephen but I stopped myself. I kept it all inside because that was the best thing to do, for me and everyone else.

'I don't know what to say, Ruby. Ruby, I don't know what to say to her.'

'Tell her we aren't going to let anything bad happen.'

This was a feeble promise I didn't know if I could fulfil, but what could I do?

Rani got up. 'Ruby. Please. I have to go, I can't breathe,' he said. His hands were shaking and he dropped the envelope with the money in it on the floor. I slid my arms from around Sita and picked the envelope up and placed it on her pillow. Sita might not want it now but I guessed she would soon. I viciously imagined her drying her eyes, picking it up and counting it as soon as we left.

The twins, stirred by the commotion, were sitting up, eyes wide, clutching one another. The baby was lying on the bed gurgling. Sita pulled the twins towards her, looking up at Rani and I with red eyes; black hair matted to her face with sweat and tears and torment. She wasn't accusing, just desperate. I felt guilty again. How had Raj thought that throwing Stephen in the river would make things better? If he had run him over and then owned up he wouldn't be in prison now and maybe Stephen would even be alive, recovering in hospital dramatically, milking sympathy for all he was worth.

We walked back along the lanes, dark and quiet now, the houses shut up. Stray dogs had started to wake, gathering in packs for a night of fighting and galloping through the slum. Soporific and cowardly by day, Delhi dogs got braver, wilder and more vicious as the night went on. We needed to get a move on and get out of here. I'd put Rani in a rickshaw and take one back myself to Nizamuddin. The thought of him coming home with me flashed through my mind.

Home alone was not appealing, negotiating my dark way past goats to get to our flat. The flat Stephen had been so proud of finding – so cheap because no other foreigners would live around the *durga*. Because they preferred being near nice restaurants and cafés and gardens to wild-eyed pilgrims, mutilated beggars, train horns and holy men. So did I. I'd like to go and sit in Greater Kailash bookshop now with a cappuccino or a Defence Colony pub with a beer and a notebook. But all I'd be able to get was an hysterically sweet glass of tea or a kebab from a chicken killed in front of me. Anger rose up inside me against Stephen. Why had he always had to live on the edge, to create such a myth of danger around himself? That hadn't really been him. He could be quiet. He liked reading and drinking in Def. Col. as much as the next person.

I thought of the Oberoi Hotel nearby. Stephen and I used to go there when we wanted a treat, though when we were there he'd sneer at other ex-pats drinking oversized bottles of Kingfisher, the paunchy consultants with whisky and sodas, or rich Delhi kids from the American school drinking flamboyant cocktails. But now I could think of nothing better than having a gin and tonic, surrounded by rich white people, feeling safe. I'd thought I was a liberal, living by a Muslim shrine in Delhi, seeing everyone equally, regardless of colour or religion, but I was just as scared of the unknown as anyone.

Rani swooned suddenly. I grabbed his arm, helping him stand. But he was frail and shaking.

'Oh, Rani, you're hit even worse than me. God. My God. It doesn't matter if you're South Indian, or British, in a slum or a bloody palace, this is fucked whoever you are. Stephen is dead.'

10

Sir Charles was staying at the Imperial Hotel, Janpath, Central Delhi. It was the most eminent of the city's many five-star hotels. A grand white colonial mansion with cool arches, green lawns, armies of servants, marble floors, strewn with Indian art lifted from all over the country.

Bored teenagers and Japanese businessmen perched on the plush pink sofas littering the lobby. Groups of tourists ogled at the luxury. I asked for Sir Charles at reception. The black-suited manager immediately flicked his eyes up.

'Ms Ruby?' he said.

'Yes – that's me.'

'He's swimming. Please, I'll show you the way,' he said, scurrying from behind the reception desk, leaning forwards in his hurry to get to the pool.

Well-heeled customers sat on the terrace under large linen parasols. A nut-tanned Euro-woman in a hot pink bikini and Dior shades was sucking hard on a cigarette. A fat, grey-haired dude in Bermuda shorts cradled a cappuccino, playing footsie with a giggling younger guy; I think he was Thai. A respectable Indian mother was loudly telling her chubby son off for not eating his croissant. There was just one, excellent swimmer in the pool. I could see grey hair and green goggles as his head turned to the side in a fast front crawl. Sir Charles.

He noticed us quickly and pulled himself out of the pool with ease. The attendant was immediately by his side with a towel and blue shirt. Sir Charles rubbed himself down elegantly, then wrapped the towel around his waist and buttoned his shirt loosely. He looked very good.

'Ruby.' He clasped both of my hands, looked me in the eye. It was the practised shake of a man who makes his way easily round the world. I saw now where Stephen's urbane ease came from.

'Please, let's have breakfast,' he said, taking me by the shoulder as Stephen used to and guiding me to one of the tables.

My heart was soggy in my chest, soaked in emotion and expectation at talking to this man. Guilt crawled around my skin with the knowledge that Sir Charles had found out about his grandson's death from my news article. He was able to act as if this was a pleasant breakfast appointment, although it was clear from the catch in his voice that he was brimming with feeling too.

A waiter moved his chair out quickly and Sir Charles glanced up slightly, nodded his thanks before ordering.

'I'll have the continental breakfast, but no Danish pastries, just croissants and pain au chocolat. Ruby?'

'Er, I'll have the same.'

'Are you sure you won't have something more? You look half starved. You're much smaller than I thought you would be.'

I shrugged.

'Apparently they do a good English breakfast here. I can't

103

imagine you have sausages often. I remember Stephen complaining he hadn't had a good sausage in months. Cecilia and I sent him some salami but it's not the same as an English banger.'

'No, no, thank you,' I said. I hadn't eaten properly for days and usually I would have loved some sausages but my mouth was still bone dry at the thought.

'Or what about an omelette?'

'Honestly, croissants are fine – really.'

'And to drink, sir?'

'Do you use leaf tea?'

'Yes, sir.'

'Good, well, I'll have an English breakfast blend and Ruby . . . ?'

'The same. My favourite,' I added, not wanting him to offer me several alternatives.

'Also, two orange juices, please, freshly squeezed, and today's newspapers, all of them,' said Sir Charles, managing not to sound pernickety.

Once the waiter had disappeared, Sir Charles seemed to deflate slightly.

'My wife Cecilia would have joined us but she isn't well at all. She's been taking sedatives and is still sleeping.' Shadows moved across his face.

'I'm sorry. How . . . When did you find out?'

'Of course it would have been a shock any way we had been told. But it was most horrible for us. We found out Stephen had died from your newspaper article. I recognised your name first, actually. Stephen had talked about you.'

'I'm sorry,' I said, the guilt rising up my throat to my face.

'Yes, the *Telegraph*. It was Saturday. The papers were thicker than usual and we were eating bacon. I turned to the international pages first, as always. "Exclusive", it said.'

'I'm so sorry,' I said.

'It was, I think, the worst moment of my life. It'll never leave me. The butter dish by my side, the smell, the steam from my coffee, holding the newspaper out in my usual position, staring at the usual typeface, the typeface I'd been reading for the last thirty years. Staring at the news that your grandson – son, really – is dead. But no, it wasn't the worst moment. The worst moment came just a second after, when I looked over at Cecilia, taking a bite of her toast. She was examining paint swatches. I think my heart broke then, knowing what I was about to do to her.'

The croissants were suddenly put down, in a quaint breadbasket with a white cloth spread over to keep in the heat. Sir Charles signed and leaned back in his chair, waiting for the waiter to clumsily lay down silver cutlery and plates, the teapot and the orange juice. I looked down at the table. There were no marks on the white cloth for me to concentrate on.

'Please, Ruby, have a croissant – they're warm,' Sir Charles said, his charm returning, passing the basket to me.

I took one and bit into it flatly.

'Have some tea too, I think it's brewed enough now,' he said, opening the pot, peering inside and passing it over.

I poured some tea. 'Sir Charles, I'm sorry. I had no idea you were going to find out about Stephen from the paper. I wasn't thinking straight. I'm sorry.'

'Ruby, on the contrary, I'm happy you wrote that article.'

'What?'

'The moment I found out about Stephen would have been most terrible, whether it had been in a phone call, or an article or anything else.'

'I was told you were furious.'

'I was furious with the police. A full investigation should have been launched as soon as they realised Stephen was

British – and the embassy should have been informed straight away, before ringing up this yoga centre. I saw Inspector Mukerjee last night and told him as much. He agreed completely, told me he'd given his juniors hell for not informing the embassy when they were supposed to. But really, Mukerjee only got going himself after your article. He strikes me as a good detective but somewhat erratic.'

Relief flooded through me.

'Stephen talked about you at Christmas you know, when he was home.'

'Did he?' I couldn't help smiling. I would never have known. I took another bite of croissant.

'But Ruby, what I really wanted to talk to you about, before Cecilia wakes up, is this search of Stephen's for his father. I, we, had no idea about it,' he said, shaking his head.

'He hadn't told anyone here but me and Rani, a friend of ours. He was just desperate to find out where he came from – he didn't want to hurt you.'

Sir Charles smiled painfully. 'I never gave him the chance to talk about it.'

'He found the whole thing really difficult. Sometimes it would all come out in a flood, but most of the time he didn't mention it at all. His father was just in his imagination mostly anyway. He knew very little. I got a text from him the day he died, talking about his father. I don't know if he'd found something out or not. I thought maybe it had something to do with his death. But then the whole thing exploded with Raj and it wasn't anything to do with that. So he died not knowing I think, without completing his mission here.'

'It's clear what happened to Stephen now; there's no need to drag his missing father into this media circus. I just wish I could have spoken with him about it before he died. I retired last year. I've kept up with Climate Change policy but other than that I've been free. It's the first time in years I've had time just to go over memories. Live in the past a little. I was coming to a conference here next month and we'd been planning a trip. I was going to discuss what I knew about his father with him.'

'Was there much to tell him?'

'To be honest with you, no. Claudia, my daughter, well, she had been difficult. Wild. She came home from India pregnant; we hadn't any idea what she had been up to. We tried to get her to tell us who the father was, but she screamed it was none of our business. We said we'd talk about it after the baby was born – we didn't want to make her ill. Only when Stephen was born did we realise his father must be Indian. We'd assumed it was just another student like herself. We should have twigged with all the joss sticks and chanting she was doing. He was such a beautiful baby. We were all delighted with him, really. Claudia called him Stephen after Anna Karenina's brother; it was her favourite book at the time. A little ill thought out, he's not a great hero of literature. But it shows how young she was, how little she really knew about characters, in books or real life. She was just a child herself and perhaps we left off asking her about the father because we weren't too sure we wanted a very strange far-off man coming into our family. We preferred to live without the truth.

'Claudia pretty much forgot about Stephen once she got to university. There were hysterics when we even mentioned that she was his mother and might come back at weekends. But in the holidays she would smother him with kisses and presents and sweets, desperate for him to love her more than anyone else. It was very hard for Stephen, very confusing. I should have stepped in, but I was very, very busy and in truth a little scared of my daughter.'

'Stephen told me she died in a car crash.'

'Yes, that's right – in South America – when he was about seven. We were devastated obviously. We loved her. My wife has never been the same since – had to spend time in hospital afterwards and is on and off antidepressants even now. But deep down I felt that this would mean Stephen had a better chance of growing up a normal boy. He was a lovely child, very intelligent. He wasn't affected too badly by Claudia's death. When he called me Daddy I let him. Later we told him his father had died with Claudia. It was wrong. We should have told him the truth, but we'd had so much drama. We just couldn't face the saga of Stephen's mystery father – and all we had were a few girlish diaries to go on anyway.

'Then Stephen dug out his birth certificate from my study – for some school project on national records. I didn't use the room much, preferred working in the breakfast room, only used the study for storing files and books. I'd only gone in to turn the clock forward for British summer time. I found him with the certificate in his hand, staring out of the window. The birds were singing and the sky was very red and the certificate said his father was unknown. How could I explain?

'I told him about Claudia's visit to India and that he could take a holiday while this project was on – I'd explain to his teacher. He was very quiet that summer and in the autumn he went to boarding school. We never did find the right time to talk about it properly afterwards. Every morning I'd wake up with the conversation I needed to have with him flickering round my mind, but the thoughts got burned away with the sun and by breakfast I was thinking about conferences, meetings, policies. My work's been very important to me . . .'

Sir Charles turned and looked out towards the swimming

pool where the Indian family was now playing. He was crying. I didn't know what to say. 'I think talking to Stephen about his father would have helped him.'

'Was it very important to him?' Sir Charles asked.

'He said it was the reason he was here in India. But you know, just soaking up the country was part of understanding who he was, I think. He'd daydream about his father, who he might be. Maybe a politician, maybe a Bollywood star, maybe a poor but noble rickshaw driver. He enjoyed making up stories about himself – he told me he had yogic blood in him. It was only the reality – how unlikely it was that he would ever find this man – that upset him. The futility of the task he'd set himself got him down.'

'Do you know if he'd got anywhere at all?'

'He had so little to go on – Claudia's address book – he'd taken it from you secretly – you know that now. There was a first name in the front – Rao – written over and over again. Some names and addresses of people she'd stayed with here. But these people had nearly all gone.'

'He found nothing out?'

'The closest he got was when he found an Indian school friend of his mother's – Laxmi Patel. They'd been in the same house at boarding school and she'd had Claudia to stay when she first arrived. Laxmi was lovely to Stephen, had him over for tea at her house. She lived in one of those big bungalows near Khan Market. Laxmi told him she hadn't seen Claudia after she'd left her house but knew she'd been living in the old Mughal city. Stephen found an address in the back of the book for an Old Delhi mansion, Haksar Haveli.'

'And he thought that might have been his father's house?'

'Yes – the address was written in a different script, kind of scratchy and male, not used to English. Everything else was in this big, loopy girlish scrawl.'

'And did he go there?'

'Yes. Rani and I went with him to help, but it wasn't a success.'

11

It had been a few weeks before Holi, and it was the first time any of us had been to Old Delhi. Stephen and I were lazy tourists. Delhi was crammed with historic monuments and tombs but the only one we'd managed to visit was Humayun's tomb, right opposite our flat in Nizamuddin.

Rani had been halfway across the world teaching yoga but Old Delhi just wasn't his kind of place – mosques and meat and hustlers. He didn't ever have any reason to go and visit. It was a world away from the middle-class New Delhi colonies where his fans lived.

The trip started off fun, jumping down the steps of the metro. The concrete gleamed.

'This is better than the Jubilee line,' joked Stephen. He looked homesick, perturbed.

We clambered out of the metro at Chandi Chowk into a crazy mash of medieval scooters and horse-drawn carts, boys with birdcages and beggars dancing on bloody stumps.

A ripple of excitement went through the crowd of cycle rickshaw drivers hanging round the entrance when we appeared from below. We were cash elephants, especially me, shiny white, towering above these wiry men. After a scrum we were hustled into the ancient cart of a black-eyed man with a ragged sarong. I couldn't believe the guy would be able to move us an inch – he was half the size of me. But he stood up on his bike and, using every single bit of his body, got up a pretty good speed.

Stephen prodded Rani to speak to the guy in Hindi, to tell him to take us to Haksar Haveli, but Rani couldn't take his hand from his mouth. A vegetarian all his life, he retched at the sight of a butcher's stall piled high with severed goats' heads. He grabbed hold of my hand and I held on to it for as long as possible. Stephen tried to show our driver the address he'd carefully copied out of his mother's book, but the man just ignored him, confidently assuming we must want to go to the red mosque, where all the tourists went. He stopped at the wide civic entrance, where families and friends sat sunning themselves on the step. Stephen poked him to drive on but he refused to move another inch, just kept pointing at the mosque and saying, 'Allah.' We eventually got out and gave him fifty rupees, which Stephen grumbled was too much, and he rode off happy.

'We might as well go up the minaret now we're here. Rani needs a rest from seeing all that meat anyhow, he can't even talk,' I said. Stephen agreed but looked edgy. He kept fumbling around with the piece of paper in his pocket, getting it out and checking the address hadn't disappeared or something.

As we walked through the courtyard of the mosque, the pigeons flew all round us. We climbed up a narrow staircase to the top of the minaret. It was the first time up there for all of us, tourists in the city we lived in. I won't forget being up high in the dusk with these two friends; clinging to the rail squashed in with white-capped teenagers, all of us staring out at the orange skyline, our hands touching, the wind making the boys' pyjamas flap.

But shadows were creeping over the city and Stephen was restless. He wanted to find this Haveli. I suggested we just come back another day but he insisted.

We pushed our way through the side streets around the mosque. It was black now, the shops lit by bare bulbs and buzzing gaslights. I wanted to stop and look at the gold jewellery and piles of glinting cooking pots but Stephen rushed Rani and me along. The crowded narrow lanes were frustrating him; tight groups of black burkas pushing around him, cycle rickshaws not caring if they ran him over. He gave up on the small inaccurate map he'd brought and started asking lazy-eyed shopkeepers directions to Haksar Haveli. They waved him off to side streets he would follow with fervour, but they all turned into dead ends: a few chickens, a water pump, a crack of light from a door, cooking smells, families shut up for the night. Rani and I strung along behind him, trying to help, whipped up but without his genuine urgency. Rani began to speak Hindi to the shopkeepers. They understood, became more alive and animated, but then mostly ended in a shrug. The streets began to feel sinister: stray dogs waking up, the odd sleeping rickshaw driver, sounds of a fierce argument in screeching Urdu piercing the black. There were no street lights.

Stephen gave up in the middle of the shoemakers' street; just dropped down with his head in his hands. Rani and I stood by awkwardly, not knowing what to do. Shopkeepers packing away their sandals and slippers looked at us oddly. In the end I crouched down and put my hand on his shoulder.

'Come on, Stephen – why don't we get something to eat? I'm starving.'

He looked up at me with red eyes. He'd been crying, but

113

he smiled. 'You're always bloody hungry. Come on then.'

Down the blackest alley yet we found a fluorescent-lit court-yard where boys in greasy brown pyjamas stirred brass vats. A smell of oil and meat fat hung in the air. Flies gathered round the strip lights, but the place was clean; there were families round the red plastic tables.

Stephen had recovered his composure by this time. He nodded to the waiters hanging around the cash register and walked past a cracked sink to sit at a table in the far corner. He lit a cigarette. I took one off him too. Rani looked uncomfortable, averted his eyes like we were doing something dirty. I felt bad and wondered how I would smell to him now if he kissed me. Stephen ordered in pidgin Hindi: chicken for us, some vegetables for Rani. The waiter curled his lip at the idea of greens. He informed us that vegetables had to be specially prepared and would take longer.

Rani said he didn't mind not having anything, he didn't like eating outside the ashram anyway, let alone at a place such as this. But his hands were shaking slightly when he lifted his glass of water to drink and Stephen insisted.

'You look like you're about to keel over, Rani; seriously, I'm worried you'll faint,' he said.

Rani tried to smile but it just came out as a creasing of the face. We all sat in silence, hungry and wary. Stephen and I smoked another cigarette hard until the waiter returned with our food.

Rani looked miserable but I dived in. I was starving. I ripped the bloody flesh off the little bones and wrapped it in naan. I looked across at Stephen; he was doing likewise. We went for the same piece, our greasy, reddened fingers locking over it. We laughed conspiratorially to one another.

I hadn't ever really eaten Indian food before I came to Delhi. I preferred pizza and pasta and sushi. But Stephen was

114

a kebab connoisseur. He always maintained the city's *khati* rolls were the reason to live in Delhi. The city loved its meat grilled on a barbecue then wrapped in bread and sold this *khati* roll snack everywhere: stalls under flyovers, hatches and five-star hotels. Stephen knew them all and we'd toured them extensively. The Khan Cha-cha hatch in Khan Market didn't look much but was high-class. Little foil-wrapped rolls of spicy chicken, light enough for the petite rich girls, perching prettily in tight jeans against their cousins' and boyfriends' scooters.

The tyre garage near our house turned into a kebab shop at night. Skullcapped boys set up their little barbecue after evening prayers, fanning the coals with waves of reeds and frying bread on an upturned wok. It was where big cars with Punjabi number plates stopped for their door-stopping wraps. We'd sit on the tyres, letting the oil and coriander sauce drip down our fingers, slices of chilli-flecked onion falling from our mouths. We'd grin at each other in the flickering firelight and agree that although the setting was hellish the food was heaven.

Our favourite *khati* roll shop had to be Nizam's, though.

It served single egg chicken rolls, double egg chicken rolls, single mutton chicken rolls, double egg mutton rolls. Not much else. The Formica green interiors, the prices and the sign telling people they could speak in Hindi if they wished hadn't been changed in decades. It felt like a strange Mughal American diner, apart from the sound system, which played happy hardcore and Northern soul. Steven told me the owner's son had studied in England during the early 90s and had got into Ecstasy and raves. He'd tried to open a nightclub on his return but it had flopped and his dad's late-night chicken roll shop was as close as he got to opening Delhi's Hacienda.

The food in that Old Delhi joint we rocked up at was nearly as good as Nizam's – and without the insane throbbing beats.

'Stephen, well done for finding this place, it's good, man. Good chicken! We'll come back,' I said brightly, trying to cover up my tiredness.

Our table was now covered in debris: screwed-up napkins, curry-crusted copper bowls full of tiny bones, a small piece of naan and a couple of soggy tomatoes on the floor. Hunger had replaced our real mission of finding Haksar Haveli for a while, but this mess was all that was left of our failed adventure.

'I didn't like it. It wasn't that good. It left a bad taste in my mouth actually, bad spice mixture I think.'

'What are you talking about, Stephen? It tasted really good. Anyway, we've got to come back to find this house.'

He reddened and looked down at his plate. 'I don't want to come back here and I don't want to look for the house either.'

'Come on, cheer up. We'll find it,' I said, patting him on the shoulder.

He just sat there, fiddling with his fork, concentrating on scraping it through a congealed piece of fat again and again, trying to rub it into the plate. Rani and I sat mute, in sharp relief against the noise and the smells and the shouts of the restaurant blurring behind us. Stephen looked up at the oily ceiling. The fluorescent bulb reflected a welling of tears in his lower eyelashes.

'I don't know, you can overdo this kind of thing you know. I'm sick of kebabs. Let's get pizza tomorrow. I'm not even sure I want to find my dad's house; I'm not sure I like it round here. I had all these ideas about what Old Delhi would be like, like a fucking Ghalib poem or something, sandalwood incense and doves wafting around. But it's not, it really stinks around here, and there's pigeon shit everywhere.'

'It smells, but it doesn't stink,' I said, trying to make a joke, cheer him up.

'It does stink, just like my fucking father does. I've always thought he'd be such a hero, but actually when you think about it, of course he won't be. Imagine, getting a young girl pregnant and just fucking off,' said Stephen.

'And he never went back?' asked Sir Charles, after I had finished telling him.

'Not that I know of.'

'How long ago was that?'

'Not so long. A few weeks ago. We didn't hear much about his father after the trip. He went quiet on it and I didn't want to pry. I think he was trying to decide what to do. He was less sure he'd find his father after going to Old Delhi. He found out that the name written in his mother's notebook – Rao – could be a Hindu or Muslim name. Stephen thought if he had lived in Old Delhi he was probably Muslim and he began to think he could even be in Pakistan now,' I said.

'If his father was Muslim and hadn't moved before Partition it's probable he didn't move afterwards. He could be living in the nice part of Nizamuddin for all you know,' said Sir Charles.

'But it was already like searching for a needle in a haystack – then suddenly it was like searching for a needle in two haystacks, with visa restrictions and a military border between them. And Stephen just seemed really disillusioned with the whole idea of his father anyhow; I don't know why this trip broke him so badly but it did, he really hadn't liked it round there.'

'So he'd basically given up?'

'I don't know – he wanted to talk to me about his father before he died. He sent me a text message saying he had a story about him. He could have found another lead. Maybe Mrs Patel had remembered something else. He could have just wanted to talk and had been overdramatic.'

'As was his wont.' Sir Charles smiled weakly.

The waiter was serving lunch by the time I left. Caesar salad for the woman in the pink bikini, club sandwiches for the Indian family. The guy with the Bermuda shorts had taken his friend back to his room. Sir Charles was due at the city mortuary to see Stephen, but suggested I stayed at the hotel and had some something to eat too. But I still didn't feel like food and he had a hotel car drop me back at Nizamuddin instead.

12

Back at the flat I wandered around in shock, the adrenalin of the last two days draining out of me. I stung all over. The doorbell rang. It was the girl from the hotel downstairs, Rajeshree, who came round to clean. She was about my age and I'd tried hard to bond with her. She'd giggle at my faltering Hindi but nod when I offered her a cup of tea. Today, she looked sombre and asked me how I was. But I didn't have the words or heart in Hindi or English to explain it all to her. I shook my head and shut the door.

All the grime and the dirt, the trail of mess Stephen left behind him because he was careless and clever and frantic was going to dry up. The toothpaste would not be crusty once I had wiped the top once again. The kitchen was already looking cleaner; the lingering smell of his soy sauce-drowned stir-fry was fading. I looked around at Stephen's posters, at the cushions he'd bought in Jaipur. What was going to happen to them all? What was going to happen to the flat? Could I live here without him? What about the rent? Everywhere I looked there were invisible outlines of him, memories imprinted on my eyes: asleep on the sofa, working at his desk, smoking a cigarette on the balcony, flicking through his music collection.

I'd had a strong sense that Stephen and I would grow old knowing each other. I'd found him with such accidental ease and not much seemed to happen easily for me. My Delhi life had fallen into place so magically I'd believed he and I to be a blessed match.

Stephen had calmed me. I'd slept well that first night I moved in with him, waking up with the early morning trains and the first light coming through my window. I lay listening to those horns, smugly believing myself to be born lucky. I didn't think I could ever feel like that again.

I wandered into Stephen's room for the first time since the morning of my birthday, before I'd had the call saying he might be dead. A pearly peppery sheen covered the surfaces; that fine layer of dust that slid over Delhi homes within hours of their being cleaned. My throat constricted. I took his laundry and his bed sheets out to the washing machine. They smelled bad but good, of Stephen. I carefully folded his clothes, his orange T-shirt, his frayed jeans, his Reebok trainers and put them back in his drawer.

There was a photo hidden in there, an old one, but colour, of a young woman. I knew straight away it was his mother. She was pale, much paler than him but she had the same gleam in her eye. Her hair was red and long and tossed back in a defiant way. It looked like a holiday, she was wearing a blue bikini by a pool. Her mouth was open wide in a laugh or a shout. She didn't look horrid or unkind but she did look like she could have been wild. I took the photo and put it in my wallet. I would give it to Sir Charles.

I picked up a book by Stephen's bed, a brand-new and hardly touched biography of Nehru and put it back with his dog-eaten

Salman Rushdie and Hanif Kureishi, his Stephen Kings, his Tolstoy. The boy read. Did any of it help him as he was dying? Or had all his reading been pointless? What was he thinking when he splashed into the river? Was he scared? Did he know he was going to die? Was he already dead? Did he think of us as the dirty, stinking water was choking him? Did he regret not finishing *War and Peace* like he kept saying he would?

He still had my copy of *Shantaram* in his room. Stephen had laughed at me when I was reading it; said he couldn't think of anything worse than reading an 800-page novel about an escaped convict on the run living in Bombay. He'd rolled his eyes every time we passed another holidaymaker with their eyes glued to one more new edition.

'It's not even set in Delhi; it's a Bombay book. Why is everyone so obsessed by it here?'

'It's not about where it's set. It's just it turns the pages on its own. I mean, you just can't put it down once you've started. Everyone loves that kind of book,' I explained.

Stephen huffed, said he'd stick with *The Brothers Karamazov* if he wanted a doorstop.

Finally, though, he had succumbed. Picking my copy up in a bored moment, Stephen didn't leave the sofa he'd been lounging on until he'd finished, twenty-four hours later. We still argued over it, though. I'd said the main character – Lin – was a good guy, had a good heart, but just acted badly. Stephen disagreed.

'Just because he's being honest about the bad things he's done, it doesn't make the bad things OK. Say if I murdered someone then confessed it and said I was sorry, the crime wouldn't disappear. I'd still be a murderer.'

'But you'd be a murderer with integrity, and that's important,' I'd said flippantly.

I winced when I remembered that conversation now. Stephen

was not a carte blanche moralist. He believed in behaving towards others exactly as he would like to be treated. Had I, had we all, acted with enough integrity after his death? Was he watching now, judging us all?

I thought Inspector Mukerjee in the end had done the best job he could, at least. He was pompous at first, vain and ineffectual too. But the whole mystery had been solved within twenty-four hours, and he'd treated me, and even Raj, despite shooting him in the leg, with sympathy. He seemed to understand people and their mistakes.

It was mid-afternoon. Baking hot as usual. I pulled the blinds down to keep out the sun. I lay on the sofa in the grey heat. I hadn't anything to do. It wasn't appropriate to begin living normally again.

I took up *Shantaram* once more, flicked through the pages. The author had spent years on the run, and now he was famous in Mumbai – people calling out his name on the street. I wondered what Mukerjee would make of his book – it would definitely appeal to his sense of drama. Maybe I would give him a copy. It would be a thank you: for getting us some closure on Stephen and for not throwing me out of the country.

The police station receptionist was signing papers. A lazy-eyed man, he waved his hand dismissively in front of me when I asked for Inspector Mukerjee.

'Out,' he said, not looking up.

'Where is he?'

The guy shrugged, continued to write. I was mildly surprised. I'm used to people taking an interest in whatever particular mission I am on and trying to help, but this guy did not want to waste one second of his time on my request.

I called Mukerjee on his mobile. It went straight to answering machine.

'He's not picking up his phone. Do you know where he is, please?'

The man glanced up quickly, flicked his eyes out to the side and back down again, trying to hide the fact that he had even deigned to lift his head to see who was standing in front of him. I blushed with annoyance as he continued on with his useless administration. This behaviour was more than unhelpful; this was uncivil, this was rude.

'Lack of communication is how relationships fail . . . It's how wars break out . . . societies break down!' I said, my voice rising.

I'd taken the bait and felt him bristle all over with triumphant relish. Indignation would fail with this man. I decided simply to ignore him and just make my way up to the inspector's office. I wouldn't be at all surprised if Mukerjee was sat there having a cup of tea, ignorant of the battle down below.

I turned to make my way to the lift.

'No!' the man suddenly shouted.

'What?' I said.

'Not allowed without permission.'

'But how do I get permission – from you?'

He shrugged, went back to his writing. I was getting upset now, my logic wavering.

'Please!' I burst out, shoving *Shantaram* in his face. 'I've brought this book to give to Inspector Mukerjee. I'm Ruby Jones; I was a friend of the boy who died, Stephen Newby? I just want to give the book to him, as a thank you for helping with the case.'

The man adjusted his glasses on his nose, peered at the book for a moment. 'Shan-ta-ram,' he mouthed slowly, before going back yet again to his papers.

'Can I leave it with you? If I can't take it up? It's a present.'

'You need permission to do that.'

'Who from?'

He shrugged again.

Fuck, this guy was insane. I sized him up. He wasn't that small. So where did the Napoleon complex come from? Maybe it came from being a man in a woman's profession. Male secretaries. Man, I would never have a male secretary: unless they also happened to be a Premier League football player or a Somali pilot, so they didn't have to worry about looking like a sissy.

I sighed loudly, with more than a touch of frustrated sob heaving up inside me and turned on my heels to make the journey back home.

'He's outside,' the man suddenly called after me.

Hallelujah.

'Where outside?'

'Garage,' he said, still not sufficiently interested in my search to look at me while speaking.

'What garage?'

'Police garage.'

This trip had been more than arduous. It felt like I was in the Sahara with no sunblock, licking off my own drops of sweat for sustenance. But I was a glutton for punishment so I went to look for the garage anyway. A small road hugged the station around to the back, where there was something that looked more like a car graveyard than a garage. Impounded rickshaws and taxis without licences sat among old wrecks the police must have removed from the road. Beyond this was a low hangar with a large sliding door standing ajar. I heard a hollow metal bang echoing round the inside of that building.

That must be the garage and that could be the inspector, banging away for some reason, I thought. Stepping inside, I was confronted by several Maruti Sazuki cars. Impounded from crime scenes probably.

The hangar was divided into sections. Moving on to the next room through a small door, I found jeeps and four-by-fours, the cars of small-time Delhi gangsters. The grating clang echoed through the hangar once more and I moved on to the final room, where the sound had come from.

This seemed to hold the cars of the city's big-time mafia. A gleaming Alfa Romeo, a Porsche, even a Bentley were parked in here. And there, right at the end of the line, was Swami Shiva's sleek black Mercedes, taken as evidence in Stephen's homicide case. And there too was Inspector Mukerjee, metal pole in hand, swinging it at the bumper. I gasped but the sound was lost as the third whack tolled round the room.

The inspector knelt down, looked at the bumper, smoothed it carefully.

'This is a beautiful car, I hate to do this,' he said to himself.

I dropped to my knees and crawled away as quietly as possible, still holding my copy of *Shantaram*. Once in the room of jeeps I stood up and walked out of the hangar. I headed straight for the road. The receptionist was standing in the shade of the entrance having a cigarette.

'You found him?'

The man was suddenly interested, after deliberately ignoring me, just when I needed to be inconspicuous. He really had it in for me. I shrugged nonchalantly.

'No. I'll come back another day.'

13

I hailed a rickshaw and told the driver just to drive south over the flyover, with no specific address in mind. The sun was getting low and making all the cars gold. Stephen always said sunset was his favourite time of day. The sun went down early and went down fast and Stephen would always try to be somewhere for it, even if it was just the roof of our building. But it was rush hour and there was no time for a sunset right now. Cars, buses, rickshaws jammed up against one another, honking and shoving and fuming. The jam lurched along in angry spurts and tension rose.

I got a bidi cigarette off the rickshaw driver. It made me light-headed but calmed my nerves. Sitting smoking in the traffic, I tried to piece together the scene.

Inspector Mukerjee had been bashing in Swami Shiva's car. Why? Swami Shiva's car was evidence. Raj had been driving it when he ran over Stephen. If he had run over Stephen there would have been dents in the car. The inspector was making dents in the bumper. He was making up evidence to go with

Raj's statement. Why would he do that? Had he made the statement up himself?

The traffic loosened up; the rickshaw driver revved his engine and asked me where we were going.

'Imperial Hotel,' I told him.

I asked for Sir Charles at reception. I heard a groggy female voice, his wife I assumed, answer the phone call up to his room. He was in the bar.

I found him hiding behind a palm, nursing a whisky, as far away from the lounge piano as possible. He was staring into space and didn't see me until I was practically in his lap.

'Sir Charles.'

'Ruby! Sit down. Would you like a drink?'

A greying waiter was immediately at his side, smiling.

'Er, yes please. Could I have a gin and tonic? Double, please,' I said.

I explained to Sir Charles what I had seen and what I thought it meant. He looked at me incredulously and then with soft eyes.

'Ruby, this is very hard for you. I know you were friends with Raj. Swami Shiva visited me today after I returned from the mortuary. He told me Stephen would often practise his Hindi with Raj, that they were friends, that you'd all been round for dinner even, at his home. Swami Shiva cannot believe it either. He's known Raj since he was a boy. He is very, very upset. I'm not sure exactly what you saw in the garage and I'm not saying you're making it up, but I'd be very careful, accusing the police of something like evidence tampering. Do you even know it was the right car? Do you even know it was an impounded car at all?' he said.

The waiter came back with the drinks. He set a mirrored

coaster down in front of me and I saw what Sir Charles and Inspector Mukerjee saw. A slightly dishevelled young woman, hair a mess, eyes wide, shirt with an inkstain on the collar. I racked my brains trying to think of something to convince Sir Charles to take me seriously.

I picked up my drink and gulped it.

'Sir Charles, I'm sorry to have to ask you this but when you saw Stephen today, did you look closely at his body?'

Sir Charles took some whisky. 'I was with him for some time.'

'There weren't any bruises on his body, were there?'

'Well, no – just one gash on his forehead.'

'And if he'd been run over, wouldn't he have had bruises on his body at least? Maybe Stephen wasn't run over at all.'

Sir Charles sat for a moment. He looked tired.

'I'm not sure, Ruby. I'm not a forensic pathologist. But I'm ninety-nine per cent sure we have the right man; that we have the man responsible for Stephen's death. Raj was setting Stephen's motorbike alight. And it's common that a suspect's statement doesn't make sense in India. Because of the way they interrogate. I don't like violent interviews but they're common practice here,' he said.

'But don't we need to find out what really happened? Don't you want to find out? If Raj is making up the story about running Stephen over, what else is he making up? How do we know he isn't covering for someone? How do we know he really killed Stephen? Don't you want to know the truth?'

'Ruby, as I said, I think we have the right man here. The idea of him walking free because of a shoddy justice system is quite awful. My wife has been battered by the death of her daughter. And now Stephen. She'll never get over this, but a swift, simple closure should give her some solace. If the investigation reopens now I don't know if her mind will hold. She can't be on sedatives indefinitely. I've been getting the manager

128

here to go and buy her a strip of Xanax each day. Do you know how that feels? The funeral is the day after tomorrow. We're burying him here because it will be quicker and simpler and we can control the media somewhat. She won't have to go through the trauma of travelling back with the body and the paparazzi circus at the airport. But if you start rooting around in the case then there will be no way of preventing this from turning into a circus. I want to bury Stephen peacefully and leave India with my wife. I would appreciate it if you don't reopen this and cause our family more undue distress,' said Sir Charles.

He threaded his empty glass through his fingers, not looking at me, watching it reflect the chandelier glints.

The waiter appeared to pick up our glasses. 'One more, sir?' he asked.

Sir Charles lifted his head up to the waiter, breathed in and asked me if I would like another drink. He was being polite.

'No, no thanks, I'm tired and I should go home to bed.'

'Would you like me to call you a car?'

'No, no, it's fine, I'll catch a rickshaw.'

I was still clutching *Shantaram* as I clambered back into a rickshaw. I called the inspector. This time he picked up. He sounded expansive and cheerful.

'Inspector, I have something I'd like to give you. Where are you? Can I come and see you?'

'Oh! Something for me? That's very nice of you, Ruby. Well, I am at home, in South Extension.'

'Can I come over and give it to you?'

There was a pause. He was clearly surprised. 'Well . . . er . . . my wife is out of station now you see. She's not at home so I couldn't offer you anything good to eat.'

He didn't sound suspicious, just slightly uncomfortable. He wasn't the kind of man to revel in having a girl come alone to his home. It crossed my mind that he might think I was propositioning him, but that was kind of ridiculous.

'It's a shame I can't meet your wife. I would have loved to. But I don't want anything to eat at all, honestly. I just want to give you this gift while I have it with me and I'm close to the police colony – it's on my way home.'

It wasn't on my way home, but he'd never know that. The traffic was so erratic a five-minute journey could sometimes take fifty. There was another pause. I don't think he was keen but I imagined he was a hospitable man, who took guests seriously and wouldn't want to turn anyone away if he could help it. I didn't want to take advantage of him but I knew if I wanted to ask anything of him, the best time to do this was when I was his guest, when he felt in a position of obligation. And I was about to ask him two very big favours.

He paused to think. 'Ah. Why not. Please come. I'll send the boy out for crisps and juice at least. It's the police colony two twenty-three A block,' he said.

Grey had begun to set in by the time my ride chugged up to see the inspector. A pink bougainvillea cast shadows over his door. It was only a little lighter inside the house, with one dim chintzy light hung dead over the centre of the living room. A pot of coffee and brass-framed photos of a Bengali wedding couple stood on a dark wood dresser, the rest of the room taken up by a three-piece velveteen suite in coral. Newspapers sat scattered by one chair, held down with an empty cup.

The inspector stood in the centre of the room, uncomfortably. He obviously hadn't been a bachelor for a long time. He wasn't used to this position. He was nervous and a little shy. I wanted him to feel like this, a little fragile. I wasn't going to mention what I'd seen, but just knowing it gave me the confidence to ask him to help me in ways which weren't totally above board. I knew now he was the kind of man to bend the rules.

'Would you like a cup of coffee? A cold drink? My wife's *nimbu pani* is excellent in the hot weather. She's visiting family in Calcutta, but I think we have a little left in the fridge. We have whisky, of course,' said the inspector. Reading glasses were perched on his nose, giving him the look of a benign professor, but I could catch a smell of stale booze from him. It seemed like he had been drinking for a while and I thought I'd join him.

'I'll have a whisky, please, Inspector.'

He looked a little surprised at my choice, but he'd offered so couldn't take it back. He placed three cubes of ice and a confused splash of alcohol in a heavy glass from the side-board. I perched on the edge of the coral sofa and took a sip.

'Thanks – just what I needed.'

His eyes widened a little. He hadn't had me down as a whisky drinker, obviously.

We sat there for a while. It really was good whisky. I took another sip.

'It's good whisky, Inspector.'

'Thank you – Red Label – not quite Gold but not bad – broke it open to celebrate closing the case. Well, of course, not closing the case, but making significant inroads,' he said. He was sweating slightly and unsure where to look, eventually resting his gaze on the book. 'What is this you have?'

'Ah, I forgot, the book. I thought you would enjoy it. It's set in Mumbai; it's a true story, it's crime. I wondered if you'd think the author should go to jail or not,' I said.

'Oh thank you!' he said, reaching out and taking the book from me.

Mukerjee peered at it through his glasses, held it close to

his eyes and then far away. He read the blurb on the back carefully. He turned it over and proclaimed the name. 'SHANT-A-RAM.'

The skin around his eyes crinkled as he looked at me. 'Thank you, Ruby. This is very kind of you. I can't remember the last time someone gave me a book.'

I felt genuinely happy to have given it to him. It was a shame that my original honest intention had turned into a manipulative ploy but one has to react to the world. There's no point in pretending we're all nice all the time.

At this point a young man with a moustache, listening to an iPod, came into the room with a large pack of Lays crisps. He opened them roughly and put them on the table. The inspector spoke gruffly to him. He looked up, sighed, brought a bowl from the kitchen, which he poured the crisps into. He left the bowl on the table but Mukerjee shouted at him again. He picked the bowl up and offered them to me. I took a handful gratefully.

'You just can't get good staff now,' the inspector said, shaking his head.

He was ashamed of not being able to host me better. I wondered if his wife and he had a good relationship. Whether she really was just on a visit to Calcutta, what the inspector was like when he was relaxed and intimate. I imagined he was rather nice, sentimental. He looked around the room.

'I should give you something too, but what . . . ?'

'No, no, Inspector, no need, though there is something I would like you to help me with.'

'What? I'd be happy to.'

'Well, it's two things really. I hope you don't mind.'

'Not at all. Please, tell me. Would you like some more whisky? Or a cup of coffee?'

'Whisky, please.'

He was warming up and poured a large one for himself and a small one for me, though definitely less meagre than the last.

'Would you mind calling your friend at the Ministry of External Affairs? I really would like to write something on the closure of the case for the *Telegraph* and need to sort out my journalist's visa as soon as possible.'

'Of course – I gave you Ranbir's number, didn't I?'

'You did, but I was wondering whether you wouldn't mind giving him a quick ring? It will be better coming from you. Perhaps he could help me tomorrow morning? Just get it over and done with.'

The inspector jolted slightly – I was being quite pushy – but after a moment agreed. He took out his mobile and had a loud and jolly conversation in Hindi with Ranbir.

'Well, that's sorted. He says come in tomorrow at nine and he'll sort out a journalist's visa for you.'

'Do I need a letter of reference?'

'No, don't worry. Ranbir will sort it all out.'

'Thanks, Inspector. That's great!'

I was genuinely pleased. It was like getting blood out of a stone, a journalist visa in India. They really don't like people nosing around. It was much better to get it sorted out before I started looking into Delhi police practices. They couldn't take it off me once I had it and if you're going to start messing around with people who make or enforce laws, you'd better make damn sure you've kept to them.

'No problem, no problem whatsoever.'

'Er . . . there's just one more thing if that's OK, Inspector.'

'What's that, Ruby?'

'I really want to go to see Raj.'

Mukerjee's face puckered. 'Why do you want to do that?'

'Swami Shiva wants me to go and see him.'

'Why does he want you to go and see him? Swami has been himself to see him.'

'Ah, Swami wants me to tell him how Sita is. Rani and I went to visit her, but she's not able to come to see Raj, is she?'

'No, not yet, not until he's formally charged. We don't want Sita trying to make him change his statement. They can do that, wives. They have an awful effect on husbands sometimes. They bring the babies. They cry. Really, it can be terrible. After Raj is in prison, she can visit as much as she wants,' he said.

'Has she got the money back from the police yet?'

The inspector blushed slightly. 'We're still trying to work out what this is. Swami Shiva says it is Raj's savings. But we need some more evidence of this. Receipts or something. It's just an envelope with money and an envelope with money always has a story to it.'

I guessed he was telling the truth. I could have very well been wrong, but he didn't seem the kind of man who would just grab money. His house was simple, there wasn't much show.

'I don't think the money matters so much now anyway. Swami is looking after Sita and he wants me to let Raj know how she and the children were when we saw them. That's what Swami Shiva told me; that's why he wants me to go and see him. You would want to know how your kids are, wouldn't you, if you had gone to prison suddenly, without saying goodbye?'

'I don't have children unfortunately,' he said, but thought for a moment. Took a sip of his whisky. Wiped his forehead with his large hanky. Stood up and turned up the speed on the ceiling fan.

'I don't see it can do so much harm. Probir can translate

for you and see nothing untoward is being talked about. I'll call him now.'

The inspector made another phone call. He didn't sound as jolly as he had with Ranbir, much more severe.

'That's also sorted. Probir will meet you at the Karol Bagh police station at eleven o'clock tomorrow morning in the reception. You can go after your visa interview. Get it over and done with,' he said.

'OK, thanks, Inspector, that's great. Thank you.'

'Now, would you like one more whisky?'

He was really warming up now. Another time I would have stayed and got really smashed with him, but not tonight.

'I think I should be getting home; it's dark and I have to be up early now,' I said.

The inspector called me a car. An early hangover set in and our conversation drained away, so we waited in semi-dark silence on the coral sofa.

I didn't go straight home, though. I had one more place to go, the ashram, to find Rani.

The gate was closed. The only light I could see was a flickering of candles round the shrine to Ganesh. I pushed my way in and towards reception. I was expecting it to be shut, that I would have to ring the bell and wake people up. I wasn't sure exactly what I would have said when they came down. But I was in luck. The reception was open and lit up.

Chewy was sitting down at the front desk, a whole cheesecake in front of him, untouched. His head was perched in his hands, his eyes were shut and he was listening to his iPod.

'Chewy?' I said.

He didn't answer. I went over, touched him on the shoulder. His eyes jerked open and his jaw clenched, but relaxed when he saw me.

'Ruby.'

'What are you doing up at this time? I thought it was lights out at nine thirty?'

'Ah, come on, you know Swami doesn't mind if we want to stay up. He only minds if we don't get to five o'clock satsang – which means you want to go to bed as early as possible anyway.'

'So what are you doing?'

'Can't sleep.'

'Understandable.'

Chewy nodded and pursed his lips. 'I've been tossing around for an hour or so. Insomnia. It creeps up on me. I used to just knock it on the head hard you know? Times like these I'd have a mug of Jack and a joint . . . and if that didn't send me off . . . I'd have another round . . . and another . . . but I can't do that here, can I?'

'Bourbon is not something Swami advises.'

'No . . . all I've got is some country music and this.' He looked down at the virgin cheesecake in dismay.

'It looks a good one, Chewy. What flavour?'

'Baked blueberry and vanilla.'

'Wow. You can't get better than that I don't think. That's bound to cheer you up.'

He shook his head, about to poke the thing. But he refrained and looked up at me instead.

'You know why I like making these cheesecakes so much? It's the closest anyone in this place is going to get to sex or drugs or booze. I'm not saying those are good things, but desire, sensuality, they are part of being human, right? This cheesecake will give you the most sensual experience possible in the ashram. You can desire this without breaking the rules. But any cook will tell you, it's not the same experience when you've made the damn thing. And I don't want a sugar hit. I want something harder. I want to have a hit on a joint or a shot. Fuck, man, I don't want to be here now. I want to be in a bar.'

'There isn't anything stopping you, Chewy. If that's what you really want, the door is open, right? You can still be part of the network. You just wouldn't be able to live in the ashram. Swami Shiva is strict on that.'

Chewy sighed. 'No. I don't really want it. This is my home now. It's just some weeks are harder than others. Do you want some cake, Ruby?'

'Not really.'

'Let's share it. It's gonna be the best you've tasted. There's a lot of emotion that went into this. And emotion is the secret to great cooking. It's the love that makes things taste good.'

I laughed. He was probably right. I was going to love a lot more when I cooked from now on. I took the fork from him.

'OK, do you want an earpiece too? It's Dolly Parton.'

'Dolly Parton?'

'A woman who knows about pain.'

We sat on the floor eating the cheesecake and listening to Dolly Parton with half an ear. You wouldn't expect such subtle sweetness from a man wearing shirts like his.

'I need you to help me, Chewy.'

'What?'

'I need Rani to meet me at the police station tomorrow morning at eleven. But I don't want anyone, not Swami, to know.'

'Why not?'

'Don't ask me about it. But can you get him there for me?'

'I don't know. Why do you want me to bring him to the police station anyhow?'

'Don't ask me now. I wouldn't involve you but I can't think of anything myself. I've been trying to think of a way to get Rani to the police station tomorrow without anyone knowing where he's going and I just can't. I'm stumped. I need your help, man. Chewy, you're clever. You're creative. You'll be able to think of something between now and tomorrow morning.'

He smiled. Chewy was a bit vain.

'And I'm sure it'll make another great story to tell people over cheesecake,' I added.

That clinched it. He grinned, took a big forkful of cheesecake and chomped. 'OK. I don't know what you're up to, Ruby, but I'm in.'

I left him on the floor, his head swaying to Dolly, finishing off his cake with the panache of someone making a plan.

14

Everything went right the next morning. At the Ministry of External Affairs, the inspector's effeminate friend Ranbir gave me tea, biscuits and a visa.

I picked up a rickshaw with a working meter, a rare occurrence in Delhi, paying exactly the right price to get me to the police station. Dad always said it was better to be born lucky than rich. These were all good signs that I was doing the right thing, or that's what I told myself.

Five minutes later, Rani turned up in a taxi. He looked dazed. But this had become his default expression recently. I didn't ask him exactly how Chewy had got him there. That could wait till later.

'Hey Rani. Thanks for coming.'

'What are we doing here?'

'I need you to help me. We're going to visit Raj.'

'What? Why?'

'I need to speak to him about something. I need you to translate.'

'Why do you need me to translate? You could get anyone to do it.'

'I want you two to speak in Malayalam. So no one knows what we're talking about. But don't say that, OK? In fact, don't say anything to anyone except Raj.'

'Ruby, what are you doing? It doesn't sound good,' he said.

'Rani, please, I haven't time, can you just trust me? Please trust me. I want the truth and so do you,' I said. Grasping him by the arm, I led him into reception where Probir was waiting for us, eating a jumbo pack of chilli crisps. He looked from me to Rani and back again.

'Inspector Mukerjee said only you. This is not only you,' he said.

'I know, but Rani's . . .' I paused. God. I really hadn't thought this out fully. This could go wrong.

'Here to . . .' Rani began.

'Pray for him,' I finished and squeezed Rani's arm tighter. 'Inspector Mukerjee said you just wanted to talk to him about his wife. I need to call him and make sure all this praying is OK.'

'No, don't bother him. Of course Swami wants to make sure Raj's spiritual welfare is taken care of too. Don't bother the inspector.'

Probir looked at me again. He frowned. He wasn't stupid, this guy; his beady eyes were bright with suspicion. He put his phone to his ear. But as he tried to call Mukerjee I heard the tinny no-more-credit jingle play out.

It took a lot of willpower not to look pleased. I tried to run with this luck.

'You're out of credit? Should I try to call him?' I said. 'If it's important for you to speak to him maybe I can call him for you. But he said that we should go this morning

140

and not be delayed. He was quite adamant.' I pulled my phone out.

'No, don't bother. Come on. He told me to take you to Raj,' said Probir, blushing.

He led us into a very bright white room with high windows. It wasn't particularly dirty but marks showed very clearly all around: scuffs on the wall; smears of dirt on the glass. The room was divided into three booths with perspex windows. At each booth was a red plastic chair, the kind that teachers used in my secondary school. Through the windows a guard and a door were visible. Rani and I squeezed into a booth together. Probir nodded over the perspex and the guard went through the door to bring Raj out.

He was wearing a worn-out prison uniform of faded pink. It must have been red or orange when new, but so many felons and so many washes had turned it damask rose. It suited his colouring. He could have been in a *Vogue* shoot, except for the whacking great bruise down the left side of his face. He walked with a jaded, broken slope and a dragging leg.

He sat down heavily across from us and I could make out all the bruise's many colours: purple, green, yellow. A vivid pink where blood had risen to the surface of his face, dark brown and crusted where the skin had broken. That iron bar hadn't only been used on the car. Raj had taken a bashing.

'Hey, Raj,' I said.

He looked at both of us expectantly, not reacting to my greeting at all.

'You have to pick up the phone,' said Probir.

There was a scuffed red phone stuck to the side of the booth, worn to white around the handset. I'd never seen plastic rubbed so thoroughly. There must have been a lot of hard conversations through that phone: in Hindi, in Urdu, in English, in Malayalam. In different languages, but all with the same desperate grip, it seemed.

'Rani, you pick up the phone, you'll be the one talking to Raj,' I said.

He did as I said but with limp fingers. Raj took up his phone too.

'You have to press the button down on the handset,' said Probir.

Rani pressed the button, it lit up and I could hear some electric fuzz. You wouldn't need electricity for a very simple connection like this. Maybe these conversations were taped. We could be in trouble if someone listened back to them.

'Probir, are these phones tapped?' I said.

He looked surprised. Then shrugged nonchalantly.

'Why does it matter to you?' he asked.

I thought he was bluffing. He didn't know any more than I did. And the likelihood there was a Malayalam-speaking policeman in Delhi who would be listening to this was slim. I'd take our chances.

'Ask him how he is,' I said.

Rani began in that sing-song language I didn't understand.

Raj shrugged, his lips drooped. He looked down at the floor, mumbled something into the phone.

'What is he saying?'

'He wants to know about his wife.'

Probir piped up. 'What language are you talking? I don't understand.'

'They're talking Malayalam; they're both from Kerala,' I said.

'Talk Hindi. Raj understands Hindi.'

'But why? This is their mother tongue,' I said.

'Because I want to understand what is being said.'

'But you can understand what is being said when Rani translates it to me,' I said.

This was completely logical. He nodded for us to carry on.

Probir might have been happy with this but I was foiled. Yes, Rani could talk to Raj in Malayalam and Probir would not understand a word. But Probir would certainly understand my English: when I told Rani to ask Raj if his statement was false; why Inspector Mukerjee had been bashing in the Mercedes; what really happened the day Stephen died. Oh fuck. I should have briefed Rani before we got here. Now I'd have to improvise.

I could soften Raj up at least. Get him really worried about his wife. He might just say something anyway if he got desperate enough to see her; that's why she wasn't allowed to come here in the first place.

'Just tell him how Sita is, Rani. Tell him about what she said when we gave her the money. About how she said she didn't want it and she wanted him back.'

Rani frowned but began. Raj's right eye began to twitch and water with emotion; his left was too scrunched up from the beating to move. He blurted out a question to Rani.

'What's he saying?'

'He wants to know about the flat. Whether Sita will be moving into the new flat. Swami Shiva said to him she would be, that he would look after her.'

'Tell him . . . tell him . . . tell him Sita doesn't want to live there without him. Tell him Sita won't take the money. Tell him Sita is in a bad way. She can't look after the children.'

I glanced over at Probir. He was looking at his watch and had his hand on his belly. It was nearly lunchtime. He had started to get bored listening to our saga. He wasn't as interested in humans as he was in food.

'Probir?' I said.

143

'Ha?'

'I hope you don't think this is rude but I'm very hungry. Would it be possible to send for some chai, maybe some snacks?'

He perked up. 'Some pakora? We do good pakora here.'

'That would be amazing.'

'I'll just go and tell the boy outside.'

We had about a minute's grace.

'Rani, tell Raj I know his statement is false. There's been evidence tampering. What really happened? Is he responsible for Stephen's death? Who is? Tell him we want to help him. Tell him Sita needs him.'

'Ah, Rani? Do you have chai with sugar?' said Probir, putting his face around the door.

'Yes, today he does,' I said.

Probir shouted into the corridor and returned to the room.

'Rani,' I said.

Rani began to repeat my questions but slowly, without my urgency. It sounded innocent enough. And Probir, I could see, had his mind on the coming pakora. Raj leaned back in his chair. Shook his head. Looked to the side of the room. He was thinking. He knocked the phone against his lips, took it away again. Took it back to his mouth, then back to his lap and bit his lip.

I was about to say something to encourage him but bit my own lip. Patience, Ruby, let the man think, I said to myself.

Eventually Raj took up the phone and spoke a few words to Rani. Rani raised his eyebrows in surprise.

'Ah, chai!' said Probir.

A boy swung the door open with his back and turned into the room with a tray of steaming cups and saucers of deep-fried bread. He put the tray down in the middle of the room and brought two cups and plates to Rani and me.

144

I felt bad having this in front of Raj, though he didn't seem at all interested.

'Can Raj have some too?'

Probir snorted, already chomping his second pakora. 'Ah no, Ruby, we're not in the hotel business here, he's a murderer.'

'Suspected,' I said.

'Good as dead,' said Probir, repeating himself in Hindi for everyone else's benefit.

'Well, we've finished here. Let's go outside and eat these,' I said.

'What about the prayers?' said Probir, narrowing his eyes.

'Ah, I've done them already, we said a morning prayer together at the beginning of our talk,' said Rani.

Rani was doing me proud today; I was very impressed with his quick thinking. We ate the snacks in the corridor awkwardly. Blew on the tea, making a thick scum appear, then sipped fast. Probir took a phone call from the inspector and walked up and down the corridor, briefing him on our conversation. He seemed happier once off the phone and popped the last cold morsel into his mouth whole.

'I will get a car for you,' he said, spurting bits of flabby bread into our faces.

'No, no, it's fine, we'll get a rickshaw,' I said.

Only once safely stuck in a traffic jam did I speak to Rani.

'Well done in there about the praying! That was really good.'

Rani shrugged. 'It was true. Raj is a religious man. He is part of the ashram. We believe in God.'

'What did he say about his statement? What did he say to you about Stephen?' I asked.

'He said we should ask Stephen's father what happened the day he died,' said Rani.

145

'Fuck. Really? What the hell does that mean? We don't know who Stephen's father is. Does Raj know?'

'He didn't say. I don't think he meant to say anything actually. I think he meant to keep quiet.'

'He cracked under the pressure of it all? The beating? Prison?'

'Yes, and the news of Sita. I told him what you told me to tell him,' said Rani.

'Fuck,' I said and slumped back in the rickshaw. I pulled out my phone. The text message. So it had meant something after all. Stephen had texted me saying he wanted to talk about his father on the day he had died. I'd known it meant something. I should have followed my instincts at the time.

Yet again I'd got in the auto without giving an address and now the driver was turning around wanting to know where the hell we were going. I understood how he felt.

'Ruby?' asked Rani.

'Well, I guess we're gonna have to try to find Stephen's father. I mean, at least we know he exists now. Haksar Haveli? Get him to take us to Old Delhi,' I said.

15

The Old Delhi goats' heads didn't seem to affect Rani so much this time round. Perhaps all we'd been through recently was hardening him up. He also knew exactly where to go.

'One of those shoe sellers we spoke to last time we were here said Haksar Haveli was near the Afghan colony round the back of their stalls. I was about to tell Stephen but that was when he gave up, sat down in the middle of the road,' he said.

This took a moment to go in. Rani had known where Haksar Haveli was all along?

'Why didn't you say anything at the time, Rani? My God!'

'He looked so upset. I didn't want him to be any more upset. He was tired,' he said.

'But didn't you see how important it was to him? He was looking for his father. That meant more than the fact he was flagging a bit.'

Rani shrugged. 'I don't like to see people suffering.'

I looked at him in wonder. The connections, the synapses in Rani's head were wired differently to mine, to most other people that I knew. He couldn't see the difference between Stephen looking tired or frustrated from a bad day, and the deep sadness inside of Stephen because he'd never known his father. I didn't think Rani was incapable of deep feelings but he seemed to have a very shallow understanding of other people's inner lives. But I couldn't really get angry with him because his intentions were transparent and he meant so well. It was all part of this fairy innocence that surrounded him.

'I thought we could come back anyhow,' Rani added sheepishly.

Well, we were back. Just without Stephen.

Old Delhi was easier in the morning. The streets were fresh. Milk was being delivered in large steel cans. The shoving shoppers in burkas had been replaced with tiny scrubbed children in boxy white uniforms and satchels strapped to their backs.

Our cyclist knew the way to the Afghan colony. It was where the best bread came from, he told Rani. He dropped us off by an earth stove where three bearded men were pummelling dough into long ovals for a crowd of chatting ladies, already loaded with shopping.

'You ask, Rani, they'll help you,' I said, thinking he'd be more effective with a crowd of women than I would.

I was right. His long lashes made all these housewives melt. They gathered around chatting and discussing exactly where Haksar Haveli was.

One shiny, tiny lady, grey hair tied tightly in a bun, took a particular liking to Rani. She forgot all about her bread, instead clutching his wrist and grinning widely. This was the kind of attention that would usually break Rani out in a cold sweat but today he let himself be tugged off down an alley. I followed closely behind. She stopped outside a large blue wooden door and rapped on it.

148

'Haksar Haveli!' she said, before scurrying off, still grinning at Rani.

Rani and I looked at each other in disbelief.

'It can't be this easy,' I said.

He shrugged his shoulders. 'God's will.'

I snorted. 'You would say that, wouldn't you?'

'Swami Shiva always says that you shouldn't struggle in life. You shouldn't get upset if things don't go the way you planned them; like that time we came here with Stephen. Swami says let everything go and everything you need will come back to you. It's about being brave. About understanding when the time is right.'

'Yeah, like the time was right for Stephen to throw himself into that river?' I said.

Rani moved back a little, hurt at my nastiness, I think.

'Sorry, sorry,' I said as I knocked on a small door, contained within a large coach entrance.

A small girl in a pink polyester shalwar kameez, her hair cut short, opened it. She looked up at us enquiringly. Rani brightened at the sight of her. He knelt down, tugged her cheek, already acting like her uncle, asking questions playfully. He was good with children. She answered nicely before turning on her heels and running off.

'OK,' said Rani. 'She doesn't know who we're talking about, she's just a little kid – she lives here with her parents and her grandparents. She's going to get her mother.'

The little girl came skipping back with a woman not much more than a girl herself, younger than me, in a green and silvery shalwar kameez. She drew her scarf around her head and scooped up the child, holding her on her hip as she talked to Rani with ease at the door, as a friend would.

She motioned for us to come into the stone courtyard. Most of the life of the house seemed to be lived here. It was bordered

149

by a verandah where two women sat shelling peas on string charpoy beds. A clock engraved with a plastic diamanté image of Mecca hung above them. On the opposite wall was a black felt and silver picture of Koranic verses. A little boy played with a red plastic truck amongst shadows of flapping cotton kurtas, hung up to dry across the courtyard. An Indian rock song wafted down from one of the top room windows and a young man looked out to see who had come in before going back to his music. There was a gentle atmosphere here.

'The grandfather bought this house about ten years ago off another family who were emigrating to America. These people are from Uttar Pradesh originally. They moved to Delhi when their trucking business began to expand. Isn't this girl lovely? What a smile,' said Rani, scooping up the girl himself now and swinging her around. She laughed. This was the most normal I'd seen him since we'd got up from the floor of the morgue, where we'd collapsed at the sight of Stephen dead.

It made me sad watching him. Rani would probably never have children. It didn't matter whether his affection for Stephen had been a passing phase or whether he really was gay. He had devoted his life to the ashram and to studying the Vedas and this meant a vow of celibacy. Maybe he would adopt an orphan like Swami did with him. It seemed a crazy world where some people sought children to look after and other children had to search for their parents.

'Do they know anything about Stephen's mother or father?' I asked Rani.

'No. This woman hasn't heard anything but she's going to get her mother-in-law, who might.'

But she came back alone. Her mother-in-law was lying down, sleeping. She couldn't wake her.

Rani set the girl on the floor. She ran over to her mother,

who absent-mindedly ran a hand through her daughter's hair and started neatening it.

'Well. I guess it wasn't the time for us to find Stephen's father. Maybe we should just take Swami Shiva's advice. Let's go. We'll bury Stephen in peace like Sir Charles wants,' I said.

Rani put his hand on my shoulder. 'I'm sorry, Ruby. I'm sorry,' he said.

Rani was kind. Even in a fug of shock and depression and growing mental strain he still thought of others first. I smiled at him and shook my head.

We turned to leave. The woman looked at our disappointed faces and screwed up her own face once more, trying to think of something to give us. As we were opening the door she suddenly shouted across the courtyard.

'She says try the beauty parlour round the corner. The old woman who runs it has been there for about thirty years. If anyone knows about Stephen's parents it'll be her,' said Rani.

'OK! Things are coming to us!' I cried.

The sign for Pearl Beauty Parlour was rusty and sun-bleached. Blue and white letters swirled round a black-haired woman waving a hairbrush. Thick curtains firmly closed out prying eyes. It had seen better days but the door was open.

'You go first, Ruby, you're a girl,' prodded Rani.

I pushed my way into a cavern-like room lit by one blue lamp. A sunk-ship boudoir. Pearly blue reflected off vinyl chairs and made great holes of navy underneath the counter. A basketful of nail polish, glinting turquoise and deep-sea navy stood against the room-length mirror. A decrepit hairdryer hung upside down by the picture of a smiling girl holding a pot of Fair and Lovely cream, for a lighter complexion.

A large, middle-aged woman in a blue shalwar kameez was

stretched out snoozing on the waiting sofa, along the oppo-site wall. I coughed loudly.

'Er – Didi?'

She didn't wake, but began snoring softly. I could hear giggling. Two young girls peeped through the bead curtain at the back of the parlour. I flashed a grin at these little mermaids, but they weren't going to wake their boss.

Eventually I went over and poked the lady. This did the trick.

'Waah!' she cried, sitting up. Her long hair, streaked with grey, flowed out all around her.

I jumped back. 'Sorry!'

She tied her hair up in a deft bun, scrutinising me, wiping her face of sleep. 'You want a manicure, a pedicure?' she asked. Her English accent was good. 'Henna – light – music!' she called into the back.

'Er, no, I just want to ask you some questions.'

The lady screwed up her face. 'Who are you?' she asked.

'You don't know me, sorry. Listen, could my friend come in? He's a man.'

'He can come in if he wants a treatment, of course he can. Haircut? Oil massage? Facial?' she said.

I laughed, which annoyed her. 'Sorry, I don't have time.'

'There is always time for making yourself a bit more beautiful. This is a beauty parlour. If you want me to help you, please come in. Otherwise let me be. I've had a long day.'

I didn't believe this but I could see she needed appeasing.

'OK, OK. I'll have a pedicure, manicure,' I said.

'With polish without polish?' She seemed happier.

'Er . . . with.'

'And your friend?'

I went outside and told Rani the situation. To my surprise,

he seemed to think this was perfectly sensible and decided on a head oil massage.

We entered the beauty parlour again together. Old Mangeshkar songs were now cranking out of an ancient tape player. The place was no longer mutely gleaming blue but loud and kitsch. Lit by a fluorescent strip, the polish sparkled red and orange, the lips of the fair and lovely girl were sexy and pink. The chairs that had looked so sleek in the dark showed up grubby yellow.

This beauty-store owner liked the look of Rani as much as the little old woman buying bread. She made flamboyant eyes at him while slashing her lips with a juicy red.

'Well, hello, my darling, my name is Rashmi. Now don't worry about a thing. I am going to take care of you today. A head massage, is it?'

Rani dipped his head in acquiescence, unsurprised and unaffected by the way he provoked this woman.

The scene irritated me much more than it should have, given the overarching importance of our visit. But every woman that fell at this man's feet reminded me of my own foolishness, my own feelings which I still, even knowing what I knew, could not shake off.

What was it about him that was so appealing? Was it his delicacy? Was it about taking care of him? There was more than that. There was an energy pulsing through him that made my skin prickle when he touched me. I could feel the nature within him, with all the wildness that comes with nature, despite his quiet appearance.

Rashmi presided over a whirlwind operation. My feet were dunked in a sloshing bowl of boiling hot water. I yelped as my girl yanked them out suddenly and scrubbed them with an ancient nailbrush, the bristles all splayed out from the many nails that they had scoured.

I looked across at Rani. His eyes were closed and he seemed to be enjoying the hands of this woman pouring warm coconut oil all over his head, talking to her in Hindi while she lavishly kneaded his scalp, throwing his hair around.

'So you want to know about Haksar Haveli?' she said in English, looking over at me.

'Yes. Do you remember a young white woman there? It would have been about twenty-six years ago.'

'How old do you think I am? You think I am over thirty?' cried Rashmi.

She was clearly over thirty. Over forty I would say. But Rani was horrified we'd offended her.

'Sorry, Auntie *ji*!' he said. *Ji* was a term of respect

'Auntie *ji*. Mister, I'm a lot more exciting than your auntie,' she cackled, sensuously massaging the nape of Rani's neck.

Rani blushed, with great pleasure, it seemed. My God, this was the most engaged I'd ever seen him with a woman. You couldn't say Rani's affection was predictable: first Stephen and now a middle-aged beauty salon manager.

I cut in. 'This is important. Someone at Haksar Haveli said that this place had been a local favourite for over thirty years and you had an excellent memory for faces and for stories,' I said. Not strictly true, but a little innocent flattery usually helped to guide people along the right path.

'Yes. That's right. My mother set it up. About thirty years ago. All the women around here come to us. I've been working here since I was a child.'

'Do you remember a young white girl? Called Claudia?' asked Rani.

Rashmi continued working on Rani silently for a couple of minutes.

'She had long red hair. Bright red hair,' I offered.

'Well, actually I knew Claudia quite well. There weren't

154

many white women living in Old Delhi, especially not in the early 80s. There were none, except Claudia. And how could anyone forget that hair of hers, especially round here! That thick red among all this black, black, black . . .' she said, shoving Rani's head to one side and slapping it.

He glanced at me sideways as my hands were being rubbed and massaged with cuticle cream.

Rashmi continued. 'I was about ten or eleven. Claudia used to come in here every week to get her hair oiled and trimmed. She liked manicures and pedicures too. I remember thinking she was very glamorous, a really grown-up woman, but she must have only been eighteen or nineteen, just a kid herself.'

'Did you ever talk to her?'

'A lot. I was a bit in love with her. She'd play and chat to me every time she came in. She spoke to me like a normal person, not just a kid. But it was hard for her I think. She didn't speak Hindi or Urdu well and none of the older women spoke English. They all loved her but their conversations never got further than "How are you?" Then they'd just start tugging at her hair and grabbing her wrist to see how thin she was. I was learning English in school and I think she saw someone she might actually be able to talk to at some point. She took it upon herself to help me with conversation; she bought me a radio and tuned it to the World Service. She told me her father always listened to the World Service. He was some kind of official, going lots of places abroad.'

The pain I felt while my little beautician took a pair of scissors to my cuticles was tiny compared to my excitement.

'So what happened?'

'Well, one day she just went, she didn't even say goodbye. I was devastated. So upset. I asked my mother about it, she just shrugged, said that's what Britishers did. She wouldn't talk about it any more than that – said the matter was closed.

I was a kid, I forgot about it after a while,' said Rashmi.

'We think she was living with someone,' I said.

'Yes, you're right; the women used to gossip about it in here. It was practically all they talked about for a time. They were scandalised. They loved it. This young English girl living with an Indian man twice her age and a Hindu at that.'

'He was twice her age?' I said.

'He was Hindu? But why did they live round here?' said Rani.

'It was more private here for them maybe. They couldn't have got away with this affair in New Delhi, I don't think – too many people who would know them,' said Rashmi.

'Would it have been that much of a big deal?' I said.

'Oh yes. Oh yes. Delhi was still very conservative then, not like now. Those girls . . . with miniskirts . . . driving around on their boyfriends' scooters. I don't know who his family was but they would not have liked it. And I think Claudia's family had friends in New Delhi who would really have been aghast.'

'They must have been in love with each other to go against everyone like that.'

'Well, I don't know. I guess they must have. I never met the man. He never came in here. He was working in South Delhi and wasn't around in the day. My mother used to go and give him massages in the evening sometimes. She liked him a lot despite all the gossiping. I think he was some kind of doctor. He gave her some herbal remedies to help her sleep once; she used to have terrible trouble sleeping. It's all the tea she drinks. I tell her now but she doesn't listen,' said Rashmi.

'So your mother is still alive?'

Rashmi grunted. 'Oh yes.'

'Would she talk to us? Is she here now?'

'Yes – she doesn't go out much. She spends most of her

time in front of the TV – she's fascinated by it. But she still loves a gossip.'

Rashmi slapped Rani gently around the head to indicate she'd finished. I held up my hands to inspect the sticky red polish that had just been applied.

Once my nails were dry to touch we all trooped through the beaded curtain to the fake-tiled lino back room, which smelled of burned roller heat. We went on through a door to Rashmi's kitchen with homely wafts of cumin, then on to a kitsch room decked with rugs and cushions. An old woman leaned back, in a white shalwar kameez, sipping red tea and watching television.

Rashmi turned to us.

'She's drinking Kashmiri tea. We moved from Kashmir when I was small.'

Rashmi began talking in a guttural mountain voice. We heard the name Claudia occasionally.

The old woman looked up with recognition and pointed to the TV.

Rashmi frowned. 'I don't know, maybe she is more confused than I thought – she says that is Rao who used to live in Haksar Haveli on TV now. But it can't be that man. He's famous, he's on TV the whole time,' she said.

We all moved round to look at the TV. Rani and I gave a simultaneous shout of shock.

It was Swami Shiva, talking about his new prison charity scheme on an NDTV chat show.

'She's made a mistake. That can't be him. That's Swami Shiva. He's my guru,' said Rani.

Rashmi spoke to her mother. She sounded like she was being harsh, but it could have just been the mountain language.

'She says it is. She is quite sure. He came on the TV a few years after he left Old Delhi and she's seen him regularly. She always thinks of the time he gave her medicine to sleep, she thought he was special then ... Come to think of it, she has mentioned this man lived in Old Delhi a couple of times before ... What is his name? Swami Shiva? We're not so into yoga and all that here,' said Rashmi.

16

We were in a rickshaw back to New Delhi.

'It's not true. I don't believe it at all,' said Rani.

'It's crazy, I know. She could just be senile, but she seemed so certain,' I said.

'No. Let's just go back to the centre. Forget about it,' he said.

I wanted a little more time to think. 'Let's not go back just yet, Rani. I need to catch my breath.'

I wanted to talk somewhere quiet, where we wouldn't be interrupted. I saw the dome of Humayun's tomb, like a single white breast sticking out of the Delhi skyline. Stephen and I always went there when we wanted to be alone. It was too sombre a place for the footballers and lovers that thronged Lodhi Gardens. Tour groups visited but never stayed long, impatient with the tomb's heavy lines and red brick, wanting to get on to the more deified Taj Mahal. It would be completely empty now, in the middle of the day, too hot for tourists, too hot for anyone.

The white marble path running to the tomb was scorching

but the courtyard garden was shady with tall palm trees. Channels of water bordered the tomb and cooled the air. Eagles and kites swung round its dome. Death was peaceful here, beautiful.

We came to the tomb room and sat on the floor, opposite the marble coffin of the emperor Humayun. Stars of afternoon sunlight fell orange on the marble floor, through the stone lattice, crossing Rani's face.

If Swami Shiva really was Stephen's father, did he know? How did Raj know? How did Stephen know? Had he really known? The text message. About his father. Had Raj killed him, not just run him over? Had someone else killed him? How much did Inspector Mukerjee know? Was Swami in cahoots with the police?

'This is impossible. Swami Shiva is not Stephen's father. Ruby, you shouldn't say anything to anybody about this,' Rani said.

'I don't know, Rani. I mean the woman wasn't mad. She seemed pretty sensible. And it makes sense that she thought Swami was a doctor, a healer. He is, isn't he? Maybe we should just talk to—'

Before I could say anything else, Rani had wrapped his arm round my neck and clamped his hand across my mouth. His skin was hot and dry. I tried to push him off but he was amazingly strong. Of course he would be. I couldn't move him at all. I kicked him. He didn't move. I struggled a bit more but I was weak. I gave up, went limp. He was suffocating me. After a few minutes he let me go and leaned back on the stone.

'What the fuck was that about?'

'I didn't hurt you, Ruby. I know I didn't. It's just . . . you don't understand that this is impossible. Swami Shiva is not just some yoga teacher who does anything he likes in private.

160

He is a devoted follower of Brahma – he is one of the most serious students of the Vedas in India. He has been following Brahmacharya, sexual abstinence, since he was a young student. He has never had relations with a woman.'

'How do you know? Do you really know that?'

'I have been with Swami Shiva every day for the whole of my life. I slept in the same room as him until I was nineteen. But this isn't the point – you've seen how much spiritual power Swami Shiva has? How people are drawn to him? Healed by him? That comes from the highest chakras. All his sexual energy is directed into this higher spiritual energy. He couldn't be the guru he is if he had anything to do with Stephen's mother, or any woman.'

'But, Rani . . .'

He grabbed my wrist, twisted. 'Just don't say anything; stop talking about it.'

'But . . .' I stopped. I gave up.

We sat in silence for a time. I could hear the birds cawing. It didn't feel peaceful here any more, not like it had with Stephen.

'Should we go and get the flowers?' Rani said eventually.

'Flowers? What do you mean?'

'Chewy told Swami Shiva and I that you wanted me with you to buy flowers for Stephen's funeral. He said that you thought I had the closest taste to Stephen's. He said you wanted to meet me at the police station because you'd be there to sort out your visa. Swami even gave me money for them. Here, take it,' he said, pulling out a wad of five-hundred-rupee notes, far too much.

I smiled despite myself. Poor Rani. He'd thought he was going to buy flowers. Instead he'd ended up in a police cell, then on a mission to find Stephen's father, who had turned out to be his own guru, the closest thing he had to a father himself. Not a normal morning, even for these strange times, even for this strange guy.

'OK, Rani, we won't say any more about this for now. Let's get those flowers.'

I'd talk to Swami Shiva directly. I'd leave Rani out of it. It wasn't fair on him. He didn't need to be involved in this.

By the time we reached the local flower seller, Rani was acting like nothing had happened and I acquiesced.

'You know Stephen loved the big flower fans, the really cheesy ones? He was so into kitsch. He loved the Ganesh at the centre with the fake marigolds all round its base and the jewels in its trunk. I think it was the Indian blood in him . . .' I stopped. I was about to describe Swami and Stephen standing in the garden admiring the statue together but decided against it.

The flower seller worked at a small desk on the side of the road near the crumbling old tomb with blue tiles, on the east side of Nizamuddin. He picked flowers from a line of big buckets leaned up against the railing of the tomb and loved to make flamboyant displays. Oranges, pinks, yellows would be fanned out in lines above some plastic trinket, designed to sit against a wall like a funny floral peacock.

Rani helped me order. A large fan of various colours for me; and for the ashram, several fans of yellow marigolds, the colour of the Shiva network. When I tried to pay, the flower seller tutted and frowned and pushed away the money.

Rani explained. 'He doesn't want to be paid for them. He remembers Stephen – he's upset. I'm going to take our marigolds now but he said for you to come back on the way to the funeral tomorrow. He wants to get some lilies to go in your fan which he'll pick up early in the morning.'

'Tell him to take the money. Death is part of his job, right?' I said.

Rani argued with him gently but was rebuffed again. 'His mother is in the yoga hostel Swami Shiva set up for widows in Varanasi; he doesn't want to charge the Shiva network,' he said.

I helped Rani back to the ashram with the flowers. I left him arranging them in the garage. There was space for them there; the Mercedes still hadn't been returned.

'I'm . . . I'm just going to give Swami Shiva the money for the flowers back, Rani,' I said.

'Hmmm.'

I'd tried to sound casual but it didn't matter so much. Rani seemed to have forgotten, or blocked out, the whole trip to Haksar Haveli and the police station. He was acting like we really had just spent our day choosing flowers. He was engrossed with checking each head now, arranging the fans in order of size. He looked like a child.

Swami was in meditation in his private quarters. As I waited for him to finish I browsed once again through the photos arranged on the wall. He might have actually got them up there for just that moment. Like magazines in a dentist's waiting room. For a man with so many responsibilities, he spent a lot of time sitting down with his eyes shut.

I had a thought. Could Claudia be up here? I searched through the wall of photos quickly, looking out for colour images, the faded, old style instead of the new, sharper digital images. And I thought I found her; right at the top of the wall in the corner. Swami Shiva was holding her up in a head-stand, a mane of red hair spreading out around her. He was smiling. They were alone. It looked like they were on the roof of a building. The sky was fluorescent orange and there were silhouettes of two kites in the distance. It was the red hair that gave Claudia away at first, but looking at her face I saw the same excitement and intelligence contained within Stephen's photo of his mother that I still had in my wallet. I hadn't given it to Sir Charles.

'Ruby,' Swami Shiva called.

I whipped round, blushing. 'Ah, Swami, the flower seller wouldn't take the money.'

'Why not?'

'His mother is in your widows' home in Varanasi.'

'Ah – well, let's donate it to her. Would you drop it in the collection box downstairs, please?'

There were several small collection boxes with the name of different projects stuck to them in reception, like in a church.

'Swami, I brought a photo of Stephen's mother with me. You know he was trying to find out what happened to her here in India?'

'Yes, yes,' Swami said.

'I thought – I don't know – you might recognise her, she could have come to the centre here maybe. She lived in Delhi for a bit.'

He kept his eyes on the photo for some time studying it, unembarrassed by the bikini. 'No, no, I don't think I know her. She might have visited my centre but it was a long time ago and there have been many students.'

'Ah. It was worth a try anyhow.'

'Yes, of course.'

Swami's eyes flicked out to the side. I thought he was lying.

'Swami, Stephen texted me about his father the day he died. Did you see him that day? Did he say anything to you about this?'

'No, no, I don't think I spoke to him that day at all,' he replied.

'Swami, could I borrow your phone very quickly? I left mine at home. I want to make a call to Sir Charles about the funeral tomorrow and I don't want to upset people using the phone in reception.'

Swami agreed immediately, pulling out a mobile from his robes.

'Please, Ruby, use the meditation room downstairs to make the call. It's quiet and private in there.'

The room smelled of incense and had a small shrine to Kali, the goddess of destruction. I sat in front of the little statue, which was dressed and garlanded. I was looking for evidence that Swami had spoken to Stephen on the phone the day he died. I flicked through Swami's address book. Stephen's number wasn't there. I went to his message folder. There were none – Swami obviously hadn't got to grips with texting. I went into his call log. He had made a few today and yesterday and on the day Stephen died. One number that day looked like Stephen's. I double-checked with my phone. It was Stephen's number. Swami hadn't thought about deleting his phone history.

I went back upstairs to Swami Shiva with his phone in my hand.

'Did you make your call, Ruby? Did you find out the details for tomorrow?'

'Ah, no actually, Swami Shiva, I didn't. I actually . . . well . . .'

I didn't know how to begin this conversation, so I took out the photo of Claudia once more and put it down in front of him.

'Swami, do you not recognise Stephen's mother?'

He looked at the photo again. Stared at it and didn't say anything.

I took down the photo I had seen on the wall, of Swami and Claudia together, and laid it down beside my picture.

'Swami, that's the same girl, isn't it? With you? You're holding her up in a headstand.'

Swami looked carefully. 'Yes, yes, it looks the same I think. I have so many pupils, Ruby. I'm sorry.'

'But look at this photo, Swami. This isn't in any centre of yours, is it? This is in Old Delhi, in Haksar Haveli.'

He looked up at me quickly. His lips went slack and his eyes went tight; he looked old. 'Ruby?'

'Stephen went down there looking for the place. Knew his mother had been staying in the house when she got pregnant with him. He didn't find it, but I did. Yesterday. I spoke to the woman who owns Pearl Beauty Parlour.'

Swami stared at me for a while. Then he simply stared out in front of him. 'She did like to get her hair oiled,' he said to himself.

Fucking hell. It's him. Swami Shiva. Fucking hell. Stephen's father. This was insane. This was so very Stephen. He must have been over the moon when he found out. He would have loved that – his dad the celebrity yoga guru. No wonder he wanted to wait to tell me in person. He'd have wanted to see the look on my face. But, God, this meant so many other questions too. My mind was racing but I tried to talk carefully.

'Were you involved with her, Swami? Did you have a relationship with Claudia?'

He didn't say anything.

'Rani doesn't believe it.'

Swami flicked his head round to me. 'Rani? Rani was with you?'

I explained to him what had happened. 'But Rani doesn't believe it at all. He says you wouldn't be so powerful, have so much healing in you, if you had ever broken your vows of Brahmacharya. He says you're not like normal people.'

'If only that were true,' said Swami.

'So he's wrong. You were involved with Claudia?'

Swami shook his head. He looked like a worried grandfather. 'It wasn't how you imagine. It wasn't sordid. It wasn't, it wasn't. It wasn't like all these horrid stories you hear in newspapers.'

'How was it then, Swami?'

He shook his head. 'Is this really the right time to talk about it?'

'I don't see any other time,' I said.

'Then wait here. I want to show you something.'

Swami left the room and came back some minutes later with a folded piece of paper. 'I've kept this for over thirty years.'

He handed it to me and I opened it. It wasn't yellowed but it was frail. It was a fax from Sir Charles to Claudia.

Foreign and Commonwealth Office
From: Sir Charles Newby, Ambassador to Laos PDR
15 June 1979

Claudia,
I have been talking to the mother of your friend Laxmi,
Padma Patel. She has informed me that you did not return
to Delhi with Laxmi. She told me you are in an ashram in
the south of India.

This will not do. I agreed to you visiting India on condition that you stayed with Laxmi and did not go off on your own gallivanting around.

I can hear you arguing with me now. You are not an adult because you are eighteen. You have not proved to me that you can make your own decisions. You were threatened with expulsion from school three times in the last year. I do not have much hope for your A level results – but you do thankfully have a place at university and I expect you to be back in England for the start of term.

Your mother is beside herself with worry here in Laos. It's been a difficult placement to begin with and the hot weather is not agreeing with her at all. Please don't add to her stress by staying down in this ashram – I would like you to go back to Delhi immediately and telephone her from there.

Please do not make me send anyone from the embassy down there – which I will have to do to stop your mother making the trip herself if she doesn't hear from you. This really will be a waste of their and our resources.

Looking forward to hearing from you on your return.

With my best wishes,

Papa

I read it and handed it back to Swami Shiva. 'Sir Charles seems to have mellowed with age,' I said.

'I was sent to give this to Claudia. That's how I met her.'

'You know Sir Charles? But he doesn't know you? That doesn't make sense,' I said.

'No, no. Let me explain. I met Claudia when she was on a, you call it, "year out" between school and university. I had just set up this first Shiva centre in Delhi. In this very building we're in now, though it was much smaller then – more basic, just a room, no running water even.

'I had been living in a rural ashram in South India with my guru, Swami Vishnu Govinda. He'd decided my future was in teaching asana practice and had sent me to Delhi to bring forest yoga to the city. Swami Govinda was, of course, a spiritual man but he watched the world too. He listened to the radio and he read the newspaper. He saw that India was changing. He told me we needed to reach out to the new middle classes, living in the cities, working in offices. To the men and women who don't have time for hours of devotion or practice.

'It had been very hard work but was going well. My classes were popular – especially, I have to say, with ladies. One of my regular students, a rich Gujarati lady, Mrs Patel, donated this building to use as a centre. One day after class she asked me to help her with a problem. Her daughter Laxmi had had a friend from her school in England to stay after their A levels. They'd gone travelling in the south of India and ended up in Pune, at Osho's ashram.'

'Osho, I've heard of him. He's the sex guru, right? The one who says you can do anything you want to. The one that got sent to jail in America.'

'Yes. But this was many years before all the international scandals about Osho and I think he was still a genuine spiritual leader. Though there were already rumours and articles in local newspapers that he encouraged group sex, drug taking, drunkenness. Osho was attracting a lot of Western attention and I wasn't sure at the time whether all these worries were simply jealousy. Other gurus missing the large donations Westerners had made to their own ashrams before leaving for Osho.

'Nevertheless Mrs Patel was concerned. Her own daughter had come home but her friend was still at this ashram. This girl's father was a powerful figure, a diplomat. He'd been on the phone with Mrs Patel and when he had found out where his daughter was supposed to be he'd been very, very angry. He'd said he would send the vice-consul down to Pune if she didn't come back immediately. He sent Mrs Patel this fax to forward on to his daughter – whom I'm sure you've realised was Claudia.

'But there were no fax machines in Pune. I knew that much. My own guru's forest hermitage was only a few miles from this new ashram. Even personal phone lines were rare there, computers unheard of. The only way of getting this fax to Claudia was by going down and giving it to the girl in person.

'Claudia was overexcitable, according to Mrs Patel. Padma's nose wrinkled up when she told me about Claudia's ecstasies over the Sufi singers at Nizamuddin, how much she'd taken to "Eastern religions".'

'She used to visit the Sufi singers? Stephen loved the singers – he loved them!'

Swami smiled, but I had interrupted him, he wanted to tell his story. His eyes weren't seeing me; they were on Mrs Patel.

'She thought that if anyone could convince Claudia to come back it would be me – a swami, a spiritual leader – but one young enough to understand her passions. What could I say? This lady had given me my centre. Of course I couldn't refuse her request. It was also an excuse to visit my guru, to visit the ashram I had lived in since I was seventeen. And to visit my old father. He'd been angry when I'd taken vows – of course he had wanted me to marry and have children. But he'd mellowed with age; after the death of my mother we had started writing to one another. He was a clever man. A doctor.

'I took a three-day train journey and went first to my father. He was melancholy and nostalgic and cried when he held my hand. He said he was lonely and wished he'd been able to have more children. It was a hard visit. But my spirits were lifted by my old hermitage, the cinnamon and pomegranates growing in the garden, the paper stars above the porch. My guru was very pleased with me. He'd heard excellent reports from Delhi. He told me I was a lucky man to have found my vocation at such an early age – I was thirty-one – but he warned me that I must keep focused, not get distracted by popularity or the world. He kissed me on the forehead as I left, something he had never done before.

'Osho's ashram was worlds away from my quiet forest. I could hear laughter and screaming as I walked up the drive. It reminded me of army barracks – a series of low concrete buildings painted white, with scrub and dust roads in between. The Murtha River ran down one side of the complex.

'Everyone was dressed in shades of orange and red and yellow. There were some Indians but mainly foreigners. Everyone was grinning. I immediately stood out in my white robes and I saw suspicion in the receptionist's eyes. She was most unhelpful when I asked for Claudia, telling me there was absolutely no one of that name in the ashram. But it became clear to me that no one here used their real names when she called out to a tall blond man named Shiva. He didn't look like any Shiva I had ever known – more like a Hans or an Olaf.

'Mrs Patel had given me a photo of Claudia with the fax and I had studied them both on the train down. She was already imprinted on my mind. I asked for the girl with long red hair and this blond Shiva knew exactly whom I meant. He was very happy to take me to her; perhaps it was an excuse to talk to her himself. I remember feeling protective of her, even before our first meeting. I have told myself since then this was a sign of our spiritual connection, but if I am honest, really honest, perhaps it was just simple attraction.

'She was in what they called a group yoga session down by the river. There were people crying and screaming, tearing each other's clothes. It was quite amazing. Then they all started hugging and kissing one another. I felt myself blushing. This wasn't yoga like I had ever seen it. Finally this group exhausted themselves and fell over on the grass, just lying around smiling, looking happy, dazed.

'Shiva led me over to a young girl with long red hair spread out behind her on the grass. She was lying back and smoking a cigarette. Everything was suddenly dazzling: the yellow sun, the blue river, the green grass, her red hair, her white skin, her blue eyes. It was the emotion of my last few days I think; I suddenly swooned.

'The next thing I knew I was staring up into the blue; worried faces, bodies dressed in orange, looking down on me. The most worried was this red-headed girl. She had her hand on my forehead.

'"Don't worry. I did first aid at Girl Guides – I got the top mark," she said. "Let's turn you on your side! Recovery position!"

'These orange people scattered like ants as she hauled me round on my side and started to fiddle with my hands. Then she lay down next to me – her face opposite mine.

'"Are you OK? This is going to stop you being violently sick and choking on it and drowning in your own vomit. How do you feel? Do you feel like that is going to happen? Don't you worry, I got the top mark for first aid," she said.

'"I am OK," I said.

'"You're not going to be sick?" she asked.

'"No, I don't think so. Can I get up?" I said.

'I remember quite liking it down there with this girl facing me and she seemed to read my thoughts.

'"It's quite nice down here, isn't it? Us two lying down on the grass talking like this. Why don't we just stay here for a bit? You can do what you like with Osho you know – that's what's so good about it here," she said.

'"OK," I replied.

'"Who are you? Shiva said you'd come to see me," she said.

'"I've come to rescue you."

'She let out a laugh like a donkey. "Rescue me! That's a laugh! I've just saved your life!"

'"I simply fainted, madam. You did not save my life," I said.

"Well – anyhow – who are you? Why are you all in white? You know you're supposed to wear orange – the colours of

172

the sun. That's why everyone loves me so much here, because I have hair the colour of the sun too. What's your name?" she asked.

'"My name is Swami Shiva. I wear white because I am a swami – I am a monk. I have renounced worldly pleasures and devoted myself to Brahmacharya and the practice of yoga," I answered.

'"What's your real name?"

'"What do you mean?" I asked.

'"OK, that's your Swami name, but what's your real name? They all call me Priya here and I hate it. I mean, that isn't what my mum and dad named me. They call me Claudia. That's my name. That's what I've heard since I was a baby. That's important, right? What your parents name you. What's your name? What's the name you started with?" she said.

'I liked that. I did. I hadn't heard my birth name for a long time and I missed it. I told her: Rao. And she said it in a rounded lovely way. I liked her saying that.

'"Anyway, Rao, what's all this business of you coming to rescue me?" she asked.

'"Madam, this place, it doesn't have a good reputation. I've come to take you back to Delhi. It's said there are . . . relations between people . . . bad things happening," I said.

'"Well, I stay away from that . . . it's a little too risqué for me," she said. She blushed and she looked very young, just a child. She sat up and tied her hair back, awkward now. "Anyway, never mind about that, who sent you?"

'I hesitated. I knew this was the time to give her the fax. I had read it several times on the train and I didn't like it. It was an angry and hard letter. I could sense the tension between the father and daughter. But that was what I was here to do – I had to keep my promise to Mrs Patel – she was important to the Shiva network.

173

'I gave Claudia the fax. She read quickly, her face dropping as she did so.

'She went very red and stood up, shaking her head, pointing her finger at me. I was a little scared.

'"You! You! You've come from my father. My God! Daddy! He won't ever let me be. He's always got to have control. I told him I was going to travel and now he's saying I have to go back. I just want to get away for a little time. And then he sent you all the way down here. You poor little man! Well, I'm sorry – I'm not going back – you can tell him that from me. I'm very happy here. You can tell him I might not be coming back to university if you like, too. He *always* thinks he knows what's best for me, but you know he doesn't. He doesn't!" she ranted.

'Well, what was I supposed to do? I didn't know her. I didn't know her father. I was embarrassed and uncomfortable. I didn't know how Western families worked. I couldn't make this girl do anything. She was fierce. But then she calmed down. Sat back down. Patted me on the hand. She could see I was nervous I think.

'"Now, I'm very sorry you made this long trip here and I don't want you to get in trouble with Daddy. Why don't you just come with me to evening meditation and then we'll have supper in the hall, it's all very tasty, and then you can stay in my dormitory, there are spare beds. In the morning you'll be fresh and happy and you can be on your way back. I will ring Mama and calm her down; she is not nearly as bad as he makes out. It's him that does it to her – making her nervous with all this entertaining he wants them to do. You can tell Mrs Patel I'll be back in time for university – that should calm him down," she said.

'Evening meditation was in a large marble hall. There were hundreds and hundreds of devotees all smiling and hugging

174

each other as they sat down. It reminded me of a drugged-up marigold field. When Osho entered they all leaned towards him, like he was the sun, feeding them. He walked through the crowd to a throne in the centre of the room, where he sat to give his evening lecture.

'I remember him scanning the room happily, calmly, before beginning. I caught his eye. Of course I would, I was the only person not in orange. I was dressed in white, like himself. His eyes met mine for one minute, they were dark and triumphant.

'I don't remember much of his lecture. I was more interested in the audience. Their eyes shone while they listened, his voice was nourishing them, helping them grow, it seemed. I wanted to have an effect like that on my students. I wanted to be like Osho, I'm ashamed to say now.

'But he was impressive. How little time it had taken him! Just a few years to gather all these people. It's taken me decades of hard work to build the Shiva network. But I hope it's a more genuine, a more honest approach to life.

'After meditation was dinner. There were bottles of wine brought over from Europe. Claudia drank rather a lot and went quite red in the face. She gave me a kiss, told everyone how I had rescued her, then led me to her dormitory and found me a bed next to hers.

'I watched her chest rising and falling as she slept. She mumbled in her dreams. Sounded angry. The next day I left as she said I should. What else could I do? I gave her the local telephone wallah's number by the Delhi Shiva centre. I told her she could leave a message at any time and I would pick it up.

'I went back to Delhi and gave a full report to Mrs Patel. She was disappointed but said at least Claudia didn't seem unhappy or in trouble. Sir Charles calmed down and said that he wouldn't take further action as long as Claudia kept her word and was back in Britain for the start of university in September.

'Over the next few weeks I found myself checking with the STD booth every day – wanting and waiting for a message from Claudia. One day the telephone wallah waved me over. Told me I had a message from an English lady. She had sounded upset. She was catching the train to Delhi and would reach New Delhi station on Tuesday, at five o'clock.

'I didn't tell Mrs Patel that Claudia was returning to Delhi. Over the next three days her red hair interrupted my meditation.

'Then it was Tuesday. I was early, or the train was late, I can't remember now. The sky was coral through the eaves of the station and I felt happy. I bought some roses. I bought them to be kind, not romantic, I wasn't thinking of romance. I remember the flowers as unusually vivid: yellow, pink, white, red, orange. Then the train came in and I saw her long red hair bobbing amongst the black, amongst the families and the businessmen and the porters and the baggage.

'I must have a looked a strange figure there – this young swami dressed in white, holding a bunch of multicoloured roses. When Claudia saw me she began crying. She buried her face in my neck and sobbed. I put my arms around her. It was the first time I had held a woman. In this busy station, where people were shouting, rushing, saying goodbyes and hellos in the setting sun, I had my most private, most exciting moment.'

'How did you end up in Haksar Haveli?' I asked.

'The old mansion had been given to my guru by a devotee of his. Not knowing Delhi, Swami Vishnu had thought that would be a good place to set up my first yoga centre. But I soon realised it wasn't. None of these upcoming middle classes lived in Old Delhi and hardly anyone wanted to make the trip there. So when Mrs Patel donated the building in Greater Kailash – a very fashionable neighbourhood – I lived in Haksar Haveli and travelled into New Delhi to teach every day.

'Claudia's time at the Osho ashram had turned nasty. She didn't tell me exactly what happened, something sexual, I assumed. All she said to me was you shouldn't trust the ones that look most respectable. You shouldn't trust people too much. I said she should go back to her parents. But she was too proud, she didn't want her father to know it had gone wrong, she didn't want anyone to know she was in Delhi. She persuaded me to let her stay with me until it was time to go back to university.

'So we went back together to Haksar Haveli. Claudia loved it there at first, wandering down the winding lanes around the old mansion. And it was good to have company. I had gone from over ten years of communal living to being completely alone in this huge house. I was lonely and didn't know how to keep myself.

'We had no electricity and I'd been living by candlelight in the evenings. Claudia went out in those first days and bought boxes of terracotta oil lamps. She loved them – said they were so cheap and so sweet. We lit them together all over the house. I called the boys in the street selling cardamom milk sweets and bought us two bowls. We'd climb to the top of the roof to watch the sunset and eat them in the fluorescent air. The songs from the mosques mixed with kites and sprays of birds. We talked until the light turned to grey and then to black, about this new city we were both discovering, about Old Delhi and New Delhi and India Gate and Connaught Place. And eventually, well, her eyes would begin to close and I'd lead her to sleep on a thin mattress in the courtyard. It was June and too hot to sleep inside. The mosquitoes buzzed around her and the bats flapped between the eaves. She put her arms out – she didn't want to be left alone – and I let myself be pulled under her sheet. I hadn't been taught how to resist this. Life outside didn't run as strictly or as predictably as in the ashram. My education was lacking in many ways.

'In the mornings, Haksar Haveli wasn't so romantic. It was run-down and shabby, the wax from the evening lamps spilt and greasy on the stone floor. Claudia was alone in this ramshackle warren of rooms, bored and lovesick. She didn't want to do anything but be with me, but I had to work. So she went to get her hair cut and her nails done and waited for me to come back, getting more and more bored. I didn't know she was pregnant. I'm not sure even she did. It was the Kashmiri woman in Pearl Beauty Parlour, Nida, who first realised. She came over in the morning to give me a massage and heard Claudia being sick in the toilet. She didn't say anything to me but went to see her in the bathroom. I'd thought Claudia was simply adjusting to the food. I was working very hard. Life was becoming difficult between us. Claudia was young and bored and felt trapped in the house. She began to throw tantrums, screaming that she loved me. I didn't know what I was doing, how this had happened. I told her to be patient, but in truth I was scared. I was a monk, and I had never ever wanted to follow any path but a spiritual one. I came back from the centre one day and there was a note scrawled in angry handwriting; she was going home. I was mostly relieved. I had fallen in love with Claudia but my path had been chosen and it did not include a woman.

'Only after she left did Nida explain to me Claudia had been pregnant. I wandered around the house, over and over again, roaming through the empty, dusty rooms, thinking of this young girl I hardly knew carrying a child of mine. I never thought I would have a child. I should have followed her, found out at least an address, but the Shiva centre was taking up so much of my time. I was going down to Trivandrum to set up a second branch.

'That's where Rani was found, outside the door of the Trivandrum ashram. And I thought he was my son, given to me by Claudia. I had thought of Claudia as a maharani, a princess, and he was found with a bracelet saying "Rani". It was a sign, a way of her telling me that this was our son and that she wanted me to look after him. So I thought everything was OK. Of course if I had thought about it properly I would have known that he wasn't quite the right age. And he is dark, darker even than me. But Rani really is my son now. Even if he didn't want to stay in the network, if he didn't want to teach or take vows or live the ashram life, he is still my son and I love him. We are a family.'

'But he isn't your son, is he? Stephen was your son. Did you know this? You spoke to him twice the day he died. I saw it on your phone. I checked.'

Swami raised his eyebrows. 'I found out Stephen was my son the day he died. I'd called him to the ashram, to talk to him about what had happened between Rani and him on Holi. I wanted to explain to Stephen how serious this had been. How damaging it was for Rani to be involved with him, both for his spirituality and his reputation.'

'Stephen knew this. I know he felt terrible about it actually,' I said.

'Rani is responsible for his actions too. I simply wanted to protect him from making mistakes he would regret later, from making the same mistake I made with Claudia. You fall in love with the wrong person and you're haunted for the rest of your life.'

'What happened, Swami?'

'He came into my quarters while I was meditating. He coughed; I knew he was there. But I needed one more minute within myself, to make my mind still, to talk to him without anger. When I opened my eyes, he'd taken the picture of Claudia off the wall and was staring at it. The same way you did. I don't know why I put it up again. I'm a foolish fond old man, I think. I couldn't bear not to have it on the wall, where it had been for so many years. And I didn't want to hide it. I didn't want to hide it.'

'What happened when he took the picture down?'

'He looked at it. He said, "This is my mother." And I asked to see it. When I saw it was Claudia I knew that Stephen must be my son. When I looked up at him I saw my own father's eyes. He had flecks of green just as my father had. He looked at me very carefully. "Are you the man in the picture, Swami?" I said I was. He continued to look at me. He asked me my name before I became a swami. My birth name. Just as his mother had done. I told him. Rao. He asked me if I was his father. I said I thought I probably was. I stood up. We looked at each other. We didn't hug. I wanted to hug him but we just stood there looking at each other. Stephen looked feral.'

'What happened then?'

'I asked after his mother. Stephen told me Claudia had died. This was a shock. I'd always had a sense she was in the world somewhere. I'd imagined her, older now but still beautiful, living in a hot country maybe. Mexico, I'd thought, I don't know why. Barefooted and laughing and brown. That red hair maybe a little bit grey. Then to find out she'd died so many years ago. That she's buried in a wet English graveyard. I couldn't speak.

'But Stephen wanted me to tell him all about what had happened between us; he wanted it all right away. The questions started: one after the other after the other. He wanted to know about his mother. It seemed like he hardly knew her

180

at all. He didn't know what had happened. He knew nothing. He knew nothing.

'But I couldn't speak. I've been explaining Hindu mysticism, the most abstract theology to students for years and years and I couldn't tell my own son his own story. I couldn't begin to heave it all, after almost thirty years, into my mouth. He thought I was being secretive, silent. He got angry. He started shouting at me that I had taken advantage of her, that I was a hypocrite. I couldn't say anything. He said he could ruin me if he wanted. I heard students moving around downstairs, laughter. I thought about Rani. What if he came and saw this? What effect would this have on him? I asked Stephen to be quiet. That made him even angrier.

'"I hate you! This isn't how it was supposed to be!" he said.

'And he just walked out. I heard his motorbike drive off. I sat for a while and then I called Raj. We went out looking for him.'

'Did you tell Raj what had happened?'

'Not at first, but as we drove around the city a rising hysteria crept through me. I'd kept this secret for so long and I couldn't keep it any longer. I told him the story, I told him what had happened. He didn't say much. He must have been shocked but he kept calm, as he always has done.

'It got dark and in the end I told Raj to turn back home. It was nearly time for evening satsang and the students, Rani, would notice if I wasn't there. Of course my meditation that evening was profoundly disturbed. I had found my son but acknowledging him would mean losing my whole life's work. There is no way people would accept me as a guru if they found out I had had an illegitimate child. And what if Stephen decided to talk without my consent? What then? Would I deny it?

'Soon after satsang, Raj said he might have an idea where

Stephen was. He said he would be back later on. He told me not to worry, to go to bed and everything would be all right in the morning. But it wasn't. In the morning we had a call from the police.'

'What had happened? What did Raj say? Did he tell you he'd run Stephen over?' I asked.

'Raj told me he hadn't found Stephen the night before. The next thing I know we're identifying his body. And then suddenly the inspector and you are at the centre and it seems Raj has made off with his motorbike.'

'You didn't know it was in your garage?'

'No, no, I didn't know. The next time I spoke to Raj was when he'd been arrested and he'd made that statement. He said he'd knocked into him as he'd been going to look for him a second time. It had been dark, Stephen had been driving too fast, he told me,' said Swami.

'Do you believe him?'

'Well, what other explanation is there?'

'What else did he say?'

'Raj asked me to look after Sita. To get her out of Dakshinpuri; he asked me to buy her an apartment. I agreed, of course. He told me he hadn't killed Stephen. He looked at me and asked me if I believed him. I said I did and I asked him again if the statement was really true or whether he'd been beaten into a confession. He was in a bad state when I saw him.

'Raj said it was true enough but he asked me to make sure he was charged with manslaughter, not murder. He said he wasn't a murderer. He didn't want his children to grow up thinking he was. I spoke to Inspector Mukerjee. Explained this. He said he'd be obliged to help.'

'I found Inspector Mukerjee bashing in the bumper of your car, to match up with Raj's statement, I assumed. It made me mad to think that Stephen didn't die the way Raj said.'

Swami Shiva raised his eyebrows. His lower lip had begun to move up and down. 'Really?'

'I went to see Raj – with Rani. I told him what I knew and he said ask Stephen's father for the truth.'

'You took Rani with you? When?'

'Today.'

'When you were supposed to be buying flowers?'

'I needed someone who spoke Malayalam.'

'And he said to ask me for the truth?'

'No, he said ask Stephen's father.'

'He told you I was Stephen's father?'

'No. He clammed up straight after. I don't even think he meant to say that but we'd been telling him about Sita. It clearly upset him to think of her so distraught. We told him Sita wasn't interested in moving out of Dakshinpuri now he was in prison. That's what she told us.'

'Why did you disturb him so much? Why did you upset him? I will move her out of there, I have spoken to her and she does want to move,' said Swami.

'But why did he say you knew the truth? The chief investigator in this case is tampering with the evidence and when I tell the suspect that I think he's covering for someone he says find Stephen's father. That's you.'

'Ruby, I have told you all I know. I had a conversation with Inspector Mukerjee, about Raj, about whether he would be charged with manslaughter or murder. The inspector told me he would make sure it is manslaughter. I don't want to speculate on actions I know nothing about but it wouldn't surprise me if this gentleman thought he was doing everyone a good turn by helping the case along with better evidence. I'm afraid this is how it often works here. Beat out a guilty confession, fix the evidence.'

'And you think that is OK?'

'Of course I don't. I just know the reality.'

I felt as if my head were going to explode.

'I think the question is now whether you trust me?' said Swami Shiva.

'What do you mean? Whether I trust you are telling me the truth?'

'I think, whether you trust me enough to keep my secret. This has been a tragedy. If Stephen hadn't died then there would have been some hard decisions to make. But I think it's my place to look after the living now. To look after Rani, to look after the students here in Delhi and round the world.'

'You don't feel you should come out and tell the truth?'

'What would be the point? Stephen will be buried tomorrow. His mother is dead. His grandparents are old. What good would it do him? Or me? He should be buried in peace, shouldn't he?'

It'd be the scoop of my life. The message Stephen sent me, he'd said it was a big story. If you call something a story you want it told. And if he'd been talking to me about it, he wanted me to tell it. I was the obvious choice. He'd wanted revenge. Did Swami Shiva stop him telling the story himself? How Stephen had died was still not clear and there was nothing to prove Swami Shiva didn't have a hand in it. But did I want to devastate the man's life? No, I didn't.

Swami didn't stop me leaving with his secret. He said he would pray for me to make the right decisions. I reeled out of the gate of the ashram and into the paan wallah, packing up his things. How late did he stay here usually? Would he know the comings and goings of that night? Whether Raj had gone out a second time? Whether Stephen had gone off on his motorbike at all?

'Stephen? *Yeh raasta?*'

The paan wallah tried hard to understand my bollocks

Hindi but I hadn't the words to ask him. You can't work out a killing in baby talk. I'd have to enlist yet another translator. God Almighty. This would be a lot simpler if I were a local. But for now it would wait till after tomorrow's funeral. We'd bury Stephen in peace, without a father, the way he was born.

17

The funeral was at eleven the next morning. I was wearing a dark-blue dress with small white flowers from an expensive French store in London. I'd brought it with me to Delhi but had never found an important enough occasion to wear it, until today.

I ordered a taxi not a rickshaw. I was shaking and kept checking my handbag, making sure my phone was on silent in case I forgot when I got in the church, but then constantly checking in case anyone had called me. I picked up my flower fan from the florist. The lilies' sickly, sweet smell overpowered the taxi. The air was close and the sky low, hot and humid.

We drove up the highway, glimpsing the Yamuna, past the Red Fort and on through Kashmere Gate station. The metro was built up high above the rubbish and burning incense of the old railway. Trams sprung gleaming and clear from the new tunnel, though clouds loomed behind. It looked like it was going to rain, the beginnings of the monsoon.

I was caught below between rusty Blueline buses. My taxi was an old black and yellow. It didn't have AC and so fumes swam in through the window and sweat patches appeared under my arms.

Eventually I was at St James', a pretty yellow plaster church. It was still two hours to the service and I was one of the first to arrive. I knew before I left I would be illogically early but the thought of being just a minute late was not acceptable to me. I prefered to have the time to think on my own.

The doors were open. My mouth was dry, my hands clammy. Memories and images of Stephen flashed through my mind. His funeral. He was really gone. This wasn't some weird Delhi game. I climbed out of the car, took a deep breath and walked towards the white plaster entrance. I wished I wasn't on my own. I missed him the most at this moment.

Sir Charles was at the church door in a tailored black suit. He looked up with instant recognition and grabbed my hand. He kissed me on the cheek.

'Ruby, good to see you.'

'You too, Sir Charles. Where is your wife?'

'She's inside finishing the flowers. I'm so pleased she was up to arranging them herself. And the music. We're beginning with a Bach choral before some hymns that Stephen used to like to sing. Come in,' he said, taking my elbow.

Sir Charles and I sat in the empty pews, a few from the back, watching his brittle wife make final touches to the huge displays of creamy begonias and peach lilies.

'I'm proud of her. She's come through for today. We're flying out tonight after the reception and I really hope she leaves the sedatives behind. I think she can; she can move on. We're supposed to be on a cruise, you know, now. Of course she doesn't want to go at all but I'm trying to persuade her that we'll join it. I've booked the flights to the Bahamas, though she doesn't know that yet. I think it'll be what she needs,' he said.

I stared up at the altar where the priest was busy blessing and preparing the Mass. I felt sorry for Lady Newby. Sir Charles invited me to sit in the front by the choir stalls where I watched the black congregation begin filing into the church. A stream of well-preserved officials greeted Sir Charles with sombre smiles and condolences. Sir Charles maintained his professional, easy-going charm.

'Gosh, it is hot today!' I heard him say in a voice that was meant to be hushed, but strain made loud. 'I'd forgotten the climate; I've been in Europe so long! Reminds me of when I was in Laos, it got fiercely hot, used to take a bath three times a day sometimes. And the funny thing was the locals loved saunas!' he continued, rambling a little, used to being a host, but not at his grandson's funeral. Trauma lay close to the surface of his chat.

His wife was standing at the door but she didn't speak, just held people's hands, trying to smile without too many tears. Swami Shiva and Rani arrived, followed by their students. All were in dazzling white except Chewy, who wore a black shirt with white orchids.

My eyes flitted around, meeting the gazes of people I hadn't seen for some time. There was a lot of this weird smiling going on, a rising climax in the room. Sir Charles was now up at the front, seating his wife, talking to the priest who was making last-minute preparations, putting the hymn numbers in the board above the pulpit. There was an organist to one side, arranging his music.

Camera crews, international and Indian channels, had been barred from entering. They were waiting in a gaggle outside the gates; I could see them still setting up as the last few mourners slid in at the back. There was a cluster of invited foreign news correspondents in the far corner looking blasé and tired. I wondered at the glamour that was supposed to

surround them. I spotted Eddie Challan, the *Telegraph* correspondent. He was wan and yellow, with dark circles under
his eyes. He saw me looking at him and nodded. Any dreams
of being invited to step into his shoes vanished then. I could
never be Eddie Challan, with his body of war-zone writing
and at least one kidnapping story.

I flicked through the hymn book. It was all English hymns.
We were beginning with William Blake's 'Jerusalem'. Stephen
had loved Blake; loved his poems. Stephen told me Blake was
the first hippy, that he'd seen angels in the seediest parts of
London.

The church was suddenly crammed. The organ sounded
out four parts of a Bach chorale and the congregation's thin
singing began, earnest and flat.

The door opened, bright blue light cracked in with the coffin.
The four Indian bearers struggled under the weight of the
oakwood coffin shipped from England. They were used to lighter,
cheaper coffins going to be burned at the city crematorium.

I was sorry Sir Charles hadn't asked me to help him find
friends to carry the coffin. Stephen would have preferred that,
I thought. Maybe even I could have done it.

Seeing the coffin was strange. I couldn't take my eyes off
it. He was in there. The scene began to blur, tears were
streaming down my face. Was he lonely in there? Could he
see himself? Was he OK? What was he wearing? I could never
have thought of this wooden box as being all of Stephen but
it was. It contained all of him and there was nothing else.

There was a sermon. The priest's English was good but he
had a lisp and it was hard to hear what he was saying. He
said something about Stephen being in heaven and how we
should all be thankful we knew him for the time we did, that
he was looking down on us. It sounded crap to me. I didn't
want to hear this. I couldn't believe that some innate good-

ness lay in such a pointless death and I didn't see why this priest was trying to convince us that it did. It just didn't. There was nothing good about it.

The priest finished speaking, and we began another hymn. 'Morning Has Broken'. Then Sir Charles stood up. He looked old. He invited us all to bury Stephen and then on to the Imperial for a reception celebrating his life.

Lady Newby had arranged a Bob Marley track to be played as the coffin was carried out. 'Redemption Song'. Stephen would have been embarrassed at something so obvious, but Lady Newby had held on to the pop star as someone she knew of herself and Stephen had played. She'd asked me just before the service began if it was the right choice and I'd said it was perfect.

The fuzz of the speakers came on as the coffin was carried out. It wobbled as the bearers brought it up and one of the lovely flower arrangements fell off. They righted it and Stephen began travelling out. But Bob Marley hadn't begun. Sir Charles and others looked around with faces of severe strain; there was no second chance at this. The music started eventually, loud, a little distorted, but something about the beat flooded me with relief. I cried again as Stephen was followed out by Sir Charles and his wife. When they had gone and the song stopped playing we all looked about us, not quite knowing what to do.

Swami Shiva, Rani and I rode with Sir Charles and Lady Newby to bury Stephen. We travelled in an old white Ambassador at the head of a loose convoy to the cemetery, past the TV cameras outside the gates. Stephen was being buried in Nicholson Cemetery, an old British graveyard.

Clouds began to roll lower over the furious sun. Splotches of wet started to smack the windscreen as we reached the peeling colonial gates of the wide, scrubby cemetery.

No one had thought to bring umbrellas. We buried Stephen in the heat and the rain. Sharp wet darts came down in sheets, churning the earth to mud and running the ink of the priest's cheap Bible. Lady Newby was shaking.

We threw mud on the coffin and Lady Newby cried. 'Bye, darling,' she said, as she threw some soil into the hole.

Sir Charles stood by her. He had a clod of earth in his hand but couldn't bring himself to throw it in. His arm kept going up and then down, tears and rain streaming down his face. The mud began to run in rivulets over his hand, seeping into his white shirt. He looked around, noticed Swami Shiva nearby looking confused.

'Swami Shiva, here, throw it to say goodbye,' he said, breaking a little of his own lump off for Swami before gently throwing in his own. They looked like weak tramps together. Sir Charles' lips were trembling; Swami's nose was running. Rain and maybe tears ran down both their faces. Stephen's grandfather and his sort-of father – two men, worlds apart, yet connected and the same. Powerful and worldly – broken by one young man.

I was the last to throw in some earth; the words stuck in my throat, I didn't know how to conclude this so I didn't say anything.

Our white Ambassadors were now brown and grimy, spattered with graveyard mud. We arrived at the Imperial sodden and dried off on thick little towels held out by waiters. Drinks were handed out immediately: red wine, white wine, whisky and soda, beer. I picked up a beer. Sir Charles took a whisky and soda and his wife had a white wine.

There were photos of Stephen blown up on the walls in the main hall. I liked the one of a small good-looking child about to dive into an outdoor swimming pool. Then at Christmas, surrounded by presents; one of Stephen on a horse, looking solemn. There was another of him as a slim teenager, before a concert, holding his violin nonchalantly. I didn't even know he had played. A photo marking his first day at university, standing at the door of his home in Holland Park, kettle, luggage, toaster, duvet surrounding him, Sir Charles and Lady Newby hugging him, grinning from ear to ear. From later that day, a photo of him sat on a little bed in his New College room, with Lady Newby looking tearful. Then just before he left for India, a party at home to say goodbye. He looked drunk, a careless cigarette hanging from the side of his mouth, smiling for the camera one of those sultry smiles of his.

'He was a charismatic young man,' said a voice behind me. I turned to see Eddie Challan.

'He was.'

'Eddie Challan – nice to meet you,' he said, putting his hand out.

'I know, I know. I've read your work – from when you were in Baghdad. It was great, really inspiring,' I said.

'Thanks – and thanks for holding the fort for me while I was ill. Typhoid. Not good. I caught it doing a few stories in Orissa.'

'No worries. I mean, I was happy to, of course.'

'Well, you put us right ahead of the game on this story and it was a big one, so thanks, I owe you one. And I'm sorry. I know you were friends with him. I hope today isn't too difficult for you,' he said, handing me his card.

I looked around the room. People were enjoying themselves now, putting their hands out happily for the canapés, smoked salmon and chicken tikka and vegetable rolls. Looking at the photos. There was a din of drinking and laughter. Some people were smoking, blowing the fumes up into the air.

'Stephen would have liked this, all these people out for his funeral. He was the kind of guy to imagine his funeral,' I said.

Eddie gave me a look. He was about to reply but Sir Charles and his wife appeared to say goodbye.

I hugged Lady Newby very lightly in case I ripped her papery skin. Her stark blue eyes locked on my face but I don't think she had any idea who I was.

I finished my drink and got another from a passing waiter, scanning the room for Rani. He was surrounded by adoring girls from the British Council, dazed and happy in dangly earrings and expensive scarves. Chewy was crying with a beer, two of the Japanese girls patting him. I felt lonely and missed Stephen. I felt a hand on my shoulder. It was Swami Shiva.

'Ruby, I'm glad you let us have this day peacefully. Would you like to stay at the ashram tonight? It's not a night to be alone.'

I had a fleeting thought he might try to murder me in my bed so his secret stayed safe, but decided this probably wasn't the case. He was simply giving me good advice; tonight was not a night to be alone in the flat. I didn't want to go home at all.

'Thank you, Swami, yes, that would be good.'

We travelled back to the ashram with a new driver, a short pot-bellied man with a moustache, in a replacement SUV. The rain pelted the car, making the windscreen steam. It was the kind of rain that could scare you if you let it. I stared out at the dancing traffic lights.

18

The lights were on when we arrived at the ashram. There was a police car parked outside and a NDTV truck. Swami Shiva looked at me. I shrugged. I didn't know anything about it. I hadn't told anyone about his secret.

Inspector Mukerjee, Probir and Mukesh were sheltering in the car from the rain. They waved at us and we all rushed together out of the wet into reception. As we shook off the rain, Inspector Mukerjee explained why they were there.

'So sorry, Swami, to disturb today, after the funeral. It's rather embarrassing but we're going to have to search the ashram.'

'Search the ashram? Why?' asked Swami.

'NDTV called and said they'd had a phone tip-off saying there were drug deals going on through the ashram. Of course, it's quite ridiculous, but you know we can't ignore NDTV, especially when the centre has been so closely connected with Stephen's case just now.'

Swami Shiva laughed out loud. 'My God. Drugs. Please go ahead and search. Drugs! I thought it was something serious,' he said. He really looked relieved. 'Chewy, would you get some snacks for everyone, please? And invite the journalists outside to come in as well. It's not a night to be waiting in the car like that. There should be at least some reward for their labours,' he continued.

Swami Shiva went up to his quarters to pray and the rest of us sat in the kitchen drinking chai and eating *chikki*, a kind of Indian peanut brittle.

'You're not really supposed to eat this in the summer; it's a winter food. But it is delicious and it's raining,' said the NDTV reporter, a fidgety girl about my age called Anita, super skinny with short black hair. She was here with her producer and cameraman. They were all pretty relaxed; the cameraman kept taking nips out of a small bottle of whisky in his jacket. Anita pretended not to notice. No one really thought there could be drugs in the ashram. If only they knew the real scoop here they'd go through the roof, I thought, biting my lip. I'd never been so silent on a story. It was killing me.

We continued to discuss winter foods and summer foods. Anita's producer told us it was very, very dangerous to eat yoghurt in the night, any time of year.

Inspector Mukerjee came into the room holding a carrier bag, his dragon eyes were huge and his mouth a grim twist. He wasn't happy.

'Could someone please call down Swami Shiva? We've found something. Heroin,' he said.

I stared at the innocent-looking carrier bag, from Khalkaji Bookshop in Connaught Place, with shocked curiosity.

'Oh my God! We've got a guru scandal!' said Anita, jumping up and into action. 'Pinkoo, call the newsroom, we'll do a live from the truck outside,' she said, racing out of the door, leaving us all stunned.

Swami Shiva came into the room. Inspector Mukerjee took

four packets of brown powder from the bag and placed it on the floor. He crouched down by it and looked at Swami.

'I don't understand,' Swami said.

'It's heroin,' said the inspector.

'What? Where did you find it?'

'In one of the lockers,' said the inspector.

'Who on earth? Really, I cannot think who could have put it there. Here! In my ashram! Whose is this?'

I knew exactly whose it was. I should have realised before. Stephen would have known too.

19

I'd found out about the drugs a few days before Stephen died, a few days after Holi.

We hadn't really left the house since Swami had found Stephen with Rani that day. We didn't go to the centre. We didn't call Rani. He didn't call us. We didn't know what the consequences of the scene, all those gold handprints, had been.

Stephen had been good about it, said he didn't blame me and that Rani didn't either. But the look Rani had given me had been black as he watched me help Stephen to gather his things before scurrying off.

Stephen bought some jasmine tea to cheer us up and we sat around the flat just drinking tea and smoking spliffs and trying to figure out what to do.

Stephen said he'd never wanted to jeopardise Rani's life, his career. He felt guilty. He had misbehaved. He'd known I liked Rani and he'd wanted to make me jealous.

'Well, you did make me jealous. I don't know if that was part of the reason I told Swami Shiva you were together. I shouldn't have said anything. But did I know you'd have gone that far? Maybe I did. Maybe I'm as guilty as you.'

'Rani is the only one who wasn't trying to hurt someone. And he's the one who's in most trouble,' said Stephen.

The knit of his eyebrows and slope of his shoulders told me he was tying himself in knots about this, much more than with his usual escapades. He looked tired. He looked ill. He didn't look like Stephen.

'I need something harder than tea and spliffs. I need some brown.'

'What?' I laughed in surprise. 'You mean heroin? Are you kidding me?'

'Yeah. Do you have a problem with that?' He leaned back on the yellow sofa, smirking. 'Most people do.'

He'd been pleased he'd been able to shock me. I tried to recover.

'Not really. I don't care at all really.'

'Have you ever tried it?'

'No.'

'Do you want to? Just smoking. I used to do it all the time when I was in school.'

'Fucking hell, Stephen. Is that not a bit extreme?'

'Fuck you, Ruby. You think you're the only one who is miserable here? You think you're the only one this thing is affecting? Stop being so fucking conservative.'

I didn't like to be thought conservative and taking heroin would prove a theory I had concocted a while ago, about drugs, about most things people are against. That people are only against things nobody has offered to them. I'll try anything once – if I'm offered.

'All right, if you know where to get it, let's go. I trust you. You won't let me die, will you? I know a couple of stories of people dying off bad drugs in Delhi.'

'No, you'll be fine. I know exactly who to get it from. Come to think of it, so do you,' he said.

'What? What are you talking about?'

But Stephen just shook his head and told me to get ready. We rode down on his bike to the traveller strip by the railway station, Pahar Ganj, where Israelis, old hippies and wide-eyed teenagers stayed. Trance music mixed with fisherman's trousers and leather sandals: an easy place to find drugs.

He parked the bike and stood there for a minute.

'What am I doing? What the fuck am I doing?' he said to himself.

'Stephen? Are you OK?' I asked him. He didn't look at me. I put my arm round him and he buried his head in my shoulder.

There was something wrong but I didn't know quite what: Rani or the drugs or his father, maybe all three. Maybe something else. Maybe me. Maybe he liked me more than he'd shown me. But I held him still in the midst of the wails of hawkers and the cows and men on scooters and travellers and rats and drug dealers. He leaned in for some time but then shook me off and lit a cigarette.

'Come on, let's do this. I know you're going to enjoy it,' he said, taking a drag and pulling out his phone.

'*Namaste*, Tito! Are you in? You're on the roof of Metropolis? OK. I'm with Ruby, we're coming up to see you now.'

'Tito?!' I said when he got off the phone. 'Are you kidding me? Is that where you get this stuff? He's a drug dealer? Are you serious?'

I couldn't believe it. Tito was one of the most genteel men I'd met in Delhi. He attended the Sivananda centre every day and many of its religious ceremonies too, which most Westerners shied away from. He had the best Hindi of any foreigner, was studying the language at Delhi University. I'd never seen him drunk, just roll the odd spliff occasionally.

'I wouldn't call him a drug dealer as such. He's got some contact for quality heroin in the north of Delhi, it comes in through the mountains, through Kashmir then Himachal Pradesh. Tito supplies it to the travellers around here for a good price. They get a product they can trust, he makes enough to continue his Hindi studies.'

'But, I mean, it's not right. He's encouraging people,' I said.

'He's making it safer for them, that's all. No one dies from bad overdoses or bad shit because Tito makes sure it is taken responsibly and sells it responsibly. He's not some scourge of society. Honestly, he's doing the whole area a favour. You've got to be realistic about this. Drugs are always going to be sold. It's better to be done by someone intelligent and dependable like Tito than someone who just doesn't give a shit about anyone or anything.'

'But he's supposed to be a yogi. He's a devotee of Swami Shiva. Yogis don't take drugs.'

'This one does. Come on. Don't determine one spiritual path like that!'

Stephen pulled me with him up to the roof of Metropolis, an art deco hotel in the heart of the hippy mess. A stylish social spot in its heyday, as the area dived so did the hotel and it was now a shabby shadow of its former self.

Nevertheless it was still the place to stay for a discerning traveller in Pahar Ganj and I'd always enjoyed its rooftop terrace. You could pretend you were on holiday, amongst the families and the bikers and the kids, drinking their beers and poring over their guidebooks, planning their way to the beaches and mountains.

We found Tito sat on the roof reading *Crime and Punishment* and drinking a lassi. He was brown and healthy and completely relaxed in his ubiquitous fisherman's trousers.

I'd never seen Tito outside the centre, except that one time at Raj and Sita's house. Stephen obviously knew him better. He shook him by the hand and gave him a hug when Tito stood up.

'How you doing, Tito?'

'I'm well. It's getting too hot though, isn't it? After Holi it always starts to get too hot.'

'I don't mind it so much. I prefer it to the cold weather,' said Stephen.

'I'm planning a trip to Himachal Pradesh, to Dharamasala, to stay in an Astanga yoga ashram up there,' he said.

'When are you leaving? It sounds a good trip.'

'Tomorrow, I think. I'll catch the train up to Pathankot and bus it from there.'

'Good job I caught you then,' said Stephen.

'What is it you want?'

'Usual, if that's OK,' he said.

Tito shrugged. 'It's always OK for you. You're not someone I worry about, Stephen.'

I hadn't looked closely at Tito till then but I saw he was older than he seemed on first impression. His black hair was greying at the temples and there were deep lines around his eyes that his brown skin hid well.

Tito had a long-term let at the Metropolis and his room was a good one, with large windows looking out across the street. Green glass rosary beads swung on the handle of the window. There was a neat bookshelf with Portuguese and Hindi titles, as well as a few in English: Seneca, Cicero *On the Good Life*, *The Prophet*, Hermann Hesse, Dickens. I liked talking about books and would have asked Tito about his choices but I was too nervous at that moment.

In the middle of the room was a very low table with a chess game set out to play and two wicker chairs.

'Please sit down. Would you like a game, Stephen? I think you won last time we played,' he said.

Stephen looked at me. I shrugged. I didn't particularly want to watch them play chess. We were there for something else. I was uncertain enough without waiting around for another half an hour.

'Next time, Tito, if that's OK with you.'

'Of course,' he said. 'How much would you like?'

'Just a couple of wraps if that's OK,' said Stephen.

Tito went to a papier mâché box on top of his bookcase and took out two cling-film packets, then handed them to Stephen. 'Would you like to smoke it here?' asked Tito.

'Yes, please. Will you join us?'

'Why not? Thank you. Should we put some music on? Ruby, what would you like to listen to? My iPod is on the floor over there attached to the speakers. Why don't you choose something while Stephen and I prepare this?'

'She hasn't done it before,' said Stephen.

Tito shot Stephen a questioning look and Stephen patted him on the shoulder.

'It's fine. She's cool, man. She wants to try it with us; Ruby's cool, you know that. Anyone can see that,' said Stephen.

Tito nodded his head and I was mollified. I was cool; I was cool with smoking heroin, of course I was. What was the big deal?

I busied myself with choosing music. Tito had a mix of Portuguese and Brazilian artists I hadn't heard of, Indian classical raga, Beethoven, Brahms and English folk music. I was about to ask him how he'd got into these English composers, but decided to leave it for another time and contented myself with playing *The Lark Ascending*, not strictly English folk but something which always reminded me of home.

'Excellent choice, Ruby, my favourite Williams piece. Please come and sit down.'

Stephen and Tito were sat cross-legged round the table with foil and a lighter laid out.

'Ladies first. Stephen, would you like to help Ruby? Ruby, nothing will happen to you. This is very good. Straight from Afghanistan through Kashmir and on to us in Delhi. Just relax and enjoy yourself.'

We sat side by side. Stephen rolled up a straw with the foil, then he flattened out a foil sheet and made a small indent in it.

'OK, hold this right close to your chin. I'm gonna put some brown on it and light it. When the drip starts running down the sheet I want you to suck it in with the straw,' he said.

The drip ran and the smoke rose; I sucked and followed as best I could.

'Come on, you're wasting it! Get closer in. That's it. Get it in the back of your throat, now hold it in, don't blow it out,' Steven encouraged.

'Do you like it, Ruby?' asked Tito.

It was not the insane high I thought it would be. It was sweet and smooth and subtle, like getting stoned, but with none of the paranoia and the nastiness. It took the edge off in a profound way.

'It's OK, yes – it's not bad,' I said.

They laughed.

'Why don't you sit back on the bed while me and Tito have a go?' said Stephen.

So I lay back on the sofa, tasting something sickly sweet in my mouth, feeling cattish, sleepy and like scratching. I watched Stephen follow his own brown drip.

I don't know how long we were there for. I think I fell

asleep. It was dark when Stephen leaned on me with slitty eyes and told me we were going home.

Tito rose from his cross-legged position on the floor with the grace and ease of a regular yogi to see us out the door.

'How much do we owe you, Tito?' Stephen asked him.

'Just give me it next time; I don't want so much money on me when I'm about to travel. You're lucky I had anything anyway, I'd moved most of it out of the hotel to prepare for going away,' he said.

Stephen took my hand in the rickshaw back and rubbed it over and over again. It was good to feel his skin and to feel the warm air on my face.

'Are you OK?'

'Fine.'

'Did you enjoy it?'

'Yeah, I guess, it was cool.'

'It's not a big deal, is it? Really? Brown. Just takes the edge off when you really need it,' he said.

I laughed. 'That's exactly what I thought about it. It takes the edge off.'

I held Stephen's hand and leaned back into the rickshaw, happy with myself. I don't generally do or think what society tells me to do or think. This trip confirmed to me that I was right to be suspicious of what editors, politicians and leaders claim. It was better to follow my instincts, to trust my friends. What was painted as one of society's great evils, heroin, had given me a pleasant evening and there had been no terrible consequences. It was no big deal, smack.

20

That's what I'd thought, but now it seemed I'd been wrong. Heroin had just turned into a very big deal for Swami Shiva and the Shiva network.

'I'm very sorry, Swami Shiva. We really will have to take you into the station for questioning. It's not simple to sort things out quietly when you have a camera crew on the doorstep,' said the inspector, holding the bag at a distance from himself.

'Of course, of course. We'll clear this up straight away. I really don't know what is going on. I want to know myself. This is incredibly serious. Chewy, will you take charge here? Call my lawyer in Mumbai, let him know what is going on.'

'Swami? What's happening?' said Rani, only just appearing. He'd been praying himself at the small temple round the back of the centre.

'Rani. Please, will you stay with Ruby tonight, keep her company? There have been some problems here and I'm going to have to go with Inspector Mukerjee,' Swami Shiva said.

Swami took me to the gate with him. 'Ruby, I am sure I

will be able to clear this up easily tonight. Please don't let anyone know where Rani is. These journalists, they'll hound him if they know. He needs protecting from this. I would appreciate it too if you kept the television off while he is staying with you. I'll explain everything to him when I return,' he said.

The new driver took Rani and me back to my house. There were more television trucks, from Headlines Today and a couple of other channels, arriving at the ashram. I pushed Rani's head into my lap as we went past and he sat like that the whole way back. I rubbed his arm gingerly. His wrists were tiny. He was twenty-eight and I could see he had a few grey hairs. How old he was in his head I had no idea. We slept side by side on my bed that night, neither of us wanting to take Stephen's bed. A few weeks ago this would have been a dream come true for me, but tonight we simply collapsed in our clothes, exhausted.

I got up early the next morning while Rani was still sleeping and switched on the TV. The Swami Shiva arrest was all over the news. 'Guru Drugs Scandal' was the strapline on NDTV. Headlines Today was running with 'Shiva Heroin Network'.

The paper flew through the balcony doors. The *Hindustan Times*' main headline was straightforward enough – CELEBRITY SWAMI SHIVA ARRESTED – HEROIN FOUND AT ASHRAM – but then they'd devoted another whole page to connections between Stephen's death and the heroin. Some bright spark reporter had discovered Swami Shiva had put down a deposit for Raj's wife on a new apartment block in Gurgaon. Questions about Raj's statement were raised in an editorial; it was suggested he may be covering for Swami Shiva. Had Stephen been on drugs the day he died? Was his death more sinister and involved than first appeared? Inspector Mukerjee had refused to comment.

It was becoming less and less clear to me how Stephen died. Stephen smoked weed, he drank, but he'd promised me he only touched heroin very occasionally and only with Tito. Tito was away. I knew Stephen had met with Swami Shiva the day he'd died, but what else?

I called Tito. His phone said he was in an out-of-service area. I knew he was up in the mountains, meditating and practising yoga in his Astanga ashram. He probably didn't even know that Stephen was dead. I didn't know when Tito would be back.

I needed to talk to someone. Sir Charles was out of the country. He hadn't been much help anyhow; he'd only really been interested in making things 'easy' for his wife. I wasn't surprised Stephen hadn't talked to him much. In the end, I dug out Eddie Challan's card and gave him a call, asked if I could meet up with him. He invited me over for coffee.

Rani was still sleeping as I left. I didn't think he'd wake up but I unplugged the TV, hid the newspaper and left a note to tell him not to leave the house. I asked the girl downstairs at the hotel to take him up some sweet lime juice and toast later.

Eddie had a garden. Not just a few pots of palms like most people in Delhi, but a proper lawn and a verandah. A sprinkler shimmered water across the unnaturally healthy grass. Behind it was Eddie, sat in a wicker chair reading the *Hindu*, sucking hard on a cigarette. He looked up as I clanged the iron gate shut behind me but didn't move.

'Ruby. How are you?'

A real answer to this would have taken too long, maybe even some therapy. 'Fine – good, thanks.'

'This story. Swami Shiva. Well, it's amazing. Have you seen it?'

'I was there when they found the drugs. That's kind of why I'm here.'

'OK. Let's go inside and get some coffee.'

Eddie's living room was large – high walls, marble floors and long windows covered in slatted blinds. Three wooden ceiling fans spun swiftly. Bookshelves lined one wall, crammed full of British and Indian histories and fiction. There was a complete set of Graham Greene and the new Gandhi biography. Along the bottom shelf were files of different newspapers. A large table dominated the middle of the room. It was a mess of papers and files and pads, held down with stones and a brass bowl full of cigarette butts. An Apple laptop sat on top of a large atlas.

A smaller occasional table was lodged against one wall, home to a more old-fashioned PC. An Indian girl in a red top and red lipstick sat working on it.

'Shruti, this is Ruby – would you mind fixing us some coffee please?'

The girl turned round and flashed me a big smile, then clopped into the kitchen on very high heels. 'Sure, Eddie.' She had an Indian accent with an American twang.

'Shruti's my assistant, translator, researcher, coffee maker. She makes great coffee.'

'Eddie, I'm going to stop making the coffee if you keep telling people that is part of my job. I've got a degree from Columbia University! I'm a journalist!' she shouted from the kitchen.

'She's angling for my job. I think she might knock me off one day – she's always threatening to lace the coffee with arsenic,' Eddie said with a smirk.

'I'm going to take it outside – it's cooler on the verandah,' she called.

Shruti brought out a brass tray with a cafetière of thick coffee, three small blue cups without handles and a plate of *pains au chocolat*.

'They're from Khan Market – I picked them up today.

They're good,' she said, biting into one. 'Do you take milk? I can get you some if you want – we drink coffee black.'

'Would it be possible for a cup of tea?' I said.

It wasn't a problem. Shruti bustled and helped us with our drinks. Eddie sat back patient and silent. He took a few sips of his coffee and lit another cigarette.

'Can I have one please?' I asked.

He raised an eyebrow and took one out for me. Shruti went for the pack straight after. We lit them together from Eddie's green Clipper lighter.

'I thought you'd given up?' he said to Shruti. He spoke to her with off-hand intimacy, the way people who sleep together, or very much want to, do.

She rolled her eyes. 'I know, but I just feel so left out!' she wailed.

Eddie laughed and turned back to me. 'So what can I do for you, Ruby? Is this visit personal or professional?'

'I guess a bit of both.'

He raised an eyebrow again, took another suck of his cigarette and continued to look at me. 'Swami Shiva is in a lot of trouble today. And some papers are connecting this drugs raid with Stephen's death,' he said.

'It wasn't exactly a drugs raid. The TV is blowing it out of proportion. There was a Khalkaji Bookshop bag with four packets of heroin in it.'

'I think it's the nature of the drug and where it was found, rather than the amount that is exciting everyone so much. But what do you think? You were there. Do you think it's got anything to do with Stephen?'

I looked at them both. I'd been happy to tell Eddie everything I knew about Stephen and Swami in return for some help in sorting all this out. I trusted Eddie, knew his work. But I didn't know this girl.

'Shruti can keep her mouth shut, Ruby. If she doesn't she'll get the sack,' said Eddie. 'Go on, you clearly know things that we don't.'

I started at the beginning. About Stephen's search for his father, about going to the morgue with Swami and Raj, about the car chase with Inspector Mukerjee and finding Raj setting fire to the motorbike, about seeing the inspector bash Swami's car, about taking drugs with Stephen, though not about who else we were with, and finally the revelation that Swami Shiva seemed to be the father Stephen had been searching for.

When I'd finished we all had another cigarette.

'God. You couldn't make this shit up,' Eddie said finally.

'Well, you could, but I'm not,' I said. 'What do I do? Can you help me?'

'I can try. I'd be happy to. I'd like nothing better than to get to the bottom of this. We'll do our own investigation – and then publish a cracking front-page article revealing all,' he said.

'Which wins awards,' added Shruti.

'Perhaps. But definitely means I get my transfer to Shanghai,' he said.

It kind of shocked me the cold way they were both looking at my story; they didn't say anything sympathetic to me at all. But perhaps I'd told it in a mercenary way myself.

My old life with Stephen, our friendship, did not connect up with sitting here in this garden discussing the 'story'. When I thought about Stephen, when I watched myself from the outside, I was amazed at what I was doing and where I was. Was it cold to be working on a story about my friend's death? But it wasn't as though I'd set out to do this, it just happened. I'd been putting one foot in front of the other ever since I got up off that morgue floor and this was where it had got me. The world had bent into strange shapes for me. Colours were more garish than they had been; the tomatoes on the side of the road unnatural and sick looking. My body was flooded with strange hormones and thoughts and I couldn't distinguish between natural and perverse. Perhaps their detached perspective was exactly what was needed to get to the bottom of how Stephen died, the colder the better.

Eddie spoke again. 'Now, there are a few basic questions we need to answer. How did Stephen Newby die? Do we believe Raj's statement or not? Why was Inspector Mukerjee tampering with evidence? Do we believe Swami Shiva? Is he telling the truth when he says that he did nothing to stop Stephen leaving when he found he was his father? Are the drugs connected to Stephen's death or are they completely unrelated? Does Swami know anything at all about the drugs?'

'Just a coincidence, I think,' I said.

'Well, you think they are but you don't know. Stephen bought heroin a few days before he died and someone tipped off NDTV that there were drugs at the ashram. They didn't go to the police and that was clever of them. This could have all got brushed under the table with such a powerful man as Swami Shiva, but the police can't do that with a camera pointed at them. Whoever called up NDTV is clever and has a grudge against Swami Shiva. Another question: who could have a grudge against Swami Shiva?' said Eddie.

'But where do we start with all this? I mean, my head feels like it is going to explode!' wailed Shruti.

'Start at the beginning. Start from where he was found. Why don't you two girls go down to Wazirabad Bridge? That's where Stephen fell in the Yamuna. Talk to people, look around, see what you find. Come back this evening and tell me what you know.'

'Haven't the police already done that?'

'They may have but we haven't. Do your own legwork.'

'What are you going to do?'

'I'm going to talk to Inspector Mukerjee. I've got a good relationship with the man. We've done a few high-profile cases together. He's refusing to make comments now and hasn't called a presser. He must be squirming like hell. I'll see if I can help him if he helps us,' he said.

21

I curled my fingers around the mesh fence of Wazirabad Bridge and stared down at the turgid water below. Stephen's last view? I pushed the fence. It was sturdy. It wasn't coming undone. I squinted at the prayer flags flapping over Majnu-ka-Tilla nearby, ragged and bleached in the sun. North of the bridge was Dakshinpuri and to the south, a temple.

I shook my head and pushed the fence again. Shruti came up behind me. She'd removed her make-up and changed into a loose cotton shalwar. Her dupatta was folded around her ears, covering her hair. She looked the model of Hindu respectability. Then she took a flying kick at the fence.

It bent back and shook, but stayed intact.

'Shruti! You could've broken it,' I said.

'Yeah, but I didn't, did I? It doesn't look like it could have just collapsed . . . and the Yamuna is so choked up and slow, there's hardly any movement. It isn't likely he'd moved far from where he fell. Something definitely happened right here,' she said.

We leaned against the fence, unsure what to do next. It was

a bleak and dusty spot, just Tata trucks rumbling past, sounding their elephant horns, the occasional four-by-four or asthmatic rickshaw. There was nowhere to stop, no reason to stop. The motorway loomed on, scrubby for miles to the north.

'The Punjabis start their dhabas about an hour away from here. There's no point beginning them any closer to the city – nobody wants to stop so soon, especially not if they're going on two- or three-day day trips,' said Shruti.

No one was selling anything on the bridge, there wasn't even a man with a kettle up here – and you can get a cup of tea in practically any nook or corner of Delhi.

'It's an astounding suicide effort to pull yourself up there – I mean, if you were feeling depressed and all. You couldn't just throw yourself off – you'd have to really mean it,' said Shruti.

'He didn't commit suicide,' I said.

She glanced at me. 'Sorry – was he a good friend?'

'He was, yeah.'

'I saw your first article; it was good. But didn't you feel bad? How could you write so soon after he died?'

I shrugged. 'I dunno. I thought it would help. Maybe it was just shock. You and Eddie were pretty cool about it too when I told you everything today.'

'Well, we're all journalists, aren't we? We don't have to pretend to be upset by a story if we've got nothing to do with it. But he was your friend, your brother here. I don't know if I could have written what you wrote.'

That hurt.

'Stephen wanted me to write something; I didn't know what exactly then. Maybe it wasn't that,' I said.

'It's done you good, though. Not that I would want a friend to die but I haven't had a byline yet and I've been working with Eddie for over a year now.'

'I didn't do it for the byline, Shruti.'

214

'I know, I know, just, you know, I kind of noticed it. Come on, let's walk over to the south side, to the temple. Maybe they'll be able to tell us something,' she said, putting her arm through mine and leading me off as if we were best pals in school.

A twelve-foot orange statue of the monkey god Hanuman stood guarding the temple entrance. In the courtyard, a gnarled banyan tree stretched its leaves out to shade worshippers. Ribbons and coloured foil flickered in the branches and incense burned at its roots, wafting holy smells around the coconuts and sweet cracked rice laid for offerings. Loudspeakers boomed chants across the sky; flashing lights in red, blue, yellow edged the roof.

Shruti read some metal signs up in the courtyard and let out a low whistle. 'Woah, it's a V.H.P. temple. I didn't realise,' she said.

'Who?'

'Vishnu Hindu Parishad. They're a far right Hindu political group. The ones who beat up the artist who painted Krishna surrounded by penises.'

'Oh yeah, that was hilarious. They're really extreme, aren't they?' I said.

'They're extreme and extremely powerful. They run all the slums around here. They're putting candidates up in the elections too – all round Delhi. They want political power not just muscle and religion now,' she said.

Shruti pulled her dupatta further across her head. She pulled another scarf from her handbag for me.

'Eddie told me to bring one for you,' she said.

We sat in the shade of the banyan tree. It was lunchtime and there were families scattered around the courtyard, eating their way through small mountains of white rice and watery curries. I watched one pot-bellied lady mix her food with her fingers and deftly pop pale-yellow balls into her mouth one after the other. Her husband leaned back, sleepy in the shade, smacking and sucking his lips before washing and praying.

'It doesn't look much like a hotbed of extremists,' I said.

'No, of course not – there are layers, aren't there? These people, well, they come for a free meal, do a bit of pooja, go home. But the managers, the priests, the politicians who work in the offices here, they're another case.'

Behind the main temple area was a red concrete complex with rooms and towers and courtyards jutting off in all directions.

'I wouldn't be surprised if they had a cache of AK-47s in the back there. And when they need to whip up a riot, they'll call on all these guys they've been feeding for most of their lives. The police didn't bother coming in here and asking about Stephen, I bet. It wouldn't be worth the trouble, even for the death of a Westerner,' she said.

'You think these guys had something to do with Stephen's death?' I asked.

'I don't know. I'm just saying if they did, we wouldn't know about it because the police wouldn't question in here.'

We wandered around, not really knowing what to do. We sat down by three priests talking earnestly in a corner. I said they looked suspicious. But all Shruti got from eavesdropping was news about the latest *Indian Idol* episode. Apparently the guy from Darjeeling had really messed up a Shahrukh Khan song last night and was out of the competition. We tried to look into the office complex but a wall of a man waved us off with a lazy flick of his rifle.

The mood changed when we reached the main temple shrine. A fervent line of worshippers scurried back and forth like ants, holding steel trays full of their pooja – five-hundred-rupee notes, gilt-edged fruits, sticky yellow sweets that kill your teeth for a week – pushing and shoving to get to the temple, banging the bell.

A commotion began at the entrance. Men dressed in white carried out what looked like a fire, something smoking, on a plinth. In front of the fire was a plastic figure of a grinning woman with wild black hair, dressed in a necklace of skulls. Around this plinth people were waving incense, ringing bells, sending it on its way in a frenzy of celebration. A band dressed in orange played trumpets and clarinets and drums in a hyper-frenetic way, loudly and shrilly. The procession was heading towards the road.

'Where are they going?'

'They must be going to the river – it looks like some Kali festival. They're probably going to throw the idol in the river. It's auspicious,' said Shruti.

'Should we follow them then?'

She grinned at me. 'Let's go – ready for some pooja?'

We grabbed on to one another and pushed our way among heavy clouds of incense, losing ourselves in the faceless women covered completely in gleaming, dirty saris, fathers in the cotton pyjamas holding crying babies, priests chanting and children pushing one another. People were grinning wildly, throwing colour, swaying to the music.

The procession danced out of the temple and onto the road, too high to care about the oncoming trucks that swerved to avoid them. We reached Wazirabad Bridge once more; the Yamuna looked as dark and polluted as it was. The plinth was moved to the side of the bridge, to the mesh fence. Prayers were performed, a priest waved fire around the plastic figurine. One priest brought out a pair of pliers, cut the fence, peeled it back. Two of the other priests threw the little goddess into the water with the fire. Everyone cheered crazily, peering over the edge to see the figurine crash into the water. I couldn't see from where I was. I wanted to, and pushed my way to the front. The fence emerged through the smoke and I peered over the edge. Bits of coconut hung off one of the concrete pillars holding up the bridge and there was a little foil stuck to the mesh. Below I could see the small broken body of the figure, still smiling inanely, the skulls intact but the head smashed, the fire out, doused in the polluted water. It was already half sunk, caught in the weeds.

Shruti came up behind me. 'The river Ganga, she's the mother river, where all life flows from. The second river, that's the Yamuna, we worship her too, though you wouldn't think it from the state of it. That's why the River Board put these fences up in the first place: to stop people throwing in poojas. Endless bits of gods and goddesses cause more problems for the river than the few poor women who want to end their lives in it. But you know these big temples, ones run by politicians, by groups like the V.H.P., they can just ignore any rules made up by the River Board,' she said.

The crowd had now scattered, returning to the temple, but we stood there in the party debris, watching until the little figurine had completely disappeared into the water. Then we walked back to the temple too.

My face was clammy with sweat and pollution. I needed the toilet. There were wet patches under my arms and on my back. I wanted to sit down. But Shruti was composed and cool and happy to stand outside the temple entrance and think for as long as it took to come up with an idea. She looked completely at home there. I was jealous. Eddie mentioned he wanted a transfer. I'd immediately thought of his job. But if there was anyone slated for the next South Asia post at the *Telegraph* it would be her. She was a local. Made much more sense than employing me.

I heard a shout. 'Paan?'

It was the paan wallah.

'Hey, what's he doing here? He's usually near the Shiva centre. I've been wanting to talk to him. Come on,' I said, pulling Shruti over.

She laughed. 'So you're into chewing paan are you, Ruby? Like a real Indian journalist.'

The paan wallah smiled, shook my hand; he was pleased to see me. Shruti chatted to him for a bit.

'What's he doing here, Shruti?'

'He's come for the Kali festival. He puts a bit of bhang in his paan, people get a little high and he makes a killing.'

'But he's usually in G.K., outside the Shiva centre.'

'He lives in Dakshinpuri, near Raj. He used to sell here before moving to the centre.'

'How come he moved there?'

'Raj told him about all the Westerners in the Shiva centre who weren't allowed smokes or drinks and would probably like a hit on his paan. He can charge three times the amount in G.K. and Raj could give him a lift in. But he's come back here for a bit now he's lost his lift and business isn't so good round there at the moment,' she said.

'So he knows Raj well?'

Shruti spoke to him; he shrugged his shoulders.

'Well enough.'

'Where was he the day Stephen died? Did he see what happened at the centre? That's what I wanted to ask him. I wanted to know if he'd seen Stephen leave that day, or Raj. Everything,' I said.

But the paan wallah hadn't been there at all that day. There had been a big festival here, the Hola Mohalla.

'What's that?' I asked.

'Another festival for the start of summer, like Holi but especially Gujarati. There's lots of Gujaratis round here.'

'Right, so there would have been all that pooja shebang on the bridge?'

'Yup.'

'So the fence could have been cut?'

'Yup.'

'And not tied up properly.'

Shruti shrugged and widened her eyes in a 'so what' school-girl kind of way. 'Guess so.'

'But there's no way of telling?'

She shrugged again. We looked around us. I felt the sweat drip down my shoulder blades and run down the small of my back into my knickers. It wasn't enjoyable.

'Look, I'm really hot. I need the toilet. I know we're on an important job but can we just go get a Coke or something? I need to chill out for a minute.'

Shruti smiled. 'Yeah, I've a banging headache. Desperate for some caffeine. Let's go find somewhere.'

She asked the paan wallah.

'OK, there's a small chai stall by the side of the temple people often go to after pooja. They've got an icebox and some chairs.'

It was a peaceful place. A tarpaulin tent strung up next to a telephone exchange hut seemed to do as a home for the chai wallah. He stood making tea on a single gas hob, powered by a red gas cylinder, and nodded to us as we sat down. A parrot stood tamely pecking seeds on a polystyrene icebox by his side. A few broken red plastic chairs sat in the shade of a frangipani tree. One man I recognised from the pooja was sitting drinking a tea and talking into a bashed-up black phone the chai wallah had wired up from the telecom line. It looked out over the bridge side of the Yamuna, which seemed a pleasant river scene from this far off.

'You can't see this place from the bridge but you can see the bridge from here – it's the tree, I think,' I said.

'Yeah, and also it's higher here. But it's still too far away to see people. It's no good for witnesses,' said Shruti.

'But it is good for drinks. Come on. Let's stop working for a second,' I said.

'What do you want?'

'Coke, please. And see if the guy sells cigarettes?'

'Cool – yeah, good idea.'

I sat down in the shade. It wasn't much cooler but it felt so nice not to be on my feet. I watched the one-armed man shoo the parrot off the icebox and pick out two wet Cokes. He shook his head when Shruti asked for the cigarettes though. She handed me a bottle and sat down beside me. I took a slurp, it was cold and sweet and delicious.

'Ah. That's good.'

'Yeah. Just need a cigarette now and I'd be in heaven,' she said.

'Look out for someone we can nick a couple off.'

We sat watching the river and waiting for a smoker to come past. It didn't take long. A guy in sunglasses, jeans, loud checked shirt and combat vest came over shortly after, shouting for a chai. He immediately whipped out a kingsize pack of Goldflake cigarettes from a camera case he was carrying.

'Ask him for one, Shruti, he looks like a journalist, he'll give you one,' I said.

Combat vests were the uniform of nearly every male journalist in India, even in the height of a city summer, where all the pockets held were cigarettes and a mobile phone.

She batted her eyelids and the guy was happy to flourish his pack towards us, enjoying the attention.

'Are you a journalist?' I asked.

'Used to be. Used to be. For Headlines Today.'

221

'Oh, cool. What did you do?'

'I was a producer.'

'Why did you stop?'

'Long hours, no appreciation, no money and always in the office; it wasn't why I wanted to be a journalist. I just decided to quit,' he said.

'I know how you feel! I kind of did the same. I'm a journalist too,' I said.

'So am I. I went to Columbia actually,' said Shruti quickly. The guy looked blankly at her.

'What do you do now?'

'I've got a film production company. We've done a couple of docs on Assam forests; that's where I'm from. It's what I love: nature, the outdoors. But we do a lot of routine stuff in the city too, to pay the bills. Weddings, corporate dos, poojas; I've just been filming the pooja by the bridge. I get a lot of work from this temple here. They're V.H.P. People say they're a bad lot but they pay well and I've not had any trouble,' he said, sipping his chai and taking out another cigarette. He offered us both the pack once more.

I took a last drag of my first, stubbed it on the ground with my sandal and took another. Shruti refused.

'What do they do with the videos?'

'They put them on the internet; they've got a website. But it's in Hindi. Anyhow it's not so interesting. You should go to my website and look at the Assam film. Look, I've got to run – got some baby competition for Dove soap to film – but take my card, look me up.'

'Aniruddha,' I said his name slowly, trying to pronounce it right.

'That's it. It means "not to be restricted",' he said.

He walked off. Shruti and I sat looking at one another.

'Who says cigarettes are bad for you?' I smirked.

'Or sitting down drinking Coke. We got a lead,' Shruti said, smiling.

Shafts of orange light cut across Eddie's lawn. The sprinkler was off now. The gardener crouched on the grass, grey in the shadow of his plants, drinking his chai. In the kitchen, Shruti plunged her cafetière with greedy eyes, preparing to investigate the website with Eddie.

'Have some? It's good – Eddie gets it sent from a friend of his in France. You can't even get this coffee in Khan Market.'

'It smells great – like it's waking the kitchen up – but it'll make me hyper. Can I just have some chai?'

Shruti rolled her eyes. 'What? Like the gardener? Why don't you go and sit out there with him too?'

I blushed and shrugged. I was never really sure what to do with comments like that. 'Fine, I'll drink the coffee,' I said.

We sat in Eddie's study, Eddie on his wooden desk chair, the two of us either side on kitchen stools, and waited for the computer to crank up.

'OK, so what exactly are we looking for in these videos, guys?' said Eddie, leaning back in his chair.

'We saw this pooja – they cut the fence on the bridge and they didn't tie it back up again.'

'It's just an idea, but if the fence were loose the day Stephen died, he could have fallen in, right?'

'He could have, but it's not exactly conclusive evidence. But anyway, it won't take a minute and anything's worth a shot. Let's have a look at this website then. Shruti, you'd better come and sit here and type if we're looking in Hindi,' said Eddie.

Shruti jumped up with eager smugness and they exchanged places with a sliding grin. I looked out of the window at the birds cooing, thinking of two more reasons why Shruti would be the next *Telegraph* correspondent and not me. She spoke

Hindi and she was fucking the previous reporter. At least that's what it looked like.

Shruti tapped in the address. The page sprung up orange with a floating picture of the temple and a couple of gurus surrounded by flowers. Wailing music started and lights flashed around the border of the screen.

'Wow, they've really gone to town. They've got a good web designer,' said Shruti.

'Good but tasteless,' said Eddie.

'Is there a section for videos?'

'Wait, I'm looking down the menu. It's a bit erratic. OK – festival dates, prayers to Shiva, V.H.P. party, send an email to temple manager. Ah, here – photo gallery, videos. Excellent.'

She clicked on the Hindi link and up came a screen with a list of video links with dates.

'Scroll down to the twenty-fifth of March,' I said.

'Here – these are all saved under the name "Hola Mohalla" – on the twenty-fifth. There's three videos from then,' she said, clicking on the first.

The first yielded no results. A black unfocused ten minutes. All we got was the sound of high-pitched female singing, juddering glimpses of saris in lamplight. Erratic zooms focused in on a flame, distorting the colours into gleaming circles on the lens of the camera. It was like some kind of weird art video. Aniruddha's camerawork clearly could not be restricted.

'You said this guy worked for Headlines Today? Sure he wasn't sacked?' said Eddie.

'He worked as a producer not a cameraman. Maybe he was better at producing,' I said.

Eddie shook his head. 'This country has gone crazy. Anyone can make money out of anything at the moment. Talent is not required.'

'What are they singing?' I asked.

'They're singing a song for the summer, praying for good weather so the grain and the mangoes will grow well. It's the evening prayers,' said Shruti.

The next tape was more promising: smokey crowds swaying around a pooja statue, similar to the one Shruti and I had followed. The light and the colour were vivid but the camera-work was again appalling, zooming in on a wobbly bit of sari then out again.

'Is Aniruddha trying to look at these women's boobs?' I said.

'Honestly? Yes, I think that's very likely,' said Shruti.

The banshee-like band began to play, making the computer speakers buzz.

'Ah! That's horrible!' said Eddie, jumping up to turn it down.

The procession was at least moving, though we were still in the midst of the crowd and couldn't see exactly where this pooja was going.

'It's like when we were there; they must be heading to the river.'

We continued to watch for about seven minutes, with the walking camera zooming in and out on various pink and yellow and blue chests. I glimpsed the road in front a couple of times and thought I could make out the bridge when the tape stopped.

The next film was a continuation of the first. Aniruddha had obviously got tired of trying to eye up the girls and had hung back to buy himself a cold drink. The top of a Coke bottle with a straw made a jerky appearance at the bottom of the screen. He had lost his original enthusiasm and this made for better filming. He didn't wave the camera around like a maniac but kept it still, resting on the table it seemed,

225

as he finished his Coke. He had set it on a powerful zoom so he was close to the action.

I could see the bridge now, silhouetted onto a pink sky. The sun was low and orange; it was a setting even this crazy camerawork couldn't fuck up. Ahead of the procession was a young priest who cut the fence with pliers, just like the time I'd seen a pooja there with Shruti. The statue was thrown in, everyone cheered and began to scatter. We saw the spark of a match and smoke floating by the screen. Aniruddha was now having a cigarette.

'I really like Aniruddha,' I said.

'Yeah, me too,' said Shruti.

'Concentrate, you two. Look at the priest, what's he doing?'

The figure was tiny but you could see he was a priest by his orange robes. He was pushing the fence back carefully and preparing to wire it up, but a small boy ran up to him, tugged on his clothes. The priest batted him away a couple of times but he was persistent. He wanted to play. Eventually the man picked him up and swung him around. They began jumping towards the temple. The fence had been forgotten.

'He didn't tie it up! That means it was loose when Stephen was on the bridge,' I said. 'Fuck, this is important.'

'It's important to how Stephen died, it's not the full story though,' said Eddie.

'But if it was loose, it means he could have fallen, right?'

'Yes. But if he really did fall in of his own accord why on earth would Raj say he dumped him in the river? Why would you take the blame for an accident like that? That doesn't make sense,' said Eddie.

'The police could have roughed him up to say all that,' said Shruti.

'But why would he burn Stephen's motorbike? I saw him do that with my own eyes,' I said.

Eddie stood up and went over to the sofa with his coffee. He lit another cigarette.

'We still don't know what the hell Swami Shiva's got to do with all this,' said Shruti.

She went over to Eddie. Standing up close, she put her hand on his stomach and leaned in to spark a new cigarette from his. I turned back to the computer while they had their moment. I stared at the frozen screen without really looking, when something caught my eye. It was a figure. Further off than the priest, right at the end of the bridge.

'Guys, look at this,' I called to them.

They came over. I put my finger by the nail-size figure.

'That guy, he's standing like Stephen. And he's got a green T-shirt on. Like Stephen had.'

'It could be anyone, Ruby, it's tiny,' said Eddie, as his phone rang.

'Eddie Challan,' he answered sharply. 'Ah! Samit! How are you? Thanks for returning my call.'

Eddie proceeded to have a chummy talk with his friend Samit and told him to come round straight away. I was kind of pissed off. It didn't seem the right time for a social call.

'Who's Samit?'

Eddie smirked. 'Your old friend, Inspector Mukerjee.'

'My friend? Sounds like you're a lot chummier with him than I am. Samit? I never knew that was his name.'

'I wouldn't say we're friends but we worked with each other a while back, known each other a long time. We went drinking in the same places when we were both younger, around the old bars in Connaught Place. I was a freelancer here, thinking I was going to write a great novel. Samit had just started as a police officer. We both liked Volga.'

'Oh man! Really? Me and Stephen used to go there.'

Volga was dark and red and cheap and the kind of place

227

where you'd say things you shouldn't. People claimed it was the oldest bar in Delhi. It certainly hadn't been redecorated since the 1950s. The seats were velvet with a veneer of yellow nicotine you could feel. Net curtains gathered up the smoke and blocked out any light. It was normally empty apart from a few solitary men sitting drinking whisky. Sometimes you could persuade the waiters to play reggae, which gave a surreal aspect to the whole scene.

Eddie smiled at his own memories of the place. 'Is the rum still dirt cheap?' he asked.

'Yeah, eighty rupees a peg.'

'It was ten rupees when Samit and I went there.'

'Ten rupees. That's insane. You must have got trashed every night.'

Eddie laughed. 'It was after a night of ten-rupee rums that Samit told me he was doing Rajiv Gandhi's security. It was coming up to the elections and I was desperate to find a story or get an interview that would make a name for myself. I bought him another rum and persuaded him to tell me where Rajiv would be the next evening – at the Oberoi having dinner. I got myself a table nearby, sent over a bottle of champagne and then introduced myself, asking for an interview. It was a short one. But I sold it to the *Telegraph* and the rest, as they say, is history.'

'Wow. Sounds like you kind of owe him a lot.'

'Him and Old Monk rum. He likes a drink, that man,' said Eddie.

The inspector arrived looking like a hangover: sweaty, pale and scared. He was clearly surprised to see me and shot me a look that made me feel like a bad penny. But then he gave a half-smile and I figured we were OK.

'Scotch, Samit? I've got single malt. Laphroaig,' said Eddie.

'Thanks. Just what I need. Could I take a cigarette from you too?'

'I don't think I've seen you smoke before,' said Eddie, handing him a glass and his packet of Marlboros.

Eddie suited smoking, Shruti too, but it didn't seem right for the inspector. He was too big and ruddy-looking to be puffing away on a cigarette. He didn't handle it well either; this clearly wasn't a regular habit.

'My wife hates it. But she's away and I've got a lot on my hands. A lot. Swami Shiva arrested on drugs charges. It's a nightmare. Half the prison thinks that he's their guru, wanting to kiss his feet and crying out all night for blessings. We've got to have round-the-clock protection, in the canteen, in the showers, in the exercise yard, in case someone tries to make a break for him.

'And then we've got you guys. TV cameras lined up outside the station, every single part of the case being analysed and gone over. I've got Shiva lawyers bombarding us with calls and letters and threats. My chief is on the phone every ten minutes and now there's even talk that Swami is connected to the Stephen Newby case. There was an editorial in *Amar Ujala* – the Hindi paper – saying Raj's statement is false and the whole thing is a massive drugs cover-up. I just can't believe these idiots. It's no such thing,' said the inspector.

'Really? You don't think the two cases are connected? You think Raj is telling the truth?' Eddie asked.

'I don't know,' he said.

'But you took the statement,' I said.

The inspector shook his head. 'I know, I know. And I didn't torture him for it either. There was a bit of beating but nothing, nothing like it could have been. And why would he lie? But there's something funny here. I'm beginning to think *Ujala* has something or someone I don't know about.'

I felt sorry for him. He looked like he was really freaking out. I decided to tell him what I knew.

'Inspector, I know you tampered with the evidence in Raj's case. I went to the station to give you that book and the receptionist told me to go to the garage round the back. I saw you bashing in the Mercedes and walked out again. But I've only told Eddie. So you're safe – kind of,' I said.

The inspector spluttered a bit, his eyes looking crazy and red. 'What are you doing here anyway, Ruby?' he eventually burst out after several spittling starts.

'She's helping me with the story. We're working on this together,' cut in Eddie.

The inspector turned his ire on to the police station receptionist.

'That man . . .' he growled. It seemed I wasn't the only one the receptionist had rubbed up the wrong way.

'Why did you do it? Why bash in the bumper?' cut in Eddie. He made it sound like he'd expected me to bring this up but he hadn't and was giving me a half frown over the inspector's worried head. I shrugged my shoulders. But I was pretty impressed with how quickly Eddie had taken up the line. He really knew how to work with people.

Mukerjee took a faltering drag on his cigarette. 'Swami Shiva came to see Raj soon after we'd released the statement. They spent a while talking in the interview room and afterwards Swami Shiva spoke to me. I wanted him to tell me what Raj had said. I was worried Raj would change his story. He'd given in so easily to interrogation, just a few hits round the head and he'd spilled everything. I thought something was going on. But Swami Shiva said that Raj had given him his word that everything he'd said was true. Then Swami asked me a favour. He asked if I could make sure that Raj would get manslaughter not murder. Raj didn't want his children thinking he was a murderer. I said I could guarantee it. I shouldn't have said that, I know. There's no way to guarantee a verdict, but it was Swami Shiva. My wife has been a disciple of his for years. I respect him immensely. It's hard not to agree to a favour.'

'Was he bribing you? Was it a bribe?' asked Shruti.

'Someone like Swami Shiva doesn't need to bribe people. He's so powerful people will do mostly anything to please him. I just wanted to please him. And I could understand Raj not wanting his children to think he was a murderer. His children were precious to him. I didn't want to take them away from him. And honestly, I didn't think he was a murderer. He didn't feel like a killer to me. Really, I wasn't sure about any of it. But I needed to close the case, it was too important to leave hanging. And every day you lose in a murder case you get further and further away from catching the killer. Eighty per cent of homicides are solved in the first twenty-four hours. Fifteen per cent of the rest are never solved,' he said.

'So you thought you'd help Raj's story along by bashing in his bumper?' said Eddie.

The inspector shrugged. 'I thought it was best for everyone involved. I didn't know Swami was going to get himself involved in a drugs bust,' he said.

'It's starting to look very messy, isn't it though? Suspect statements, evidence tampering, deals with key witnesses. The kind of thing that ruins a cop if it gets out,' said Eddie.

'We've known each other a long time, Eddie. I am not perfect, I know that. But I am far, far better than many officers in Delhi. I don't steal, I try to catch the right man and I don't take bribes. Often. And I'm here, being honest, asking you for help,' said Mukerjee.

'We all know how it works but it's pretty bad, evidence tampering. Not something any self-respecting journalist should turn a blind eye to.'

'Will you help me or not?'

Eddie looked at me. I shrugged and nodded. He replied with the same gestures.

'Another peg, Samit?'

'Why not?'

I didn't feel I had the luxury of moral high ground with Inspector Mukerjee. My behaviour would not stand up to close scrutiny either, I didn't think. Not after the article I had written, not after the way I had given Rani and Stephen away to Swami Shiva.

My overriding feeling was, as it had been from the beginning, that I wanted to find out what had happened to Stephen, and now to Swami. These two cases were connected because Stephen was Swami's son. But was there a possibility that Swami had had something to do with his son's death? Finding this out was more important than the bashed-in bumper. And Eddie owed the man. So did I. He'd got me a visa, it was because of him I could stay in the country.

22

It was late and dark by the time we were ready to leave Eddie's but we had a plan in place to try to figure out what had really been going on – with Stephen and with Swami. We worked together. The only thing Inspector Mukerjee didn't know was that Swami was Stephen's father. That was too big a scoop to risk telling him. None of us mentioned it.

And I didn't let any of them know that Rani was staying with me either. Eddie mentioned several times how good it would be to find him and interview him but I kept my mouth shut. I'd promised Swami Shiva to keep Rani away from people.

The first thing that we'd all agreed needed to be done was establish whether that was Stephen on the bridge. If it was, that meant Raj's story was definitely false. The sun had been setting and, according to Raj, Stephen had been dead by then, stuck in a traffic jam under a towel with a brain haemorrhage. I gave Aniruddha a call and he invited me over to his studio early in the morning to have a look at the original tapes.

After that, I would meet Shruti – we were going to go and find the paan wallah in Dakshinpuri. We'd got in trouble from

Eddie for not getting his name or his number so all that was left was for us to just go down there ourselves and search him out. Inspector Mukerjee and his juniors had had no luck in the slum, trying to find out who made the call about Swami Shiva and the drugs. He thought us two girls might have some better luck, especially if we knew someone. I thought about suggesting talking to Sita too, but she had been so devastated last time I had called round I didn't think I had the emotional energy to face it.

Eddie was going to do some straight interviews on the story with big players – the mayor of Delhi, the temple manager about the loose fences, the head of the Yamuna River Board – for our article.

Inspector Mukerjee was going to keep on questioning people down at the yoga centre. He picked up his car keys to make a move but then paused. 'I wish I hadn't let Raj and Swami talk in Malayalam. I was in the room when they spoke but I have no idea what they were saying. I'm going to stop interviews in any language other than English, Urdu and Hindi from now on.'

'When I went to see Raj, there was a buzzing sound on the end of the telephone line. It sounded like they were being tapped. Are they recorded, those conversations?' I said.

The inspector raised his eyebrows. 'I think I would know if they were, wouldn't I?'

'I dunno, would you?'

'I've never heard of it at all. But I'll check with the tech bods. The IT department are always getting up to mischief. They are all about fifteen, it seems, down there. Always wanting to start wire taps and bug people,' he said.

Eddie gave me a lift back home to Nizamuddin, saying he wanted to stop at the wine and beer shop on the way anyhow, in Khan Market. There was chaos outside as usual, possessed men struggling to get at their whisky, which was kept behind bars and passed through the grating in brown paper bags, the occasional ex-pat sauntering up and pushing through the fray for a bottle of imported Chardonnay.

'Anything you want?' Eddie asked as he got out to buy some more gin for himself.

'No, I'm fine.'

'Sure? Bottle of wine? They've got some nice French ones in there.'

'They're really expensive.'

'My treat.'

'You don't have to do that.'

'I get paid a London salary and I live in Delhi. I have expenses for living away from home. I have a very, very comfortable life, Ruby, and I don't know how long this kind of thing can last, so we may as well make the most of it while we can.'

So I arrived home to Rani with a bottle of Châteauneuf-du-Pape in my hands.

He was lying in a ball on my bed when I arrived home and turned on the light.

'Rani, are you all right? Did the girl downstairs bring you anything to eat?'

'She did. She brought me some juice and a chicken kebab. I didn't eat the meat, I just ate the bread.'

'She thought she was being nice to you. They don't understand vegetarianism here.'

'Where have you been? I haven't had any money to get back to the centre. I don't really know why I am here anyway. I don't have a phone to call anyone on. They must be worried. Swami Shiva will be very, very worried about me.'

Rani was this big yogi superstar, but he was completely lost without his guru. He hadn't taken in any of what had happened last night. He believed in Swami Shiva completely. Nothing would budge his faith. I was scared for him. He was staying with me and I felt I was responsible for him, by default it seemed. There was no one else to look after him. But I did want to take care of him. My feelings for him were changing. Whereas before I'd idolised him and loved him as some perfect being, I loved him now for his frailties, for his weaknesses. And he was a last connection with Stephen, which made him all the more precious.

'Don't worry, Rani. Listen, Swami Shiva's in a bit of trouble. Did you see he had to go with the police last night? But we're going to sort it out. I'm working with Eddie Challan from the *Telegraph* and Inspector Mukerjee. We're going to find out what happened. We think someone is trying to get Swami Shiva into trouble.'

'But why would anyone do that?'

Rani looked perplexed and worried. He was fiddling with his hands, fidgeting, the way I noticed he did when he was stressed. His movements were getting quicker and quicker. I had no answers to calm him down. I thought maybe I should give him some of Eddie's wine.

'Listen – I know it's against ashram rules but I don't think I've had a tougher two days and I imagine you haven't either. Eddie gave me this bottle of wine. Why don't you have a glass, with me? It'll help you sleep and it will relax you.'

Rani looked unsure.

'You're not going to get intoxicated after one glass, Rani. Nothing will happen, I promise.'

'OK then, Ruby, I trust you,' he said.

I was pleased he said that. It felt like we were growing closer together.

We lit a mosquito coil on the balcony and sat the bottle down between us. Rani went very red after half a glass and started giggling. He seemed fascinated with himself. I drank and smoked and enjoyed watching him. We both laughed.

A wedding band started up its caterwaul music down below, announcing the bridegroom coming to collect his bride. The groom was young, dressed in a gold suit with a necklace of money. We watched him process on a white horse, surrounded by dancing family, waving dynamite sparklers.

'He doesn't look like he rides horses often, does he? He's kind of awkward,' I said.

'He's nervous – he will be alone with his bride for the first time tonight. But he'll be fine. It'll be easy for him,' said Rani.

Rani's confidence in the groom surprised me. He didn't have any experience of women – or sex. Except that one afternoon with Stephen – and no one really knew what had happened between them. Those gold handprints could have been all it was. But maybe he wasn't as innocent as I'd assumed.

'How do you know, Rani?'

'Well, it's easy if you're married; you have a wife. You don't have to struggle with your desire. He's nervous now but tomorrow he'll be happy. And he won't feel guilty.'

'Do you have to struggle much, Rani?'

He shrugged. Looked down at his glass and took another sip.

'Are you struggling now?'

'Ruby,' he said in a low voice, rolling the empty, stained glass around in his fingers. We stayed silent, listening to the raucous band for a while. I suddenly felt very tired.

'Come on. Let's go to bed.'

He swayed a little as he got up. He looked lovely, smiling, holding on to the balcony banister.

It was our second night in the flat together. We shared my bed again – neither of us wanted to sleep in Stephen's room still.

Rani kept his clothes on. I had a shower and got into an oversized, frumpy cotton nightdress from Lajpat Nagar, the kind of thing Indian housewives can spend all day in. I'd bought it with Stephen as a joke. I gave us both night sheets to cover ourselves.

I lay stiff in bed, sweating. It was really too hot for nightclothes or sheets. I would usually just lie there naked but I couldn't with Rani there. I opened my eyes in the dark; there was a slight orange glow from a street lamp near my window. I listened out for Rani sleeping but all I could hear was the sound of the horns and the whooshing of the fan above my head. I turned my back on him, curled up. The hairs on the back of my neck prickled. I lay still like that for what seemed like hours. I must have drifted off eventually because I woke with a start when I felt Rani's hand on my shoulder. I opened my eyes. It was pitch black now – the shrine lights were off – and the trains were silent. I heard myself breathe out in shock. He moved nearer to me, I could feel him up against me, his breath on my neck. I could feel something pressing on my leg. He had an erection. His arm came round my waist and pressed me against him. He kissed my neck. I stiffened. He moved his hand up to my chest. Kissed my neck again. I went lax, turned towards him. He kissed me on the mouth and I let him. I reached up to his hair.

A peal of train horns woke me up. Light flickered in my opening eyes. It was later than I usually woke and the bright high heat had already begun. I woke slimy with sweat and with no sense of rest. I wasn't sure if it had been a dream. I was screwed up naked in a bed sheet. I could see my nightdress at the corner of the bed. The pillows were on the floor. It was sticky between my legs.

I put on the nightdress and wandered into the living room.

Rani was practising a locust, his legs high in the air behind him.

I sat on the sofa and lit a cigarette, watching him and trying to process the situation. The ashtray had three cigarette butts from the night before; I remembered lighting them off the mosquito coil and Rani chastising me gently for the bad habit. The empty bottle of wine had fallen over, perhaps knocked by a bird or the morning newspaper, and rolled into the living room leaving a line of wine, dried now to a dark, blood red. These were the remnants of the night before, which, like the fingermarks on my glass of gin the morning after Stephen had died, told me I wasn't dreaming.

And here we were. In the middle of this nightmare; my dream come true. Watching him there, practising his yoga in my living room, I felt I was in love with him. It wasn't the far-off crush I'd had before, but a real stomach love, the kind that makes your legs twitch and your throat hot. The kind of love you only feel from going to bed with someone you're desperate for.

I felt guilty. I hoped what we'd done wouldn't damage him, wouldn't make him lose his power. Finding him with Stephen, gold prints all over his body, had been like finding a wet butterfly unfurling. Butterflies don't last long though, their wings become dusty and broken.

But then, perhaps we'd both needed it. The sex had been quick and clumsy. It could have been his first time. But it had been a real release from the pain and hurt and death and confusion. To be that close to someone was something I had been missing, more so now Stephen had died, but before too. I hadn't had a boyfriend in Delhi at all. I'd needed all my energy and focus for my work, to survive, to get on. Stephen had cared for me, loved me in his own way, but he hadn't been my lover and I'd begun to feel dry and empty. Now I was here with Rani and I felt full of life.

He collapsed out of his locust and told me off once more for smoking. I blew out a smoke ring. I could smoke if I wanted. We looked at each other but we didn't say anything about the night before. My stomach lurched again.

I said I would be back later, that I was working on the story about Swami and Stephen. I got changed, went downstairs to order some more food for Rani for the day and hailed a rickshaw to Aniruddha's studio.

23

The sounds of Akon wafting from Aniruddah's place, by the South Delhi ring road, was a welcome breath of fresh air.

He opened the door with a fag in his mouth and another loud checked shirt, blue, green and yellow this time.

'Come down! So happy to help in a mystery! How exciting!' he said.

We jumped down the stairs of his office to a high-tech studio.

'Wow, this is nice, man! You must be making quite good money to put this all in,' I said.

'Well, to be honest with you, my dad footed the bill for it. He's in steel you see.'

Aniruddah gave me a meaningful look. I shrugged.

'I'm rich. Stinking rich. Really I don't need to do anything. I'm just being noble. Only way to work in the media, isn't it?'

Journalism certainly wasn't paying for me at the moment. I hadn't thought about it since Stephen's death but I was going to have to seriously consider how on earth I was going to afford to make ends meet in a few weeks. The money Guy

Black had promised me still hadn't come through, which I would have to call him about.

'So what's this concerning, anyway? Sounded really mysterious on the phone? You want to look at the Hola Mohalla tapes?'

'Yeah. It's, well . . .' Should I tell him anything? I hardly knew him but he seemed a good guy. I decided to be honest. 'It's about Stephen Newby.'

'Who?' said Aniruddha, absent-mindedly going through a wall of tapes in a slick glass cabinet.

'Stephen Newby – the British guy? In the river?'

'Sorry – not sure. What happened to him?'

I couldn't believe it. Anyone in Delhi who wasn't blind, dumb or deaf would know who Stephen Newby had been; it had been wall-to-wall coverage since my article. But this guy had managed to avoid it. I started to suspect his news producing might not be any better than his camerawork. Maybe wealth wasn't really the best thing for a journalist. Nice guy though.

'Ah, here we go – let's have a look at them,' he said, pulling out three tapes.

We sat in a darkened booth as Aniruddha played around with the panel of dolly mixture buttons. He had three tapes, all ninety minutes, although he'd only used a few minutes on each. I didn't know much about camerawork but I figured that was a bit of a waste. This guy seemed to have absolutely no idea what he was doing.

But the equipment was good. High resolution on a big screen meant I could see so much more detail than on the small internet video. We came to the part where the priest had begun tying up the panel and then forgotten about it while playing with the child. I saw the figure I thought was Stephen on the bridge once more. He wasn't wearing kurta pyjamas and he wasn't part of the temple crowd.

'Can you zoom in on him?'

'Not while the tape is running. But if we freeze it we can.'

He flicked around with the panel and froze it just as the priest swung the child up in the air, framing the distant figure.

'There, stop,' I said.

He zoomed in, but not in the right place. The screen was filled by the child, laughing. The close-up had pixellated the image somewhat, but not as much as I'd expected.

'It's a great picture. It hasn't fuzzed up at all,' I said.

'This is high def. Top range. Wait, I've got the wrong place though, let's try it again.'

He got it right the next time. I could see the guy had long hair, jeans, beads and a green T-shirt. It was Stephen.

'That's him. That's him. Fucking hell. That's Stephen on the bridge. Zoom in again.'

He zoomed and got his torso. He was scratching his arm and leaning against the bridge.

'It's Stephen. He's on the bridge and he hasn't been run over. Shit, this is insane. Zoom out again. Let's see if we can see his bike,' I said.

'What are you talking about, Ruby? Who is this Stephen guy?' asked Aniruddha.

I looked at him. I could explain, but I didn't think he'd mind if I didn't. He wasn't the most curious of people.

'It's a long story – can I tell you another time?'

Aniruddha shrugged and zoomed out. There was no bike.

'Fuck. Fuck,' I said.

'Are you OK? Do you want a cigarette? You look like you've seen a ghost, man!' said Aniruddha.

I stared at my friend on the computer screen. He looked like he should be on TV. It gave me some moment of hope.

To see him there, on the bridge, alive, not bashed up by a motorbike accident, made me think he could still be breathing somewhere out there. Then I remembered the morgue, his waxy face, and realised this wouldn't bring him back. It just meant we were closer to knowing what really happened. Closer and further away.

'What the fuck happened to you, man?' I said, touching the screen.

'Who, me? Nothing, I just spilt some kebab sauce down my shirt yesterday. Shit, man, is it that obvious? I thought it mixed in all right with the green,' said Aniruddha, scratching at his chest.

'Sorry, Aniruddha. I didn't mean you. I was kind of talking to myself . . . or to someone else at least. Thanks for your help.'

Aniruddha got his driver to give me a lift to Dakshinpuri in his huge four-by-four, filled with filming equipment. I texted Eddie and Mukerjee, to let them know what I'd seen. That it was definitely Stephen on the bridge.

I met Shruti on the outskirts of the slum. She had a scarf wrapped round her head and had once more transformed herself into a demure Hindi maiden.

'How do you do that?' I asked, giving her a peck on the cheek. 'Change your look so quickly – one minute you're a vixen the next a little kitten.'

'That's an essential change for a woman to get ahead – don't you remember last night? I just had to make some more coffee for Eddie to be fine!' laughed Shruti.

Eddie had been pissed off with us the night before – Shruti and I hadn't got the paan wallah's mobile number, address or even his name. He'd shaken his head in disgust, saying, 'What exactly did they teach you at Columbia, Shruti? All that money? For what? A New York accent? And you should know better, Ruby. You've done local papers. So what are you going to do? Walk around Dakshinpuri asking for the paan wallah?' I'd just shrugged shamefacedly but Shruti had worked magic in minutes.

We walked down an alley to begin our search for the paan wallah when Shruti got a call. She started. 'I have to take this.'

She moved off and I waited. She was chewing her nails as she spoke.

'Who was that?'

'Oh . . . it's just someone I know at the *Telegraph*. Guy Black.'

'I know Guy.'

'You do?'

'Yeah, I met him before I went to India. He wanted me to send him stories that Eddie or the wires weren't picking up. He's got this thing about exclusives.'

Shruti grimaced. 'I know. I know. I'm trying to get a piece in with my byline through him. But he called to say what I'd written wasn't right.'

I was kind of surprised. So he was working with both of us. I had no idea. I wondered if Eddie had. 'What was it on?'

'V.H.P. actually. I wrote up a piece about the fences being cut. But he said it didn't quite work when we only had a fuzzy video as evidence and no quotes. He said keep working on it. But he said what he really needed was an interview with Rani. He said he could give me a full page and a picture with that.'

'Be careful what that guy promises. He said he'd give me two grand for that article and I haven't seen any of it. And does Eddie know about this? Shouldn't you go through him?'

Shruti blushed. 'Eddie doesn't respect me as a journalist. I've been trying for the last year to get something through

245

him and he just has me do translations and add to his stuff. He says I have to learn more. But how much fucking more do I need to know? All my friends from Columbia are working in the US at TV stations and I'm stuck back here doing piecemeal shit. I want a break.'

I knew how that felt. I put my hand on her shoulder and smiled at her. 'Look, come on, lets find this paan wallah. He could give us both the break we need.'

She smiled back and we went on into Dakshinpuri. But I was wondering if there was enough of this story for both of us to get a break.

It wasn't so hard to find the paan wallah's house, even without his name. We walked along the lanes into the heart of the slum, picking on a benign-looking man, sitting smoking a bidi cigarette. Shruti asked him if he knew the guy who made paan outside the Hanuman Temple. He thought for a moment, took a drag on his bidi and shouted into a nearby house. A woman ducked out of the door with a ladle in her hand. She thought for a minute before pointing towards a small store, squeezed between two houses, just a counter made from bits of wood. Her husband got up off his haunches and padded over to the shop where he had a chat and bought a pack of biscuits. His wife brought a steel plate out of the house and he placed the biscuits out carefully before sharing them between us all. He told Shruti the shopkeeper knew the guy we wanted, bought paans from him for festivals. He lived a few streets down. A small boy scurrying past was hoodwinked into taking us directly to the paan wallah's home.

We chased after this child who flicked between chickens and goats with the ease of a practised master. We were panting along and about to lose sight of him when he stopped abruptly in front of a very clean plaster home painted bright turquoise.

It wasn't a plush residence, even by Dakshinpuri's standards. There was no front yard as Raj's house had. It opened directly on to the lane. Nearby was an open sewer round which pigs played. A jasmine around the entrance of the house fought off the stench and gave the place something of a garden feel. The boy shouted into the dark doorway. A reply came out and he nodded for us to go inside.

My eyes adjusted to the darkness and I saw the paan wallah sitting on the floor in a checked dhoti. He was reading a Hindi newspaper. He smiled his big smile. He gestured for us to sit with him and shouted out to someone. A fat woman in a pale-blue sari entered the room with two thin cushions. She smiled at us, smacked the cushions hard and placed them carefully down in front of the paan wallah. He asked for chai.

I just sat there as Shruti talked. There wasn't much I could do but smile and try to look nice. The conversation was short and sparse. They seemed to have finished even before the tea was placed down before us. The cups were tiny pink enamel and thin. We blew on the tea in silence. It was good, thick and sweet, but it was awkward just sitting there. As we got near to the end of our cups, Shruti made our good-byes. The paan wallah sighed and said something that made her shrug.

'Get his name, Shruti,' I said, just as we were leaving.

'I have. It's an easy one to remember: Prasad Prasad,' she said.

'Didn't seem like you got much out of this Prasad then?' I said as we made our way back.

'He said he had no idea about who could have made the call.'

'Did you ask him where the STD booth is? We could have gone there.'

247

'He says there are several. He said he couldn't explain to me where they all were.'

'He wasn't very helpful, was he? I'm surprised.'

'It's a small place. Everyone knows we came to see him. He said that we shouldn't have come actually. He said we should have gone to see him at the temple. But it's not a day that he would have been at the temple. There's no festival today.'

'So he knows something but won't say anything. Is that it?'

'He wasn't that obvious. Really I don't know. He was polite and friendly and all, but very careful. The only thing he mentioned, when we were leaving, was he'd seen the man with the tattoos from the Shiva centre around Dakshinpuri a few times.'

'Do you know who he's talking about?' Eddie asked once we were back at his.

'No idea,' I said. But of course I did. It was Tito. He was up in the mountains now, at his Astanga institute. I didn't know what to do. I didn't want to shop the guy. If I told Eddie about him and his dealing, Inspector Mukerjee would find out and they'd investigate him and he'd get put in prison or chucked out of the country.

'We've hit a bit of a block. Let's hope Samit's day has been at least as productive as yours, Ruby. Then we might know something.'

It had been. Mukerjee arrived at Eddie's with a flash disc containing an audio file of Swami and Raj's conversation. The phone in the interview room was tapped and all conversations went straight into a computer as an audio file. Nothing usually happened to the interviews, conversations with families and wives about children, school fees, rent, weddings, deaths. They were recorded because some bright spark in the

248

police IT department wanted to try out wire tapping without going through the legal loopholes required in the real world.

The inspector had got the files from some computer guy but hadn't listened to them. He needed a Keralan to translate them and, as I'd thought, there weren't many Keralans in the Delhi police. At least not ones the inspector could trust.

'Listen, I have a Keralan friend. We could get it translated,' I said.

'Who is it? He needs to be trustworthy,' said the inspector.

'He is. He's from the ashram actually, but staying with me. You can trust him to keep quiet about all this.'

The inspector shrugged. 'Time's ticking away. We'd better get going. Do it. Here, take it,' he said.

I arrived home to find Rani meditating. He seemed well and steady. We still didn't mention what had happened the night before. He asked after Swami Shiva and said he was worried about him and missed him. I reassured him they would be reunited as soon as Swami left the police station.

I'd bought a couple of Cokes from the hotel on my way up. Rani cracked the bottle open and began sipping it exactly as he was, in lotus position. He looked like a model in one of those Coke ads that try to make out the whole world – tribesmen in Africa to Arctic Eskimos – is drinking Coke from dawn till dusk.

'Rani, I found out today that Stephen didn't die the way we thought he did.'

I could see cogs whirring in his head as he processed this. After a few minutes his face formed a tight frown. 'What? How? How do you know?'

'I've seen some footage, filmed by the temple, which shows Stephen on Wazirabad Bridge around sunset the day he died. He wasn't run over like Raj says.'

'Why would Raj lie about that? Get himself into trouble? How did Stephen die? I'm confused,' said Rani.

'You're not the only one. But listen, I think we might be able to find out with your help. Remember when we visited Raj and we had to speak in the phone – do you remember the buzzing sound?'

'Not really.'

'Well, they were recording our interview onto a file. I've got the file of Swami Shiva and Raj's interview with me. Can you translate it?'

'Well, OK, I guess so.'

'I don't know what we're going to hear. It could be something that's bad. Are you ready for it?'

He sucked on his Coke, thinking. 'What do you think I am going to hear?'

'I just don't know. Maybe nothing. I don't know how much Swami is involved in this. But if Raj was going to tell the truth to anyone it would be him, right?'

'Yes. Yes. And you know I believe in Shiva *ji*. I won't hear anything from him I wouldn't want to hear. I've known him all my life.'

You've known him all your life, but you don't know all of his life, I thought. But I didn't say anything. Rani had complete faith in Swami Shiva – he called him *ji* now – using his honorific title just as his honour was most in doubt.

I carried on, plugging the flash disc into my old computer. The file came up as an MP3, with the date, two days after Stephen died, 27 March. I double-clicked it and it loaded as a wavy solid mass on the screen.

'OK, you ready, Rani? What I'll do is I'll play a bit and then stop it. You tell me what has been said and then I'll write it down,' I said. He nodded.

Swami Shiva's mellifluous low voice began, answered by

Raj in abrupt sentences. I paused it after thirty seconds.

'Swami Shiva is asking Raj if he is OK, if he's been beaten badly. Raj is saying no. He's saying they didn't string him up or electrocute him. He made his statement in a short time.'

I wrote it down and pressed Play again. Rani frowned. I stopped the file.

'What?'

'Swami Shiva is saying he doesn't believe Raj's statement. He doesn't believe that Stephen was run over and he doesn't believe Raj threw him in the river. He wants to know what really happened. Raj is saying that the statement is true enough. Swami Shiva asks him who he is trying to protect. He wants to know if he is trying to protect the Shiva network. He wants to know where Stephen went after he left the ashram that day. He wants to know where Raj thought he had gone that night. Swami *ji* thinks he knew where he was going.'

'OK, so Swami Shiva is telling the truth when he says he doesn't know what happened that day, when Stephen left him.'

I clicked Play on the file and stopped after another chunk.

'Raj is saying again that his statement is true enough. That he didn't kill Stephen but he is responsible for his death partly. Swami Shiva wants to know how. They are both getting upset. Swami says he's known Raj since he was a child, he says he loves him and trusts him with everything.'

I pressed Play once again. Rani's face then contorted badly. I stopped the file.

'What, Rani? What does he say?'

Rani had his head in his hands.

'What, Rani?' I went over, put my hand on his shoulder. 'What is it?'

251

'Swami Shiva says he wants to know what happened to Stephen, to his son.'

There was a thought in the back of my mind that this might happen, that Swami might say something about Stephen being his son.

'I'm sorry, Rani. He told me the evening before the funeral. He said he found out the day Stephen died.'

Rani still held his head in his hands; after a while he spoke through them. 'Carry on with the file. I want to hear what else is said.'

'Are you sure?'

Rani nodded through his hands and didn't take them away from his head for the rest of the interview.

'Raj asks Swami *ji* if he is going to tell people that Stephen was his son, if he is going to make a statement. Swami says no. He says there is no point now Stephen is dead. That it will hurt those who are still alive. He says he is worried about Rani, about me. That I am his son too and he must look after me. Raj says you protect your people, I will protect mine.'

I could hear the rising emotion in all the voices, their pitches getting higher and their patter quicker; in Swami, in Raj and in Rani here with me. I stopped the file again.

'Swami Shiva wants to know who exactly Raj is protecting. Raj asks him to trust him that this is the best way for everyone. He asks Swami *ji* for one thing. For his charge to be manslaughter not murder. He doesn't want his children to think he is a murderer. He is worried that the car does not look like it's been in an accident. Swami *ji* says he should not worry. Raj asks him to get Sita and the children out of Dakshinpuri and help them with the flat they want to buy. Swami agrees. Now they're praying. Swami Shiva is saying a prayer over him.'

The file ended there. Rani and I were left with the buzzing of the computer and the train horns.

'Sorry, Rani,' I said.

24

We sat side by side on the sofa. The lights in the shrine shut off and the flat was suddenly darker. That meant it was late. Past midnight. It hurts to see anyone upset, in pain and it was grim to see Rani broken up like this beside me.

'Do you want to talk about it, Rani?'

He looked up and his eyes were wide.

'Rani, do you want something to eat?'

'I'm not hungry.'

I put my arm round him, rubbed his back. He put his head in his hands once again. Then he began talking.

'I tried so hard for him. I never asked for this life, but I tried so hard for Swami Shiva. I believed in him and what he taught me. He told me I was a son sent to him by God. But I wasn't, was I? Stephen was his son. He never let me near women. When I was a child the women in the kitchen used to mother me, feed me. When I started calling them "sister" Swami stopped me going into the kitchen. I made vows of Brahmacharya before I even knew what desire could be. And I never knew anything else but ashram life, never knew anything but this discipline, this stoic love. He made me scared of women, of passion. I only thought of God – of reaching Brahma – of studying the Vedas and practising my asana. I tried hard for him. I never touched myself. I never did. I lay in my bed filling up with this madness. Stephen was the first person who touched me. I cried. I cried when he touched me because it felt so good and I'd been told it wasn't, that it was unnatural and bad. He never told me I was human, that everyone fails sometimes. It was only discipline and meditation and not giving in. And all that time he was hiding a son, his own mistakes, his own passion.'

'You know he's been in the police station for the last day or so? They found drugs in the ashram but there is no proof that they are Swami Shiva's. He's being released today. You can talk to him about all of this.'

Rani let out a short laugh. 'I'm not going back there – I'm not going back to the ashram. I'm not.'

'But, Rani, what are you going to do?'

He looked at me simply. 'Stay here with you.'

I hugged him. The idea scared me but it was good too. I needed someone for the future. I couldn't survive on my own here. But I couldn't just take him from the ashram, from his old life, with an easy conscience.

I put my head on his head as lovers do and he let me. I quietly tried to explain to him what had happened with Claudia and Swami Shiva, so he'd have some sympathy with his adopted father, but he told me to be quiet. The silence was exhausting and eventually I suggested we go to bed.

We lay side by side as the night before for some time. I wanted something to happen. Rani grabbed my hair and pulled me over to him. He was frantic and quick and left me shocked. Afterwards, we lay there together under the sheet but we didn't hug or touch each other. Rani clearly hadn't watched many

Hollywood romances or Australian soap operas, which is where my friends and I first learned how boys and girls are supposed to act when they are together.

In the morning I woke to find Rani already up. He was sitting on the sofa in his clothes, watching TV. I sat down next to him and wiped the sleep from my eyes. He was watching NDTV; the reporter was Anita, doing a live outside the Shiva centre.

'You plugged the TV in?'

'I want to know what is happening.'

'Swami Shiva is being released from questioning today without charge but his name is now connected not only with the death of the Britisher Stephen Newby but also heroin. These scandals aren't going to simply disappear for a guru who'd been known for his strict living. And where Rani Shiva, his young protégé has gone, no one knows. Many centres across India and the world remain closed. That's a lot of people missing out on their daily yoga. Anita Karnad, NDTV, Delhi.'

I logged on to my computer and read through the interview we'd transcribed yesterday evening. It was good evidence that Swami Shiva was Stephen's father and that Stephen had found out the day he died, but it didn't take us any further into working out what happened to him. Or who had made the call to NDTV about the drugs. It seemed like Raj knew more than he was letting on. He needed to be questioned again. And Tito needed to be questioned. If I talked to Tito I'd know what had happened. But there was no way to get in touch with him. I'd looked up the institute on the web, to find a number and call him. But it said that guests at the ashram had no contact with the outside world. There was not even a landline number for staff. You had to write to ask to stay. The only way I could talk to him was by going myself to Dharamasala.

I didn't want to leave Rani on his own but I knew it was

the only way to move the story on. I checked online for a plane ticket – there was a flight in the afternoon. It was expensive. Two hundred pounds return. I checked my bank balance. Fuck. Guy Black still hadn't transferred any of that money into my account. I needed it. I was five hundred pounds off the bottom of my overdraft. I checked the time. It was five in the morning in England. But fuck it. I needed the money now. I rang Guy. He answered in a voice too groggy and confused to be pissed off.

'Guy, it's Ruby.'

'Ruby. What are you doing calling me at this time? You know what time it is, don't you?'

'Yes. Sorry, Guy, but it couldn't wait. Look, I'm running out of money here and I need to book a flight. You told me I would get two grand for that article and I haven't seen a thing yet.'

'It takes a few days to go through, of course, got to be checked over by finance,' he said, still sleepy.

'OK. That's fine. I've got a credit card that can see me through for a bit. But I just need to know that it's going in for definite.'

'You'll get paid, of course . . . It might not be quite as much as agreed.'

'What? You said two grand.'

'I was a bit . . . perhaps I shouldn't have said that much. If I am honest I don't really have the authority to decide payments. The foreign editor is making a bit of a fuss about the amount. Says it's too much to pay and anyway we've burned some bridges with the Foreign Office because of it – and he's not happy about that at all.'

'But why did you say that to me, then? Guy, that's not fair.'

'Ruby, come on. I've heard you're working a bit with Eddie now. That must be making you some money? You wouldn't be doing that if it hadn't been for my help.'

257

'Your help! You weren't helping me. You were helping yourself. And you got me into shit, Guy. And now you're saying you're not going to pay what we agreed.'

'Ruby, I can't believe you're haggling over your friend's death like this. Really. What would Stephen say if he knew you were so bothered about a few pounds?'

That took my breath away. 'How much am I getting paid and when, please, Guy?'

He sighed. 'Seven hundred. It'll be in by the end of the month. OK?'

'Fine.'

I put the phone down and bit my lip hard like it was a stick. Guy was unbelievable; he cared so little about other people. He'd accused me of making a name out of my friend's death, a guilty thought which had sat in my stomach like a stone since the morning the article had been published. But at least I felt every little bit of what I did; shitting on people was like water off a duck's back for him.

I booked the flight, then rang Eddie and Inspector Mukerjee, told them about the disc, emailed them both the transcript. I said I'd be out of town tonight looking into a lead, but back tomorrow morning. Eddie jibed at me for being elusive, wondered if I was going to try to find Rani. I shrugged it all off.

Rani was watching TV as I left. I kissed him goodbye.

He grabbed my hand. 'Where are you going?'

'I'm going away just for the evening. I need to go see one of Stephen's friends who's in the Astanga ashram in McLeod Ganj. I'll be back tomorrow. Are you going to be OK?'

'Yes. OK. I'm going to stay here and watch the news.'

Seeing him sitting there, cross-legged, watching TV like a normal person made me want to cry. He was changing so quickly, it must hurt. I rushed over and hugged him.

'Rani, I love you.'

It's dangerous saying 'I love you' to someone. It brings with it responsibility. I'd learned in the past not to be too free and easy with the words, but when I felt like saying them I couldn't help it and I felt like saying them at that moment. Rani didn't seem that surprised. He looked at me and then at my collarbone, poking through my shirt. He put his lips round it and kissed it.

'Ruby, of course, I know.'

The trip to Dharamasala can be beautiful. You catch a train to Pathankot from Old Delhi, then a bus or a taxi through small valleys, past winding streams and rivers, apple orchards and waterfalls until you arrive at the small mountain town. Then it's simply a question of a rickshaw, larger and more grunting than those in Delhi, up the hill to the Tibetan colony of McLeod Ganj, where the Dalai Lama has his residence.

I didn't have so much time and just took a taxi from Dharamasala airport to McLeod Ganj and booked into the Green Hotel. It was cooler here in the mountains, fresh and clean. I had on my jeans and my trainers and that felt, in its own way, great. I walked down the dirt lane to find some food and to ask about the Astanga institute. Shack cafés strung with glowing paper lanterns lined my walk, where white Buddhists, yogis and trendy monks sat around drinking ginger tea, smoking spliffs and playing chess. One was much the same as the other and after ten minutes I settled down. It was a glorified shed inside. There were a few books stacked by the window: Paulo Coelho's *The Alchemist*, a dog-eared copy of *The Tibetan Book of Living and Dying* and *Mein Kampf*, which I thought was a bit odd. A young Tibetan woman came out of the kitchen and gave me a grease-splattered menu. It was a choice of omelettes, noodles or *momos*. I chose meat *momos* and a masala chai. I smoked a cigarette until the steaming plate of anaemic-looking slugs was plonked down in front of me. I ate them fast; I was hungry. I had a few sips of the chai but it was far too sweet and the glass was dirty so I just drank some water from my bottle and smoked another cigarette, looking at the posters and flyers that had been pinned all over the café. They advertised a variety of Eastern delights: Ayurveda courses, Buddhist meditation, reiki healing, full body massage, herbal highs, Tibetan cookery classes (those I would definitely stay away from), missing people adverts and many, many yoga classes. A wide-eyed blonde couple came into the café. They ordered vegetarian *momos* and apple juice. He had a beard and she had long hair plaited loosely. They talked quietly as they waited. He began rolling a spliff. They seemed pretty sane for hippies.

'Hi, have you been here long?' I said.

'Yeah, yeah, about four months,' the man answered, taking a drag out of his joint.

'We're studying Buddhist scripture at the Tibetan institute,' the woman chipped in.

That seemed one of the saner things you could be doing here.

'Where are you staying?'

'Green Hotel, we've got a long-term let there. It's a bit more expensive than staying with a family but we like our own space.'

'Where are you from?'

'Germany. We've both just graduated from teaching college, we'll be teaching religious education.'

'Aw. That's cool!' I said. I liked teachers, they reminded me of my dad. 'Could you help me? I'm looking for a friend. He's staying at the Astanga institute here. Do you know it? I think it's supposed to be pretty good, pretty intensive.'

'It sounds like the Sri Pattabhi Jois ashram. It's a little way out of town, going up to the villages,' said the woman. 'It's residential. You have to go for a month minimum. You can't just do classes so we've never been, but people who come back from there rave about it.'

That sounded like the place.

'Do you know how I get there?'

'It's getting a bit late now, but people usually catch a rickshaw there. It's about a hundred rupees,' the man replied, passing me the spliff.

I took a few puffs gratefully and said thanks. I walked down to the centre of the small town. It was about ten at night and most of the cafés were shut up. The one bar was crammed and blaring out U2. Several rickshaws were parked outside.

The drivers were having their own kind of party and reeked of cheap whisky. I saw a bottle of fake Johnnie Walker in one man's hand, with only a slither of liquid left. None of these guys was a wise choice of driver along steep mountain lanes at night, but I didn't have a choice. I was catching the morning flight back to Delhi. They all fought over which of them was going to take me to the ashram and the thought struck me that they could do anything to me in the dead of night and no one would know. My mobile didn't work up here. I decided to take my chances with the oldest of the lot of them, a bent-backed man who looked like he'd lost interest in the opposite sex some time in the sixteenth century.

His rickshaw was almost as old as he was. It wheezed and chugged up the hills so slowly that had he gone anywhere near the edge of the mountain, I could have easily fitted in a cup of tea before jumping out of the rickshaw. Slow but safe, at least.

I arrived at a series of low wooden buildings, built in a

simple Tibetan style, set slightly into the mountain woods. A single light glowed outside a carved main entrance. I pushed the door but it was locked. I rang a bell outside. After a few minutes, I heard sounds and a middle-aged black woman in a white turban opened the door. She was very thin and very toned and her eyes were very wide.

'Yes, hello? This is very late to be coming to the ashram. Are you booked in to stay here?' she said in a rolling South African accent.

'Er. No. Actually I am here to find someone, Tito . . .' I realised I didn't know his second name. I was a terrible journalist. Terrible. 'He's Brazilian . . .'

'Yes, I know Tito. He's been here a couple of weeks. But he's doing an intensive course; he's not supposed to have visitors. He's not even supposed to be talking unless it's necessary. But look, come in, you're here now. Let's try to sort this out,' she said. She wasn't super-nice but she seemed fair.

She opened the door wide and I stepped into a dark wooden entrance room with a large desk, which had candles and flowers on it. The air was suffused with lemongrass, just like the five-star spas in Delhi. This wasn't some charity joint; this was high class. Tito must be making some money from his drug dealing. Of course he was. Crime pays. The woman sat down at the desk and pulled out a leather-bound A4 notebook. Her cheekbones glowed in the candlelight.

'Hmmm. Yes. Here he is – Tito Alfonso – came in from New Delhi. Staying for a month. Brazilian, yes, you are right. He is here. But as I said, he's not supposed to be receiving visitors. Sri Pattabhi is very strict about this. We get a lot of people coming here to detox, to get off drugs and we can't just have anyone wandering in.'

'That's ironic,' I said, without thinking.

'What did you say?' she said, frowning.

'Sorry, nothing. I was just thinking out loud. I'm sorry, what is your name?'

'Cheryley.'

'Cheryley, I understand that this is unusual and I'm sorry for turning up so late at night but I don't have very long. A good friend of Tito's has unexpectedly died.'

Her mouth went into an O and her eyes became softer. 'You should have said, I'm sorry. Come this way,' she whispered.

We walked down a narrow corridor with doors down each side. Cheryley opened a room up and clicked on the light with an orange silk cord. There was a narrow bed made up with white linen with a set of white clothes folded neatly at its foot. More flowers and candles sat on a small desk.

'The ashram is divided into men and women. I will have to wake one of the swamis to go and get Tito. You can't visit that part of the ashram yourself. I can arrange for you to meet in the common room. Please, make yourself comfortable while you wait. You can shower and change. You must have had a long journey.'

I sat down on the bed and closed my eyes. Perhaps I would have a shower. I suddenly felt very dirty here, my hair greasy and my clothes sweaty and creased. By the time Cheryley returned, I'd cleaned up with soap and oil and put on the white cotton trousers and T-shirt lying on the bed.

She nodded approvingly. 'You look like you are staying here now.'

'God, I wish I could. Another time perhaps. When all this is over.'

She squeezed my hand but said nothing, leading me into a square room lined with bookshelves. The middle of the room was sunken. Cushions in orange and red and yellow were scattered around.

'This is where visitors come to read and relax when they

are not practising yoga. Please, make yourself comfortable. I will arrange for some tea. We usually serve white tea but is there anything else you would prefer?'

I had never actually heard of white tea. I suspected it wouldn't be a patch on a normal cup of tea with sugar and milk, but I didn't say this, of course.

'Thank you, you're very kind. You're making this as easy as possible for me. I'm grateful.'

Cheryley smiled and put her hand on my shoulder before leaving the room. I sat down on one of the cushions and waited. Tito soon came padding in, dressed only in his white trousers, his chest brown and supple.

'Ruby? This is, this is . . . Is everything all right?'

He had an open, nervous look on his face, as if he trusted the world too much to let the fears which one feels when woken in the middle of the night take him over. I was sorry to break this trust down.

'No, no, Tito, it's really not all right.'

He sat down opposite me and took my hands. 'Tell me, what has happened. Tell me how I can help.'

I told him about Stephen's death. This took some time for him to take in. He was very upset. I waited. Then I told him brief details of what had happened since then. Raj's arrest. Swami Shiva's secret and the terrible effect the whole thing had had on Rani. The tapes where we heard Raj practically admit covering for someone and Swami talk about Stephen. I told him about the drugs. How someone had called NDTV and the scandal it was causing. That Swami had been taken in for questioning and the network was in crisis.

A young girl entered the room and carefully placed two thin china bowls full of steaming clear liquid beside us. Tito took his up and blew on it. I did the same. We sat there for some time before he spoke.

'I am so very, very sorry about Stephen. I'll mourn him. But later. I need to clear up some of these problems.'

'Can you?'

'Yes. But I'm going to have to leave the country. I don't want to go to jail.'

'You live here. This is your life.'

'Yes, but I do deal drugs. I can justify it to myself but in the end it's a crime and I knew I may have to run one day. It's the price you pay for a job I can say I enjoy and think is useful. I'm good at it and responsible.'

I didn't know what to say to this. Tito was making heroin-pushing sound like teaching or being a doctor. I decided it wasn't the time for a debate. People think some weird things.

'It was your stash they found in the centre, wasn't it?'

'Yes, yes, it was. And only one person knew it was there, the same person Raj is trying to protect.'

'The guy who rang up NDTV?'

'It's not a guy. It's a woman. Sita, Raj's wife.'

'Sita?! Raj's wife?'

'Yes. She knows everything. I got the heroin through her and she got it through the Tibetan colony Majnu-ka-Tilla. She'd been working as a cleaner there, in one of the guest houses and got talking to the people who owned the place, got involved in this side business of theirs. We talked about it when I visited Raj. She thought I'd have good access to foreigners. She couldn't sell it in Dakshinpuri. We struck up a business. It worked well and I got to practise my Hindi.'

'Fucking hell. Did Raj know?'

'I don't know. She tried to keep it from him but he's not stupid.'

'But why would she call NDTV?'

'Revenge? To try to get Raj out of prison? To push the blame for Stephen on to somebody else? Why is Raj trying to protect her? Most probably because Stephen was on drugs the day he died. This would make sense. You know Stephen was talking to me that night when you both came over to mine. The night before I left for the mountains. He said he was having a bad time and would like to know where to get something if he needed it, while I was away. I let him know that if he needed anything he should talk to Sita. He should visit while Raj was at the ashram and no other time. He was shocked, of course. But agreed to keep it quiet. He may have gone to see her that day; the colony is very close to the bridge, isn't it? If the fence was loose and he was on the bridge out of his mind, he could easily have fallen in.'

'And Raj is taking the blame because he doesn't want Sita involved?'

'That would make sense, knowing what I know of them both. He would do anything for her,' said Tito.

It was 2 a.m. Tito suggested we meet early morning, for the 6 a.m. yoga class. I said I'd give it a miss and meet him afterwards but he was keen, saying it could be the last class he would take in India. He had a computer and wireless in his room and said he would book the same flight as mine back to Delhi and another back to São Paulo.

I got his full name and email address before we left each other: Tito Cezar Alfonso – Titoca@gmail.com. Then I tossed and turned in my beautiful bed for the few hours that I had to sleep.

Tito had filled in the missing piece. Stephen's death was an accident. He'd been on drugs it seemed. He'd died fucked on brown and fallen in the river like one of those shitty idols, his head smashed in on the concrete just like theirs. It was no one's fault but it was everyone's fault. It was the priest's fault for not tying up the fence. It was Sita's fault for selling him the drugs. It was Tito's fault for telling him where to get

266

them. It was Swami Shiva's fault for reacting so badly to his son. It was Sir Charles' fault for ignoring his grandson's history for so long. It was my fault too, for not looking out for him more, for not telling him it was wrong to get smacked up like that. I was selfish. He'd been lying in the morgue that morning and all I had been thinking of was my mango milkshake. It was all such a nasty mess.

25

As soon as I'd arrived back in Delhi I went over to Eddie's and told him what I'd learned about Sita and the drugs. He shook his head for a while then said we were ready to write the article.

'Are you going to tell Inspector Mukerjee about this? I promised Tito I'd wait till he was out of the country.'

'We don't have to. He's a good detective. He's going to work it out himself. The audio interview we translated has given him a new direction. He knows Raj is hiding something. He knows the phone call about the drugs came from Dakshinpuri. He's put two and two together already and thinks Raj is connected to the call. He's not quite sure how yet. He's thinking about the money he found at their house with Sita. Let him work on it a bit. I'm trying to decide whether to include his evidence tampering in the article.'

'You're going to shop the inspector?'

'I wouldn't put it like that. I'm going to include everything I know.'

'But he's your friend. You said you'd help him.'

'I have. But we didn't make a deal about what information I could use. I need a really good story here to give me leverage with the editors back home and police corruption is sexy anywhere. It also wouldn't be a bad thing if I was in a bit of trouble with the authorities here – speed up a transfer – it would make sense for them to move me quickly,' he said.

Fuck, Eddie was lethal. No wonder he'd done so well. I didn't know if I ever wanted to get that strategic. I'd prefer not to get so far and be a bit softer, I think. But then I'd already started on my own back-stabbing path with my first *Telegraph* article. And I wanted another. And like Eddie I wanted this next story to be as good as it could be, even if that meant shopping someone we'd been working with. You could justify it as the truth, honesty, holding institutions to account, but really, a large part of it was ego, wanting to be the hero writer.

'Anyhow, Samit is going to "re-interview" Raj today. He wants him to tell him who made that call. He wants to know how Stephen and the drugs are connected. He might know about Sita, he might not. But the story sounds better coming out of his mouth than some random Brazilian hippy. I said you'd go down and take notes as they go along. Then you come straight back here and we start working on the story for tomorrow's paper,' Eddie said.

The interrogation rooms were in the bowels of Karol Bagh police station.

I was sitting behind a mirrored window in a soundproof room, watching Raj strung up, swinging gently from side to side. Probir was leaning on the wall, picking his teeth. We were all waiting for Mukerjee.

The inspector wore sunglasses into the room. He gave a roar and smacked Raj hard on the legs with an electric rod. Raj jerked around like a puppet. Over the next hour the inspector screamed and shouted at Raj while prodding currents through his body.

When saliva was running down the side of Raj's hanging mouth and his eyes were rolling and yellow, the inspector began to simply pummel him with his fists. Blood flew from Raj's nose and splattered the inspector's Ray-Bans. Perhaps why he wore them in this windowless room.

'Take him down. Give him one hour,' the inspector said, marching out of the room without bothering to inspect the results of his handiwork.

He came to see me.

'I'm sorry you had to watch that. It didn't yield much in the way of results. Often we get suspects to answer questions while up there, but Raj wasn't able. He said he'd speak though. And I told him we knew most of it already; so he couldn't protect his family by keeping quiet.'

'His family?'

Had Raj given Sita up already?

'We always tell a suspect he can't protect his family by keeping silent. Even if their family have got nothing to do with the case it's a good line to use, guaranteed to shake a man up. It's one surprising thing about this job. No matter what dirty criminals we're dealing with, they pretty much all love their family, would do anything for their wives, their children. It's heart-warming in its own way,' he said.

An hour later I watched a second interview, from behind another mirrored window. This room was a more conventional set-up with a table and two chairs.

Raj was slumped back, thin and broken. The inspector puffed on a cigarette. The smoke wafted into Raj's eyes and made him retch slightly.

'*Bolo*,' said the inspector. Talk.

Probir sat beside me and translated what Raj said.

'You say you know it all anyway. Is this going to save my name? You'll put something on me even if it isn't murder. I didn't run Stephen over. I'm not sure exactly what happened to him. All I know was that I came home to find his bike outside my door. My wife said he'd been to our home upset. He had been on drugs, she said. I went looking for him but couldn't find him, so I drove the motorbike back to the ashram, caught a rickshaw home and came to work in the morning as usual. When I got to work there had been a call from the police about the body.'

'Stephen was on drugs? How would your wife know that?'

'She's an intelligent woman. She knows about the world.'

'Did she say what kind of drugs? Why did he go to your house at all? Because he wanted more drugs? Were you dealing, Raj?' asked Mukerjee.

'No.'

'You're trying to protect someone who was?'

'No. No, of course not. It's nothing to do with me or my family.'

'Raj, don't make me beat you again. You were involved in this or you wouldn't have tried to burn his motorbike. I'll ask you another question. Whose drugs were they that we found in the centre? Do you know that?'

'Yes, I know. The man with the tattoos, they were his. He goes to the Shiva centre. Tito. I don't know his last name. He stays at the Metropolis in Pahar Ganj, I know that, I've dropped him there.'

'Probir? Check it out and go down to this hotel. Get him in here. Where did Tito get the drugs?'

Raj was silent.

'Raj, we know anyway. So tell us. Tell us.'

Raj refused to talk.

Mukerjee waited for some time, then got up with a grunt.

271

He came into the interview room and spoke to Probir and me in English.

'He's admitted he didn't run Stephen over. He's said he didn't kill him. Probir, did you translate this for Ruby? We're going to go now and search his house for drugs, OK? His wife had that packet of money. Trace that for drugs and finger-prints too. The way she screamed after me for the case, I wouldn't be surprised if she was involved. She's a money lover,' said the inspector.

Mukerjee was right about families. Raj would never give his wife up but let out Tito's name in a flash. The inspector had good instincts. He had practically got the whole story just then. He might have some luck with a raid on their house, but Tito, I knew, was already on a plane back to Brazil.

I left the station for Eddie's to write up our investigation as Mukesh and the inspector were making their own way down to Dakshinpuri.

26

I walked in round the back of his house to find Eddie making coffee himself in the kitchen.

'Shruti's not here? She's not writing with us?'

'No, no, she says she wants to write a separate article, an interview with someone from the centre,' he said.

'Who?'

'I'm not sure. Just let her get on with it,' he said.

I shrugged. I was surprised. This was going to be big and she'd been so keen to be involved. She'd helped too with the translating and everything.

'Ah fuck, I've burned myself. Ruby, do you know how to use this damn coffee maker?'

I laughed and helped him out, though I wasn't much better and we both settled for tea in the end.

We worked steadily, phoning people, checking out facts, finding quotes.

Eddie was in contact constantly with Inspector Mukerjee, who was out raiding Delhi left, right and centre: Pahar Ganj,

Dakshinpuri, the V.H.P. temple. Now he had his story he was on it.

He saw us as a team, was grateful for our help and kept us updated with all the latest developments. Sita had been found with four packets of heroin in the house. The same batch as in the ashram, it appeared. Her mobile phone showed two calls between herself and Stephen the day he died. She'd been arrested. The inspector had the envelope with the money in it fingerprinted. Stephen's fingerprints came up on several notes. Sita's prints were on every single one. Raj and Swami were in the clear.

We tried to ring the V.H.P. temple on the bridge several times for a statement on the fence cutting, but all we got was some tinny Hindi chanting.

'Listen, Ruby, you're going to have to go down there again and get this in person. Tell them you're from the *Daily Telegraph* newspaper and that you need an interview with the manager. Tell them it's regarding evidence that Stephen Newby died because of a loose fence, cut by one of their priests. Don't leave without a statement,' he said.

The entrance to the temple's office complex was guarded by a wall of muscle who said his name was Nakul. I fluttered my eyelashes. He was bored and I managed to raise a spark of excitement in him, enough for him to trundle off and give Eddie's card to the temple manager.

The office of the temple manager was a medium-sized room with pictures of various swamis and gods covering the walls. The windows were dark and there were mounds of paper and Indian bureaucracy filling up shelves. A small, thin, white-haired man was writing intently behind a large desk, also covered in bits of paper and office mess. Looking up, he peered at me suspiciously from behind large glasses. It was hard to believe that this man and this place were part of the same religion as the Shiva centre.

'*Behto,*' he said.

I knew this meant 'sit'.

'Thank you, sir,' I said.

'No English!' the man cried out, raising his finger to me. 'English is not the language of Bharat! Do you know what Bharat means? It means Mother India! You cannot know the spirit of Bharat without speaking Hindi. Do you speak Hindi?'

'*Thora, thora,*' I said. Little, little. It usually drew a laugh from people, but not this man. He merely frowned.

'Why you come to this country without learning Hindi? Why do you think people should speak to you in English? English is not the language of Bharat!'

'Er, I'm learning now, sir. *Apa kaise hu?*' I asked him how he was, falteringly.

He leaned back in his chair and peered at me.

'This is no longer your country – you should not expect us to speak English.'

Beads of sweat were appearing on his forehead. I glanced over at the door. Nakul was leaning against his rifle. Another man, with one eye significantly larger than the other, had appeared and was lethargically spinning a pistol round. I could almost touch the violence. It's always there, simmering under the surface of Delhi life: in the road rage beatings, servant killings and family shootings. This little manager seemed to have a particularly short fuse. He burrowed his beady eyes into me and pursed his lips.

'Chai *dedo!*' he shouted. Nakul duly went off to the kitchen to get some tea.

'You are not Eddie Challan. You are a girl.'

'I'm his assistant. Sorry, sir, I don't have my own card to give you.'

275

'Why have the *Telegraph* sent their assistant to see me? Why have they not sent their correspondent? They should send their correspondent to me.'

This little guy had a big ego.

'Ah, Eddie told me to send his regards to you actually. Said you were very well known and this temple was famous for its political power. He very much wanted to come down himself but he's stuck in a police press conference all day and the story is urgent. For tomorrow. He thought it would be more respectful to send me in person than simply call up the temple. He also specifically wanted to get an interview from you – no one else.'

It was amazing how easily people believe flattery. I didn't even know this guy's name, but he didn't seem remotely suspicious of all this. He leaned back in his chair and pushed his chest out in satisfaction. Nevertheless, I thought I'd better cover my tracks. It was a bad habit of mine to see how far I could push it with people.

'Sir, would you mind just giving me the spelling of your name? Eddie was very keen to get your name exactly right, as it'll be high up in the article. We might even box up a quote from you.'

'Yes. Yes. It's N-A-R-E-N-D-A. That's my first name. And then P-A-T-E-L. That's easy enough, isn't it?' He was becoming friendlier, more expansive now.

'Yes, sir. Thank you, sir.'

'Now what are you here about? If it is about the painting and that terrible artist I am not talking about it. The men responsible have been cleared.'

'No, sir, it's not . . . it's not about that.'

Nakul came lumbering back from the kitchen with two steaming cups of tea, a sugar bowl, a cracked plate of yellow Indian sweets and a packet of cashew nut biscuits.

'Please take, no formality.' The man gestured, holding out the plate of sweets like an eager auntie at a tea party.

'Sugar? I am diabetic so we make tea without,' he explained apologetically before barking at Nakul. 'NutraSweet *dedo*!'

I heaped in a teaspoon while making clucking noises about the man's diabetes.

'I'll have one biscuit though – just one won't do any harm. Please, you must try one of our sweets. They are made here,' he said, holding one out for me.

'*Shukriya*,' I said. Thank you.

The man plonked the plate down and became fanatic once again. '*Shukriya! Shukriya!* That is Urdu! That is not Hindi! You say *dhanayavad*! That is Hindi!' he screeched.

I was starting to think madness was a prerequisite for religious leaders in India. That Swami Shiva was the exception rather than the rule.

'Sorry, I live in Nizamuddin, it's a Muslim area, that's what they say there,' I explained.

He wrinkled his nose with distaste. I thought I'd better cut to the chase before his mood got worse.

'Sir, we've got evidence that this temple has been cutting the fence on the bridge and not tying it up again properly. This is against the law.'

The manager looked at me with bemusement. 'Of course we have been cutting it. For river poojas. They are very popular. We tie it up again usually. I don't know, maybe the priests were too full of God one day if it didn't get tied up.'

'It's illegal.'

Mr Patel shrugged. 'The police don't care. It doesn't do much harm. Some of them come to the festivals.'

'So you're admitting it?'

Patel screwed up his beady eyes and directed them at me. 'What's this about?'

'There's video evidence that on the day of Hola Mohalla, a priest from this temple performed a river pooja and didn't tie the fence up properly.'

'And?'

'Have you heard of Stephen Newby? The British man who died?'

Narenda Patel shrugged.

'Stephen is seen in one of your videos, on Wazirabad Bridge just before he fell into the river. It looks like he fell in the Yamuna because of the loose fence. There's no other way. Do you have anything to say about this? We would like a statement from the temple in our article.'

The manager pursed his lips. Then sighed. 'The English man? The same age as my grandson. My grandson is married with three children. What was that boy doing alone there in the first place? What festival was it again, please?'

'Hola Mohalla.'

Patel barked at his assistant, who lumbered off once more. We sat in silence for some minutes. It was very hot in the room. I ate another sweet. It made my teeth ache. Nakul came back with a thin boy dressed in white with an orange bag around his shoulder. He was young, maybe nineteen, with a fluffy moustache. He looked scared.

'*Ha ji*,' he stammered and bowed slightly to Patel.

They began talking fast in Hindi, the older man speaking sharply to the young priest, who was going whiter and whiter and stammering much more. He began crying and knelt down on the floor.

Patel barked at him to get up, which he did immediately, trying to stop crying.

Patel took off his glasses and rubbed his eyes. 'You probably didn't understand half of that, did you? This is the priest who was in charge of the fence that day. I'll tell you what he said. This is off the record and then you can take down my statement. Don't try to use anything not in my statement. Eddie will understand. It'll come back very badly for you if you do. Not many people mess with the V.H.P. and survive.'

Patel explained the young priest, called Shiva, had just been initiated. He was from Bihar and had travelled down to work in the temple about two weeks ago. It had been his first festival. He'd been given the job of wiring the fence up but had forgotten. I knew why he'd forgotten, because he'd been playing with a small child. I felt bad for him.

The young priest suddenly piped up with some desperate plea. It didn't amuse Patel, who threw a paperweight at him with a sudden ferocity.

'What did he say?'

'He says he's sorry. They don't have fences in Bihar. They don't ever need to tie them up.'

Patel nodded at Nakul, a small gesture but a violent one and I knew that this boy would be beaten badly. Nakul took the boy by his elbow and pushed him from the room.

'What did you say to him?'

'I told him he'd got the temple into trouble. That he'd killed the boy from the Shiva network. The student of Swami Shiva, that he'd have to pay for that.'

'It wasn't his fault.'

'It was his fault. He needs discipline. And it's bad for the V.H.P. to cause problems with the Shiva network. They have their own power. Now, you want a statement to use in your little article, do you?'

As I took my pen and paper out I heard a muffled scream.

'The temple completely denies any responsibility in the death of Stephen Newby. The mother Ganga and the mother Yamuna are the source of all life. Worshipping them is essential to the

Hindu faith. Stephen Newby was blessed to be found in the Yamuna,' he said.

It didn't make sense to me but I wanted to go. I didn't like the atmosphere there and didn't want to think about that young priest.

Eddie was waiting for the final statement when I got back to his house. He didn't like it very much but I told him if he wanted someone to go back he could go himself.

There was one last thing Eddie had to do before sending his copy. He called Mukerjee for his own quote.

'Listen, Samit, we're going to write up that there could have been evidence tampering by Delhi police. Do you have anything to say about this?'

I heard some far off roaring but Eddie stood his ground.

'And I have helped you, haven't I? I'm not going behind your back. I'm just doing my job. And I'm asking you for a response.

'Look. It's not going to do you much harm. There's nothing but some eyewitness statement that you're obviously going to refute. It's just a small suggestion; think of it like a sprinkling of paprika on a *chaat* snack. We don't need it. It's not going to stand up to any close investigation. But it's going to add a little piquancy. So do you want to give me a quote or not?'

He did. Eddie wrote down a few lines. I was surprised to hear the inspector actually say goodbye to him in a normal voice. It seemed he took it pretty well.

I played typist as we put the final version of the article together. Eddie walked up and down the room dictating. He made sure both our bylines were on it. We sent the piece about five in the evening.

SHIVA SCANDAL REVEALED — *TELEGRAPH* EXCLUSIVE

By Eddie Challan and Ruby Jones

Stephen Newby Death Drugs-Related
Mystery father appears to be Swami Shiva
Driver lied to protect his heroin-peddling wife
Police colluded with false statement and tampered with evidence

Raj Kumar, the driver charged with the death of Stephen Newby, has admitted his statement is false. He did not run over Stephen and he did not throw him into the Yamuna.

An exclusive investigation by this newspaper has revealed that the Stephen Newby death was a tragic accident, which sparked off a series of cover-ups and crimes by members of the international Shiva network and the Delhi police. That an accidental death can reveal so much scandal, suggests India has a long way to go before it is the open and modern society it likes to project to the rest of the world.

The day Stephen Newby, 28, died, he discovered the identity of the absent father he had been seeking in India: the international yoga guru Swami Shiva. Although Swami Shiva has since admitted that Stephen was his son to this paper, the guru had initially pressed Stephen to keep this secret, fearing it would damage his reputation, his network and his protégé, Rani Shiva, who is now missing.

Stephen left the Shiva centre that day for Dakshinpuri, a slum resettlement colony near Wazirabad Bridge. A number of calls were made between Stephen and Sita Kumar, the wife of Swami Shiva's driver, and it now appears that Raj Kumar's original statement and the reason he tried to burn Stephen's motorbike was to protect his wife.

Stephen had gone to Dakshinpuri to buy heroin from Sita.

She had been running a small heroin-dealing business with another regular at the Shiva centre, Tito Alfonso, a Brazilian living in Delhi. The police have raided both Alfonso's hotel room and the Kumars' home. Four packets of heroin, from the same batch as discovered in the Shiva centre, were found with Sita. Alfonso had vacated his hotel room and is now in Brazil.

Sita Kumar is currently being questioned by police and has already admitted in the face of overwhelming evidence that Stephen smoked heroin in her home that day. He left shortly afterwards, for a 'walk', she said.

Locals around Dakshinpuri have now come out as witnesses, saying they saw a bike matching the description of Stephen's parked outside the Kumars' residence. A friend and neighbour of the couple, Prasad Prasad, said Raj arrived late in the evening and, after spending half an hour inside his home, drove off with Stephen's motorbike, arriving back much later on that evening.

Videos from a local temple covering a festival on Wazirabad Bridge show pictures of Stephen in the background. Always fascinated by Indian rites, perhaps Stephen had noticed the commotion and had gone to have a look. The videos show two priests cutting the fence to throw a goddess statue into the river as sacrifice. They do not tie the fence up again as they are supposed to. Stephen, drowsy from the drugs, must simply have fallen into the river, maybe leaning on the fence he thought was secure.

His death was an accident but the Hanuman V.H.P. Temple will now be answering serious questions about the way they conduct their festivals. Delhi mayor Sheila Dikshit told this paper in response to the revelations that she would be: 'urging Delhi police to put an end once and for all to the river poojas which have been illegal now for some years'.

She called the practice of river poojas a 'cheap crowd-puller, designed to pull in voters, which destroys and pollutes the Yamuna, makes our bridges unsafe and has caused the death of a promising young man'.

Ms Dikshit refused to comment on the revelation that Swami Shiva is Stephen's father. Although Swami Shiva is not directly involved in either the drug deals or the death of his son, his reputation and his network have already been damaged by these scandals. He was released from prison yesterday and will find attendance has plummeted across his network. Regular donors to the centre have told this paper that they will be stopping their association with the centre now.

Although Stephen's death was an accident, there is damning evidence that Swami Shiva and the inspector on this case, Samit Mukerjee, colluded to let an innocent man take the blame for Stephen's death.

Although neither knew the full story, both were suspicious enough that Raj was not telling the truth to talk about making sure the charges would be manslaughter and not murder. Despite Stephen having no bruises on his body that would correspond to a road accident of the kind that Raj described, Swami Shiva's car has several dents in its front bumper. The police deny in the strongest possible terms that these appeared after the car was impounded at Karol Bagh police station.

Rani Shiva, Swami Shiva's protégé and a close friend of Stephen Newby, has not been available for questioning. Nor has Stephen's grandfather, Sir Charles Newby, who is currently on a cruise in the Caribbean with his wife.

It remains to be seen who will actually come to trial in the case of this young man's death. Possibly no one. It is certain that no one will stand accused of murder, but there are many people responsible for his demise.

Eddie took out his bottle of Bombay Sapphire and we had a drink on his lawn.

'It's good, Ruby. Well done. You've worked well. This will be very positive for you. It's a great cutting; you're bound to get more work from it. Shruti missed out today. Silly girl, she can be so perverse sometimes, really,' said Eddie.

'What's up with her?'

'She's upset I'm leaving, I think.'

'You're still looking for a transfer out of here?'

'Yes, soon. In the next few months.'

'Will they advertise your job?'

Eddie laughed. 'Good God, no. This isn't the kind of job you advertise. This is a reward post. It'll be one of the war correspondents who've have had enough of putting their lives on the line, probably; that's why I got it. Or maybe a big-shot reporter in London who wants to get out of the UK for a bit.'

Not me then. Of course it wouldn't be me. Of course. Why would it? Disappointment. Hurt pride. Embarrassment. Clarity. Fear. All these emotions frothed up together in my belly as I did my best to keep a poker face.

I could see clearly now I'd thought I was worth more than I was. So I'd had one scoop. So had Eddie, with his Gandhi interview. And it had taken him another twenty years to get the job of South Asia correspondent. Why on earth did I think I could skip a couple of decades? I felt tired and worried. It had been a real hope that had kept me going through the last few days, that out of this mess I could get a job with the paper. I needed to survive, to move on. I couldn't simply take a Caribbean cruise to get over Stephen's death. I needed to work. Now more than ever.

And this new correspondent, he wouldn't know me. He wouldn't be so happy to have me pitching ideas, articles. He'd want to make his own name. What was I going to do? I had nothing. Well, I had Rani. We'd work something out together.

I deflected my own disappointment by projecting it onto Shruti.

'Do you think Shruti might like a go at a job like that? Is that why she is pissed off, 'cause she wants it?'

'Not a chance. All that girl wants is to leave this place! She's desperate for me to take her to Shanghai!'

'Really?'

'Our relationship hasn't been . . . ah . . . purely professional. It's complicated. But I can't get her a job in London and I don't want her to come to Shanghai with me. It's been fun here but I have an ex in London I want to make a go of it with. She's waiting for me.'

Eddie got his driver to drop me home and said he would let me know what the reaction was to the article in London – and from Mukerjee. He didn't mention payment and neither did I, from some kind of false pride that I regretted once in the car back. I could do with being paid for this. I had Rani to look after now. Was I going to have to support him? How would we survive? I wanted him to stay but didn't know if I could manage it.

I found him lying on his back on the sofa, his arms holding his head, looking out on to the balcony. A thin evening light streamed onto the floor and slid over his torso and face. He was listening to some Indian ragas of Stephen's. I was surprised he'd worked out how to use iTunes. He was really making himself at home here. I went and sat on the edge of the sofa.

'Rani, I'm back.'

He had his eyes shut and opened them slowly. 'I see.'

'How are you? Did the girl bring you up some food yesterday? I told her not to give you meat.'

'Yes – a couple of girls came here – and the food was better.

They gave me dhal and chapatti. It wasn't bad. More spicy than at the ashram. I could get used to it though. I quite liked it.'

I took his hand. 'Listen, Rani, I've been thinking. You know, it's been really good for me, to have been with you like I have for the last few days. And you know how much I feel for you. I've liked you so much since I met you. But I don't think it can work, us together here. I think your real place is with Swami Shiva and teaching yoga. I know you're angry with him now but really, you don't want to throw away your whole life on a snap decision made at such an upsetting time. If you spend much longer with me here you'll not have a choice – people will know you've lived with a girl and it'll be impossible to go back to your old life.'

Rani closed his eyes. 'I've made my mind up about this. I'm not going back to the ashram. It would be living a lie. Maybe one day I will be able to see Swami Shiva but now I can't. I've decided to make my pilgrimage in the normal world.'

'But what will you do, Rani? How will you cope? The truth is, I really haven't very much money. I can hardly support myself, let alone two of us. The rent is paid on this place up till next month but I don't know about afterwards. I'm so stressed living here and I just . . . I just don't think I'll be able to cope with looking after us both.'

Rani looked at me in surprise, then softly. He took my face in his hands. 'Ah, Ruby. You don't need to worry. Look at you. Come on! It's going to be OK.'

He put his arm round me. I could feel a tear well up in my eye and then roll down my face. It was quickly followed by another. I was crying. I wasn't used to someone being this kind to me. Stephen had loved me, looked after me, but he had been tough. He hadn't been a gentle person. Rani was.

'Ah, Ruby. Don't cry. Come on. It's going to be fine. I know

286

I am a bit mental in your eyes. I don't think the same as other people, I know that. It's the way I've grown up. But I'm not stupid. I've been all over the world, I've taught yoga to prime ministers. I know I've made a lot of money. I don't want it back. It's all in the Shiva network and it's all been put to good use. But I know I can make more, a lot more. I've been thinking. I'll teach privately. I know the embassy pool will pay me enough to keep us both easily. And there'll be more. Don't worry. You don't need to look after me. I'll look after you.'

I didn't want to speak so I just nodded. It sounded good.

27

Eddie's and my article came online around ten in the morning. It wasn't the main headline. That was some spat on MPs' expenses. I was disappointed. But I guessed the government was slightly more important to British readers than Stephen, a swami with a roving eye and a small amount of drugs in a Delhi ashram. We were headlined on the World pages, however. Eddie had a photo but we both had our names.

There was a picture of Stephen graduating from Oxford. They'd also made an effort at 'multi-platform' journalism by linking to footage from NDTV. The clip was of Swami leaving prison, dressed in pressed white robes with Probir and Mukesh at his side. It was hard to see him through the debris of news: the cameras, anchors, the microphones. Journalists shouted at him for a quote but he looked straight ahead. Probir, on the other hand, couldn't help a coy wave at the cameras. He thought he was on the red carpet at Cannes or something, pouting and turning his head from side to side so every camera got a good picture of him.

There was also a sidebar article to our main feature. An

exclusive interview with Rani Shiva – by Shruti Soni.

I felt my pupils expand. I couldn't believe it. She'd kept it a secret from both Eddie and me. She must have interviewed him when I was away in Dharamasala. My God. I scanned through the article quickly. It was a verbatim Q and A.

Q: Rani Shiva, journalists everywhere have been clambering for an interview with you in the last few days. Where have you been?
A: I've been here.
Q: Why have you not come out to comment on your guru's fall from grace?
A: No one has asked me.
Q: Could you give a comment to this newspaper?
A: I don't want to be disloyal to my former guru but a devotee of Brahma cannot have a son. Swami Shiva is supposed to be a devotee of Brahma but he is not now and I cannot call him my guru.
Q: What about the drugs charges?
A: I don't know about those really. I don't believe them. I spent all my time with Swami Shiva.
Q: Attendance is down at the Shiva network, although Swami has been released from jail now without charge. Will you continue to work there with him?
A: No, my time with the Shiva network is over. I will no longer be connected to the ashram or its work.

My first feeling was some kind of overwhelming relief that Rani really did mean to stay with me and not go back. Seeing his break with Swami Shiva in print made it a reality. But then I got angry. How the hell had she managed it? And why hadn't Rani said anything? But perhaps he had. He told me two girls had called round while I was away. One of them with food, the other must have been Shruti.

I called up Eddie. 'Have you seen the interview with Rani?'

'Yes. I'm mad about it. The girl should have said. It makes us look stupid, saying that we don't know where he is then having a fucking sidebar interview with him. That shouldn't have happened. No way. There should have been more co-ordination on the desk. It's that Guy Black, pushy little toerag. He worked separately with Shruti on this and brought it to the editor just as the paper was about to go to bed. Of course they would run it but they didn't cross-check our article where we say his whereabouts isn't known. The editor is fuming about it this morning; makes us look like idiots, really it does. I tell you, she hasn't done anyone any favours this girl. You can't work like this. It's not even very good. Doesn't show any talent,' he said.

'What are you going to do?'

Eddie sighed. 'I'm not sure, to be honest with you. It's a good excuse to let her go. We've been . . . well . . . we've been arguing.'

I didn't pry. It was their business. 'How's Inspector Mukerjee?'

'Angry. But he's not as angry as you would expect. A lot of good stuff came out of those raids yesterday. They got a huge stash of drugs from Majnu-ka-Tilla and that place has been a problem for years. They've cleared both the Swami Shiva case and the Stephen Newby case, so his boss is willing to overlook the evidence tampering – everyone accepts it happens anyway. Even the mayor isn't bothered – she's more interested in stopping river poojas. She's an environmentalist. It's more of a visual mission too, shows voters she's cleaning up the city. And it gives her an excuse to go after the V.H.P. She's told the police to start investigating river poojas and V.H.P. activities after this and Mukerjee's going to be heading up that team. It's good for him. Political. He'll probably make a bit of money from it. By the way, he told me to tell you he's begun the book – *Shantaram* – and he really is enjoying it,' said Eddie.

Rani wandered into the room as I was saying goodbye to Eddie. He was enjoying a mango. The juice was dripping down his face and fingers.

'Hey, there's a guy downstairs selling Alphonso mangoes. They're great. They're so ripe. I got a box. Go get one, in the kitchen.'

'Rani, what the fuck were you doing giving an interview to Shruti? Why didn't you tell me about it?'

'What?'

'Look.'

I showed him the article. He looked surprised but then shrugged.

'She came over when you were away. Said she was working with you. I thought it was OK.'

'She was working with me but I didn't know about this.'

'But what's the problem? It's true. I meant it. I'm not going back. I'm staying with you. It's my responsibility now.'

He handed me a piece of mango. The juice went over my wrists and down my arm. He kissed it off and I put my hand through his hair as I watched him.

28

I made a move down to the Shiva centre with a printout of the article. They might as well know about it as soon as possible, and about Rani.

It was very quiet in the garden of the centre. I could hear a cuckoo in the tree. The usual pile of shoes and sandals outside the door of the mid-morning class had dwindled to just two pairs. I recognised Chewy's battered Havaianas and a pair of Jesus sandals. There was no one in reception to check my membership card. I wandered into the main hall assuming there would be no one there either.

But I was surprised to see a class about to start after all. Swami Shiva was lying out in corpse pose, the first position of yoga, at the top of the room by the shrine, where Rani would usually be. There was one young girl with black hair lying to the side of Swami Shiva. I picked up a mat and joined them.

A huge om suddenly vibrated round the room. It sent a shock through my body.

'Feel the power of the om run through you. Connect with

om, the life force, feel your individual problems disappear. Over the next hour, concentrate on the space between your eyebrows. Feel the energy pour into you as we practise the asanas,' Swami Shiva intoned.

He took the three of us through the thirteen asanas as thoroughly as if he'd been in front of the usual jam-packed hall of devotees. First the headstand, then the shoulder-stand, the plough, the bridge, the fish, the forward bend, the cobra, the locust, the bow, the spinal twist, the crow, the triangle, the standing forward bend. As always, I felt horrified at the beginning of the class at the thought of an hour and a half of concentration, of stretching and working every bit of me. But Swami's rhythmic voice rolled through me and I soon lost myself in the movement. I looked gently down on myself. At the end of the class, Swami moved through our bodies, relaxing each muscle, each internal organ, with his voice. My shoulders, my neck, my stomach, I could feel them instantly obey him and loosen up.

We finished with a prayer. I stayed where I was with my eyes shut. I had meant to go to this same class on the day of my birthday. It would have been an excellent beginning to the day. I had been about to get ready to go when I'd got the call about Stephen. Maybe this was that class. Maybe it was still my birthday. I began willing this. I prayed for it. I visualised Stephen sitting by my side, the Japanese girls opposite me, their backs perfectly straight, making me jealous.

I opened my eyes in a burst. It was still just me and the girl with black hair. I noticed grey hair had crawled further up Swami's beard. That's what having children does, I guess. We all sat there for a while longer before Swami Shiva bowed his head and left the room. He didn't look at me or acknowledge me at all.

I went to look for Chewy and found him in the kitchen,

putting the finishing touches to a ginger and pineapple cheese-cake. He was smashing biscuits in a bag with a rolling pin – violently.

'The secret is to use American ginger nuts in this cake – or Arnotts if you can get 'em, they're Australian, the best. The Indians though, they don't know how to make a proper ginger biscuit. I get students to bring me packs from the States. It doesn't matter if they get crushed cause I crush 'em anyway,' he said, thumping down the rolling pin.

'Where has everyone gone? Have the residential students left too?' I said.

'Fucked off, haven't they? They've no faith: no faith in yoga, no faith in Swami Shiva. After all he's helped them with and taught them. The Japanese girls have swept off on some tour of Rajasthan palaces; the Israelis have gone to Goa. Those three English women teamed up and booked themselves into a five-star hotel in the Maldives. And I tell you, I never saw them look so happy. They went round with faces like wet weekends the whole bloody time they were here, saying the food made them bloated. They weren't bloated – they just ate too much and were fat to start with! The only one who's here is the little Iranian girl who arrived yesterday. I told her what had happened but she just shrugged and said he was a reli-gious leader, what did we expect? At least he didn't torture and kill students, she said.'

'You're still here. Why?'

'It's not a big deal! Swami Shiva is human! Does it make him evil that he could love a woman? I'm here in this ashram and I love women! I love women so much! Those hot little Japanese girls drove me wild. I got hot every time I saw Kiki hanging up those tiny lime-green knickers of hers to dry.'

'How is Swami Shiva?'

'I think he's surprised all the students have left. I felt so bad telling him, Rube. And then there's Rani. We've all seen the article this morning with his interview.'

'You've seen it? What? But Swami Shiva just taught that class without saying a word to me.'

'Swami Shiva has depths you and I know nothing about. He said the Shiva network will carry on as normal and there was no difference in following the path of yoga with thousands of companions or completely alone. He said he'd take all the classes till Rani was ready to teach again. I said we could get a teacher from any of the other centres to come here – any of those US yogis would kill to teach in the first Shiva ashram. There's a waiting list as long as my arm to come here. But Swami said he wanted to teach himself now. He hasn't done that for years, Ruby. Years and years.'

One of the Keralan cooks, glistening and wide-eyed, long hair tied up in a green cloth, put her head round the door. She chatted to us in Malayalam, oblivious to the fact that neither of us spoke a word. We kind of understood anyway. Swami had finished his prayers; lunch was ready.

'You're joining us, Ruby?' said Chewy.

'Yes please, thank you,' I said.

We ate in the kitchen on the floor by the cookers. The ladies had prepared several different dishes and these were subtler than the usual ashram dinners that they prepared for crowds. We ate in silence. The lady with the green hair-cloth crouched on her haunches by us, proffering each dish in turn. Eventually she got bored of us refusing and filled up her own plate, signalling for the other girls to do the same. They sat a little apart from us, eating with steady concentration.

Swami Shiva didn't talk until we'd finished eating completely and all washed our hands.

'Ruby, I read the *Telegraph* piece online this morning. Is

295

the interview with Rani accurate? Does he really want to leave the network?'

'Swami Shiva, I am really sorry. I left town for one night and that's when Shruti got the interview. I didn't know anything about it. But, yes, from what Rani has said to me, he's going to continue to teach, but privately.'

The irises of Swami's eyes expanded and then shrunk small. He blinked a few times and closed his lids completely. After some time he opened them again and looked at me calmly and steadily. 'Where is he going to live?'

I blushed. 'I think he'd like to stay with me, Swami.'

'Well. That is good. To know he is with a friend. Obviously, this is a great sadness for me. But this is karma at work. I will continue to be here, teaching and running the network. Please tell Rani, Ruby, that it would give me great joy simply to see him and talk. If he would like to visit us here I would be very happy.'

'I'll tell him, Swami. I'll come again tomorrow myself whatever.'

Chewy was in reception listening glumly to his iPod as I left, Kenny Rogers apparently.

I bought coconuts from a stall on the way home. I knew Rani loved coconut water and there were no sellers round the shrine. It was a South Indian thing and most pilgrims were from Pakistan and Bangladesh and the North – harder terrains. We sat on the balcony and sucked them through straws as I tried to persuade Rani to come with me to the centre the next day.

'Rani. What about forgiveness? What about that? Isn't that something you believe in? You're being so rigid in your morality you're forgetting the reason you hold the morals in the first place.'

'What do you mean?'

'Religions, morals, codes of living – they're supposed to make you a better person, right? All these systems should make it easier for us to live with each other and make us more humane. But you're just concentrating on the rules, not the humanity. Be a bit gentle. Be human. Forgive him. Go and see him.'

Rani looked out over the shrine, at the birds flying around the dome. 'You might have a point. I'll see him. But not yet. Not yet. I need time. I need time to get my head in order. You go. You go and see him and that'll help.'

I was early for the class the next morning. There was one more pair of shoes outside. As I slipped off my own sandals, a thin boy pushed past me, grabbed the chappals and ran off. He was strong. I thought I recognised him but the most overwhelming impression he left was a real stink. Urine and body odour and gutters hung in the air. I didn't know anyone who smelled like that.

I found Swami Shiva lying at the top of the room in corpse pose.

He looked very peaceful. I wouldn't disturb him with the bad news that Rani would not be coming today. I was early. I'd just lie down and wait for the class to start.

I lay there for some time, breathing in and out, letting out the strain and tension from my body and filling it with oxygen and energy. I tried to imagine my mind was a feather looking down on me. It was a while before I opened my eyes again. There were a few others now, also in corpse pose, waiting for the class to start. Chewy was there, wearing a shirt with pink flamingos and green giraffes, as well as the Iranian girl and a middle-aged Indian man with a pot belly I'd seen in a number of classes.

I looked at the clock on the wall. We should have started twenty minutes ago. Maybe Swami had fallen asleep.

I got up slowly and crept over to him. 'Swami,' I whispered, trying to wake him.

He wouldn't wake up. His eyes didn't indicate awareness of my presence. I shook him again.

'Swami?'

I put my hand on his stomach. He was not practising abdominal breathing. I put my hand on his chest, checked his pulse. He wasn't breathing at all.

'He's not breathing!' I said.

Chewy sat up. 'What? What are you talking about?'

He leaped up and crouched over Swami Shiva. The other two students sat up with nervous looks on their faces but hung back. Swami continued to stay in corpse pose. Not moving a muscle.

'He's dead. He's not breathing. He must have had a heart attack,' said Chewy.

29

The next hours were blurry. The Iranian girl began sobbing loudly. Chewy tried to comfort her though he was shocked white himself. He patted her on the back but could not stop staring at Swami Shiva. The Indian man called the police and the doctor. I called the hotel downstairs from my flat and tried to tell them to get Rani to come here. But they couldn't understand what I was saying. I wasn't sure if this was because of my Hindi or because of the extreme high pitch of my voice. They didn't seem to recognise me. I shook my phone at the Indian man and asked him to speak for me.

The police arrived first. Mukerjee; he'd been called off his new temple-raiding duty for this special case. He raised his eyebrows when he saw me.

'At first I thought you just make a habit of being where trouble is, Ruby. If you're not careful I'm going to start suspecting you of causing it,' he said.

He came with a forensics team. He was serious and he was focused.

'Is that necessary?' said Chewy. 'This is a holy place, not a crime scene.'

'We need to make sure we know exactly what happened, sir. This guru, he had practised yoga his whole life. He was a powerful swami, it surprises me he just died of a heart attack.'

We were told to wait in reception. Rani arrived while we were sitting there chewing our nails. He was wearing a pair of jeans and a T-shirt of Stephen's I'd given him, while his kurta was in the wash. They were loose on him, he looked like some teenage skater – except for his face, which was lined and crumpled.

'Ruby? What's going on? I had a message saying Swami Shiva was dead!'

I nodded.

He looked at me and then Chewy. 'Chewy?'

Chewy nodded.

'But how? I don't understand. How?'

Inspector Mukerjee came out of the hall holding a yoga pillow.

'Do you know whose this is? We found it stuffed behind the altar. The doctor here says Swami Shiva died from suffocation. We'll need you all to be questioned at the police station. This is a murder investigation.'

30

I found myself in the same interrogation room in which I'd seen Raj, with the mirrored window. It was a more civilised experience for me. I was given police chai that had now become a familiar synthetic taste. Inspector Mukerjee sat opposite me.

'Ruby Jones,' he said.

'Inspector.'

'Just tell me what you know. Tell me anything you think can help with this.'

I racked my brains. I had been the first person in the hall. I knew that. Had I seen anything else? Anyone else? I had. That boy. And I had recognised him.

'Oh, fuck, Inspector. I saw someone run off from the centre, just as I was arriving. It was the boy from the V.H.P. temple. The guy who'd cut the fence; I remember his face. He was dirty, he really smelled.'

It was something. Inspector Mukerjee headed straight out for the temple. I went to find Rani.

He was at the centre, preparing Swami Shiva's body for cremation. I watched him working through the window of

the hall. He'd done a lot in the hour I'd been at the station.
He had washed himself and changed into fresh white clothes.
He'd done the same for Swami. He'd also moved the body
around to face south and lit an oil lamp at Swami's head.
There was a look of quiet concentration on Rani's face. His
movements were smooth and slow as he began to smear ash
on his guru's forehead.

He bowed low before the body and prayed for some minutes
before getting up and making his way out of the hall. I moved
back so he wouldn't see I'd been watching him. It had looked
like a private ritual. I greeted him in reception.

'Rani. I'm sorry.'

He put his hand on my shoulder. 'I need to go and fetch
some water from the Yamuna. Holy water is needed for the
soul to attain liberation.'

'Do you want me to come with you?'

'No, no. I want to go alone. You go home.'

'Will you come back after?'

He frowned, looked me in the eye. 'No. I'm going to have
to stay here to watch over the body and to greet mourners.
There'll be many, many people here over the next three days.
Then we'll have a cremation on the river.'

'Are you going to come after that?'

He continued to look at me straight, but his mouth twisted.
'I don't think so. I don't think so. I think I'll have to stay here
now, Ruby. I'm sorry.'

'No. It's the right thing. You're needed.'

I cried in the rickshaw back home. I got a call from Mukerjee
as I neared the flat. They thought they'd found the young
priest and wanted me to identify him. I turned around and
made my way back to the station. I was grateful for something to do.

I watched him through the same old mirrored wall. They'd

got the right guy. He'd been found under a flyover in South Extension, where Bihari labourers congregated. Patel had thrown the boy out after Nakul had beaten him. They had tough discipline in the V.H.P. And it looked like he really had been the one to suffocate Swami Shiva. Forensics had matched his fingerprints to the pillow and found his hair on it too.

I didn't want to watch another interrogation and went as soon as I could. I met Eddie coming out of the station. His eyes were wide.

'Ruby! Can you believe it?'

'No.'

'Swami Shiva dead. And that boy. Responsible. Really, I know I've said it before but you really couldn't make this up.'

'Hmmm.'

'Where are you going?'

'Home.'

'You don't want to stay with me? I'm going to talk to Mukerjee. Find out exactly how this kid from Bihar ended up killing one of India's best-known gurus.'

'I'll read about it tomorrow. I just want to go home and sleep for now.'

31

According to the *Telegraph*, after it had been discovered that the young priest was partly responsible for the death of Stephen Newby, the boy had been beaten and thrown out of the temple. He'd been disorientated, shocked. He ended up with some Bihari labourers taking bhang. They'd watched a small TV wired up to a Hindi news channel. There had been a news special on the Swami Shiva scandal. It built up Swami Shiva into a villain who'd molested one of his students, got her pregnant and then hidden the evidence. The homeless priest's new friends suggested he go after Swami Shiva, take revenge for Stephen. It would even up his karma. After more bhang he too thought this would be a good idea. He'd found the centre, wandered in and found the man himself in corpse pose. It had been easy for him. He'd taken a nearby pillow and stuffed it over Swami's face. Swami Shiva had been so deeply in meditation he would have hardly felt a thing.

The Indian papers all ran full-page obituaries of Swami Shiva on their front pages. The British obituaries online were long and had obviously been prepared years in advance. Swami

Shiva's indiscretion with Claudia was simply a small footnote, Stephen a little mark on an otherwise incredibly praiseworthy life.

Eddie's obituary in the *Telegraph* portrayed him as a man genuinely devoted to his path; who brought yoga and meditation to thousands of people around the world; who explained Eastern morality to the 'lost West' without superiority or smugness. The *Indian Express* claimed he was an international politician with a party of millions around the world. The *Hindu* wrote a huge amount about his work in the Middle East, calling him a peace envoy for India. The *Hindustan Times* suggested minting a coin with his image. The finance minister declined to comment on this but Delhi's chief minister promised a city holiday on the day of his cremation.

The streets were closed the day of his funeral. It reminded me a little of Holi. The city felt empty, until my taxi reached close to the river. A steady stream of cars, rickshaws, pedestrians were making their way to Nigambodh Ghat, round the back of the Red Fort. It was the oldest funeral ghat in Delhi. It was always busy, bodies burning throughout the day and an electric crematorium there too now. This day, however, there would be just one traditional pyre set alight.

As the roads choked up I showed a special funeral pass Chewy had dropped off for me the night before, to allow me to enter the inner ghat area. He'd told me Rani would have come round himself but he was preparing Swami Shiva's body and was busy with funeral rites. I'd tried not to look too upset at this.

'Ruby, can I ask you something?' Chewy had said, sitting down on the sofa. I'd asked him in for a cup of tea.

'Sure.'

'Anything happen between you and Rani?'

I'd blushed, shrugged unhappily. Chewy put his hand on my head.

'It's the right thing for him to do, Ruby. The network wouldn't survive if he didn't come back. He can save it and Swami's reputation. He's not been touched by any of these scandals. He's thinking about more than himself, he's thinking of all the people that follow him,' he said.

I shook his hand off me and shrugged my shoulders. 'I know. I know.'

Chewy himself was leaving though.

He'd told me he was packing up to go back to Hawaii and stay with his old mother for a bit. She was excited. Fattening a pig up for his return, even though he had told her again and again he was vegetarian. Two of the Japanese girls had arrived back from Rajasthan to pay their respects to Swami Shiva and were now going with him. One of them was Kiki with the lime-green knickers. He wanted to know if I wanted to come too. I told him I didn't know what I was going to do. But I'd suddenly realised I didn't want to stay in Delhi any longer.

'I don't want to pay the rent on the flat on my own. I can't afford it. But then I don't want to go home. I might as well stay in India if I've got this journalist's visa. They're so hard to get and it's valid for a year. Maybe I'll go somewhere else. Maybe Mumbai. Maybe Hyderabad.'

'Why go to a city? They're so full of people. Expensive. Every damn city is the same. Why don't you go to Goa?'

I'd laughed. 'Trust you, Chewy – that's like the closest place to Hawaii in Asia!'

Chewy had shrugged. 'I know how to have a good time, isn't it?'

'I'll sleep on it, Chewy. Thanks for the suggestion. I'll see you at the funeral.'

Delhi police beat a path through the crowds when they saw the pass and I could see Chewy sitting a few rows in front of me. We were both in a VIP section, among swathes of expensive saris and crisp kurtas. I recognised some of the mourners: politicians, actors, writers.

I could see Rani too but he was too far away to see me or acknowledge me. He was standing by the pyre, on the funeral ghat itself, knelt down in prayer. Swami Shiva was lying on top, in yellow robes and covered in flowers. There was a video screen up for the crowds at the back to see what was going on and it focused in on Rani's solemn, lively face. After some time, he raised himself up and nodded over to a priest waiting by his side. Hindu chants began to crackle out of loudspeakers, announcing the beginning of the funeral. Rani slowly walked around the pyre, sprinkling water as he went. After the third time round he nodded at the waiting priest who brought him a flaming torch. He put it to the feet of Swami Shiva. The air was dry and the pyre lit up with immediate life. The tin chants stopped and I listened to the loud crackling of the fire.

The sun beat down on the crowds as we all watched Swami's body burn and melt in the flames. We sheltered from the ferocity of both the flames and the sun under umbrellas and scarfs and hats. A slight breeze relieved the heat but sent the smell of burning flesh towards me. I put my hand over my mouth. Rani stood close by in prayer, not affected by the sun or the fire or the smell. He looked very strong indeed.

It took about two hours for the pyre to collapse and the body to disappear into the debris. The ash wouldn't be collected until the night. I began to make a move as soon as other people did; the smell was making me feel sick. I wanted to give my condolences to Rani, but knew he would not be leaving his position for some time and that he would be a public figure for at least thirteen days, the mourning period.

307

I woke up early the next morning, with the first light. I walked out onto the balcony where white specks floated round me. It had rained during the night and the air was a little cooler. I thought of the pyre, soggy and ashy and Swami all gone. I thought of Stephen and decided to visit his grave.

The light around the shrine was still foggy and morning white as I left. Capped men were picking out big yellow breakfast breads from their ovens with iron rods. Rickshaw drivers were drinking their morning chai. They called to me, asking where I wanted to go, but I didn't want to disturb their breakfast.

I crossed the trunk road separating Nizamuddin West from East and wandered down a lane skirting the red walls of Humayun's tomb. Men were lying asleep on its grass banks, dotted around, sheets covering them, like colourful corpses. A sadhu wandered past me, hair wild but eyes benign. I kept walking, past a one-armed man who made tea on a bend in the road by Guru Granth Sahib Gurdwara, then on past a small Sufi shrine, painted blue and green. Flags flew among the shrine's trees. Old Muslim hippies were washing themselves. I'd walked here with Stephen a few times. He'd pointed out this little grotto and told me a story about a holy man who'd lived under a tree on this spot. Childless couples would come to be blessed by him. When he died the son of one of these couples built the shrine. And now people cry and tie little pieces of string to the railings and pray for children. The little lane emerged on to the main road again and I hailed a rickshaw to take me to the graveyard. I bought some flowers from a seller at the entrance, pink Busy Lizzies.

The sun was high in the sky by the time I arrived at Stephen's grave. The stone stood out among the other mossy memorials, sleek black marble from Italy. It was the freshest grave there by years, most others were from the time of Empire. It was a privilege to be buried here, like it had been a privilege to swim in the embassy pool. I sat under a banyan tree close by and watched two gardeners busily remove his funeral bouquets. Pots of jasmine prepared for planting stood nearby. They'd smell beautiful. I walked over and gave them my fresh flowers. They smiled at me, took them and arranged the blossoms in a pattern on top of the gravestone.

ACKNOWLEDGEMENTS

Thank you – in no particular order – to Ritesh Pandey, Harriet Sergeant, Tim Crook, David Ambrose, Charlie Viney, Sophie Lewis, Shakti Bhatt, Filipe Moura, Sarah Courtauld, Jon Weil, Emma Beswetherick, Markia Ohtani, Jess Hamilton, Jitender Shambi and Dominic Charles.

Do you love crime fiction?

Want the chance to hear news about your favourite authors (and the chance to win free books)?

Kate Brady
Frances Brody
Nick Brownlee
Kate Ellis
Shamini Flint
Linda Howard
Julie Kramer
Kathleen McCaul
J. D. Robb
Jeffrey Siger

Then visit the Piatkus website and blog
www.piatkus.co.uk | www.piatkusbooks.net

And follow us on Facebook and Twitter
www.facebook.com/piatkusfiction | www.twitter.com/piatkusbooks

piatkus